PRAISE FOR
THE MUSIC BOOK

"On page after page, you hitch a ride as O'Leary asks an existential question: does 2 plus 2 in fact equal 4, or is there a missing element, a spiritual or cosmic element, that can bend reality at any given moment, that can transport you to a different time, a different place, or perhaps lead to orgasmic ecstasy in the moment itself? Where will this journey lead for the main protagonist: to a fulfilling relationship? to discover the twenty-first century heirs to the Seattle Sound? to overcome personal doubts to create his own timeless art? O'Leary offers up all these possibilities in this masterful tome."

—Stephen Tow, author of *The Strangest Tribe: How a Group of Seattle Rock Bands Invented Grunge*

"*The Music Book* is all about Acting into Being; existing immersed in the ache of needing to be heard, begging to be read, things to make and do, saved by music beyond drink and despair and doubt. It stretches out patiently at the cusp of real life like a trembling, thought-obliterated fan in a scene-entry dive watching their favorite yet unknown band at the low angle of the stage on a torrid, parched Tuesday night. Will we all make it to a spiritual Friday or Saturday headlining slot? What happens if we do or we don't? Read *The Music Book* and deeply understand those stakes, either way."

—Chris Estey, Big Freak Media, Light In The Attic Records, KEXP Blog

"The Music Book is very successful at transporting [the reader] to that world...captures the power of music...a really entertaining book."

—Margaret Larson, New Day Northwest

"The Music Book is the most aptly titled novel since On the Road. [It has] passion and frustration. Lyricism and criticism. Beer and bass guitar and barstool banter. And love. Lots of love. The real music in The Music Book is the sound of O'Leary's heart—beating loud as a kick drum."

— Joe Oestreich, author of *Hitless Wonder: A Life in Minor League Rock and Roll*

THE MUSIC BOOK

DAVE O'LEARY

An Infinitum Publishing Trade Paperback 2nd Edition
Published in 2017 by Infinitum Publishing
a division of Infinitum Limited based in:
London, UK, Vancouver, BC, New York, NY, Baton Rouge, LA

infinitumpublishing.com

Cover Design by Elizabeth Martin

This is a work of fiction, though the musicians and radio personalities in the book are real people. All other names, characters, places, brands, media, and incidents are either the product of the author's imagination or are used fictitiously. Any resemblance to similarly named places or to persons living or deceased is unintentional.

Print ISBN 978-1-937634-05-6
EPUB ISBN 978-1-937634-06-3

Library of Congress Control Number: 2017936846

This book is dedicated to the letters A, B, C, D, E, F and G.

When I die
I want it said of me
that I played
the Blue Guitar
to the merriment
the sorrow
the irritation
of others,
that the "woo woo!"
of the crowd
was heartfelt
and unrestrained,
that reality did
change
flash
soar
with the notes
and the words
and the
love.

PROLOGUE

THERE WAS AN A CHORD and then silence.

And then applause.

I looked up from the stage at the sixty or so people in the South Heidelberg, a little underground place in the neighborhood of Ohio State University. It was dungeon-like down there. The walls were mostly uneven white stone dirtied with the grime and haze and graffiti of being a campus-area bar for forty years or more. The few lights were dim, even by dive bar standards, the ceilings low, the pool table never functional. The stage was actually a step down from the audience, which could make one feel small on crowded nights. It wasn't the most popular music club in town, not by a long shot, but we gigged there often because they let us play from ten until two with no opening band, no quickie forty-five minute sets, no triple bills. The nights were all ours, and we'd let passages and solos and rhythms go and see where they wound up. Time and space were filled with music. I grabbed one of the two Rolling Rocks on my amp, took a swig, let out a sigh, felt the nerves ratchet up like they always did between songs. There was a shout from the crowd.

"Third Stone!"

The next song was a cover, Pink Floyd's "Pigs (Three Different Ones)." It had a little bass intro over some chords on the keyboard so there would be no guitars or drums for fifteen or twenty seconds. That meant the focus would be on me, and that was a scary thought. I was a musician, but I'd never been comfortable in the spotlight for it brought a kind of nakedness, a fear of being seen, of making a mistake, so I looked down at my Fender Jazz bass. It had a wood grain finish, black pickups, black inlays on the neck. My left arm tightened up a little, and I had the thought, *Shit. I'm going to fuck it up.*

When the place was absolutely quiet, Stephanie started the song. I looked over as she eased into the keyboard, repeated chords, brought the volume up. I was mesmerized. I wanted to be out there in the audience. I wanted just to *listen* to her roll along those keys. Right in front of the stage there was a woman with black curly hair. She had her head tilted back and her eyes half open like she was trying to read the notes on the ceiling. She was swaying, and I just watched her for a few measures before remembering I had a responsibility. I knew the keyboard intro couldn't go on forever, that the bass was supposed to come in high up on the neck. I steadied myself, readied my fingers, played a few notes, the *wrong* few notes. I felt a sense of panic as I suddenly didn't know what key I was in or even which one I was supposed to be in. I swayed a little, took a step forward and probably looked drunk. My mind went blank, my face red, but I tried again, played the wrong few notes again. The neck of the instrument suddenly didn't make any sense to me. It was just a piece of wood with some metal strips on top, a few dots on the side, four pieces of wire running the length of it. It was a bass guitar, but really, what *was* this thing in my hands, and what the hell was I supposed to do with it? The keys continued, but all eyes in the audience were on me, wondering what I was doing, waiting for something to happen. I knew how to play, really, but in the moment it seemed I'd forgotten. I swayed a little more and took two steps forward, nearly falling down.

Stephanie's boyfriend, Deon, was working the door, and he just stared in disbelief at my little dance, figured I was drunk and might pass out, that the show would be over right then and there with no Pink Floyd cover to end it all in grand fashion but rather with a head-line in the *Columbus Dispatch* the following morning: "Bass Player Passes Out, Bumps Head, Show Ends, Future of Band Uncertain." I steadied myself and looked over at Stephanie. She was still playing those chords, grooving in her own way to the music she was making, head down, brown straight hair hanging over a white shirt. She seemed unconcerned with my two fuckups. She had confidence in the music, that I would get it right because I always had before.

I stepped over to my amp and turned the volume up just the slightest bit. The crowd was still hushed, and then finally Stephanie's chords enveloped me, soothed me, did their thing, said to me in their own strange language, "It's all right." The redness left my face, and I took a swig of beer and felt like I was drinking the music. *Maybe John Lennon was wrong*, I thought, *maybe this is all you need*. I smiled. Music. Maybe the intro could go on forever, and we could all groove and listen with our eyes half-closed and let the chords take us places.

A few more measures went by, and with my eyes on Stephanie rather than my bass, I tried it again, and this time, I nailed it, played a few high notes, added a little vibrato, sustained one for half a measure, and then descended down to an E on the seventh fret of the A string as the guitars came in, Kevin chunking a low E on his SG, Matt letting his Les Paul ring out a little higher, and the cymbals crashed and everything descended to a B a couple times around and then the singing about those different kinds of pigs. There were cheers, cheers that meant there would be no headlines in the morning, just another small band playing in a small bar. We were jamming, rocking, moving bodies and souls, but it was only for sixty people. Maybe I should have passed out, taken a tumble for the band, a cut above the right eye, a bloody nose. Maybe the world would have taken notice.

We finished the song to much applause and more shouts, "Third Stone… Third Stone!" Deon came up to me. "That rocked, man. Glad you didn't pass out." What could I say to him about what really happened? Instead I just smiled, "Thanks," and there were post-gig beers and after-hours shots and handshakes and hugs. No one in the audience mentioned those awful notes or my awkward steps, but of course the band would tease me for years to come. Even long after we broke up, there were references to it. "Man, I thought you were going to do a face plant right there, or maybe that you'd do another twist and fall into my drums," Frank would laugh when we met for beers or the odd solo recording project. It seemed everyone just thought I was drunk that night, so I let them, and though I should have, I never told the guys in the band the truth, never told them that I was often filled with doubt, that I some-times wondered if I was somehow not qualified to step on a stage.

It happened during every show, those moments when something unwanted crept in, a kind of uncertainty, a hesitation that meant a few wrong notes from time to time, or a few panic moments when I suddenly felt flushed and nearly fingered the wrong note or hit the chord change a little off time. And it wasn't because I couldn't play, but just because I worried about it, so in the middle of a song, in the middle of a measure, the question would come, "What's the next chord? E? A? Shit!" I *feared* it. Stepping on stage was a scary thing, so I froze sometimes, and swayed and lurched forward and had to hold the bass steady and ask, "Why do I put myself through this?"

But over the years, I always thought that, fuckups or not, at least I wasn't a critic. That seemed the worst of all things, worse than any embarrassment a few bad notes might bring. The Critic. I had my fears, but it was not for me to be stuck only commenting on the creative endeavors of others, to wait and wait while artists and musicians did their bits, good or bad, in confidence or in fear, to change the world, and then only to react, never to put forth one's own voice in the effort to create something new.

That gig was in 1995 when I was finishing a degree in English literature. It was an easy major. I read books and wrote a few short stories, a few essays, had enough extra hours after classes to pursue music. I wanted to get my own thing down in my own voice with a pen or a bass or a guitar, and even though I was in Columbus, Ohio, it was one of the greatest times of my life, even when the music was off by a few notes because that woman who was grooving and looking at the ceiling hung around after the show, walked up to me with a couple shots in hand even though the bar was closed. The Southberg was like that, another reason we played there often. She handed me a shot of cheap tequila. "That was cool. I've never seen anyone play that song before." It struck me then that she hadn't realized I'd fucked up, that maybe it was something known only to the musicians in the audience. "Thanks. Cheers." We did the shots, and I knew already that she would go home with me. It was the music, "Roadhouse Blues" or maybe "White Rabbit" or our Pink Floyd closer, or the grooves and the lengthy improvised jams of our original songs working their way though her body. If she'd simply seen me at some random bar, she would not have done that, the grooving and gazing, the shots and the sex. She was moved before we ever said so much as hello. It was the rhythms, the riffs, the art of it all, and all of it in the moment, for live was the thing since it brought the possibility of all else.

The following morning at my place I woke to find her leafing through some of my journals and stories. She was flipping pages, pausing to read a few sentences, then flipping some more. "Sorry. I just saw these here and was only glancing through. You didn't tell me you're a writer too."

"Yeah, I am," but it wasn't really true. I didn't want to call myself a writer until I'd published something, and I somehow knew that wasn't going to happen anytime soon. I did consider myself an artist though, and there was, of course, a certain amount of ego that went into that, even with all my panic in some moments, so let's say I was the doubtful artist, fearful but plagued with a belief in the self, a belief that one's own voice, one's own perspective, is important, is valid, is able to change the mindset of others, to encourage reactions and beliefs and feelings that will be remembered or that will help us forget, that will lift, destroy, resurrect, even damn.

"I'd like to read one of these some time," she said. "What do you write about?"

"Fear."

She smiled. "Interesting." She put the journal down, and neither of us said anything more about it. Instead, we went out to McDonald's for breakfast and talked of other things. Afterward, in front of the trashcans, I asked for her phone number. We'd both just thrown our wrappers away, and she was wiping ketchup from her hand—she was a ketchup-with-scrambled-eggs kind of person—"Can I have your phone number?" I'd thought she was expecting the question, maybe hoping for it, but she said, "I'll call you. What's yours?" So I gave her mine. She memorized it and promised to call that night, and we hugged before going our separate ways. At home, I played guitar all day while waiting for the phone to ring. I'd play a song and pause, play a song, pause, play a song. The phone never rang. I never heard from her again. I kept on playing guitar and pausing, but she didn't come to any future

Third Stone shows. She didn't knock on my door at 1:00 a.m. with a six-pack and a smile. Nothing. And it was like it had always been. Music filled up the space in my life.

It still does.

And these days, there are the moments like this one where I pause at three in the morning to pick up my blue Fender Stratocaster and pluck the entirety of Radiohead's "2 + 2 = 5," and the song, the notes, my fingers on the strings and the pick in my hand stir up the matter in my life. There's recording too, and listening, and yes, writing about music, capturing the feeling when the sound has diminished, trying to remember the meaning of the moment. There is also tinnitus, which means my ears ring all the time. I'm not sure when it started, can't remember if it was gradual or if it was just there one day. Maybe I'm just use to it. It makes me afraid though, never having complete quiet, and so the great worry is that the ringing will increase and increase until it ceases, until I go deaf, because that will mean not being able to hear a D chord cranked to eleven. I'd still be able to feel the vibrations, but I'd have to imagine the sound, recall some past chord from memory, never knowing for sure if I have the right one, if whatever is in my head isn't a D at all but maybe a G or an A. I have my doubts even now when I can still hear, and so I question, sometimes, my ability to play, to make music. Maybe when I place my fingers just so on the neck and strum, it is a D, but not a D as big and bold and awesome as it could be. Maybe I'm missing something. Maybe all the Ds in the world are different, mine somehow less. And so I worry, and I wonder, and I lie awake at night counting down the days and hours until the volume is cut. I shouldn't because I *know* the sound, I feel it in my bones as they say, but I fear the loss that would mean 0db, and I fear it in the same way I fear waking up alone, or the same way I fear that I might eventually die that way, alone, maybe a quiet heart attack in my sleep after a night of beers and notes and song titles that defy logic, for the loss of hearing is a kind of death, a shutting out of the world, and that's why I see so many bands now. I'm stocking up, preparing for the possible silent emergency, anticipating the memory of sound, trying to fill the empty space.

PART 1

Chapter 1

"YOU CUT YOUR HAIR," I say, looking at her exposed neck. She smiles, grabs a bit of it, runs her fingers down its length, twirling it around her thumb. It used to hang just below her shoulders. Now, it hangs not even an inch past her ears, but the effect is good, the neck ready for the nuzzle of a forehead. "I like it."

"Me too."

"Thanks. Here you go," she says placing a Manny's Pale Ale in front of Greg. She pauses, smiles at him, then sets the same in front of me. She pulls a napkin and a pen from her apron and scribbles numbers on one side and then the other while we drink. She looks around the bar to make sure that no other customers need anything and then flips the napkin a few times going over her calculations. "You guys ever use much math these days besides adding and subtracting?"

"Hell no," Greg says. "Counting coin is about all I ever use it for. Computers do all the tricky stuff." This is our usual hangout, the Beveridge Place Pub in West Seattle, when we want a few drinks after he gets off work at the bank and before I go to a show. He works as a teller for lack of ambition, says he just counts the money of others. Before that, he was a waiter at a fancy place downtown, which he says is the same except for the additional bit of bringing them food. He's done construction work too, and some warehouse work, driven a delivery van for a dry cleaner. He's floundering in his thirties, maybe his whole adulthood, going from job to job, a little aimless at times, very much so at others, but seeming not to worry about it as the years drift along. I'm the worrier in this friendship, or rather this beer-drinking partnership. We first met in this place about six months ago when I was scribbling thoughts in a notebook and sipping a pint of Manny's. He sat next to me and ordered the same. He took a good long hit from his beer, looked over at me, offered his hand. "I'm Greg." I figured he would ask about what I was writing, but he didn't. I liked that. Instead we talked about the beer.

Manny's is brewed by Georgetown Brewing Company, a Seattle brewery located just south of downtown, and its red and gold label is quite the common sight in the taps of dive bars and high-end joints alike in the Pacific Northwest. It's something hoppy enough for beer snobs but without the bitterness that turns many away from craft beers. "I read an article about it once," Greg said. "The guy, Manny, he used to work for Mac and Jac's when they were just getting started, and he'd drive all over the city convincing bars to put it on tap. Did pretty well, too."

"I never much liked Mac and Jac's."

"Me neither." He took a sip of his beer. "I had a girlfriend once who thought that if you didn't like the taste of hops, it meant that your taste buds hadn't fully developed."

"I'd have to disagree with that."

"Yeah, it was a pretty dumb thing to say. Anyway, Manny was upset that they didn't bring him in to be a partner since he'd done a ton of legwork to get the beer into bars around the city and build up the company, so he quit and traveled a little before coming back to Seattle to take a job he hated."

"I do understand that bit about having a job you hate."

"Cheers to that." We drank. "Then he met this guy named Roger, or wait, I think they were roommates. Anyway, it doesn't matter. They weren't happy where their lives were going so every night over beers Roger tried to convince Manny that they should start their own brewing company."

"And they did. Happy ending."

"Indeed. Hell, I should probably do something like that. They seem to be doing pretty well for themselves."

"If you need a partner, let me know."

When I got home that night, I stood outside and stared long at the stars telling myself to quit my job, that I should just write and play music and see what would come of it. I didn't, of course. Quitting a job is a scary thing so I had to applaud Manny for his courage and his beer, and thus, as I looked up at the sky, I decided to drink his namesake pale ale whenever it was available on tap.

The bartender this afternoon is Katie. She's worked here for about half a month, came over from a different bartending job. At one point, she was thinking about going to culinary school, was saving for it, but she gave that up in favor of just living. "I was tired of scrimping and saving all the time. Screw that. The paths we choose and the things we save up for should make us happy." She was right, of course. Greg and I raised our glasses to her, "To being happy." If only it were so easy. Joy comes in moments, but it's a damned hard thing to sustain, something akin to playing the Beethoven sonatas. Few get there, and even fewer truly succeed.

Looking down at her napkin, Katie says, "I'm thinking about buying a car so I'm trying to calculate down payments and interest and how many payments things work out to, but it just isn't happening. I remember spending hours in high school going through this kind of stuff and never getting it right even then."

"Fuck that. Use a calculator or a computer," Greg says. "You can do that stuff online, you know."

"Yeah, I know, but I'm here."

"It isn't that hard on paper. It's like paint by numbers. Just plug in the right values and you're fine."

"Easy for you to say. When's the last time you ever used a formula for anything?" Funny that she asks, because I've lately been running over one on those late nights alone in my apartment when the guitar leans quietly in the corner, or not so quietly on my knee, and I wonder at the title of the song, "2 + 2 = 5." Is it possible? What do things really add up to? No, that isn't the question. It's *music*. What does *music* add up to? A life, all the moments we spend alone trying to get something down, a few chords, a few notes, a melody, something magical, a song, a moment that transforms and changes things. It's temporary, yes, but permanent too. It adds up to something more. 2 + 2 = 5. I won't mention that now, though. I'll drop that on them some other time.

"It is true," I say, "that most people don't do much beyond the basics of math. It's all computers."

"As I just said."

"But there are practical, everyday uses, stuff besides car loans."

"Such as?" she asks.

I think for a moment and then begin. "Well, let's say there's a party hosted by two people, and one of them made a punch that is 40 percent alcohol and the other made a punch that is 60 percent alcohol. And furthermore, let's say they decide in their infinite wisdom that the optimal alcohol percentage in their punch should be 52 percent. Now, the question then becomes how many liters of each punch should be mixed to produce 20 liters of a 52 percent alcohol party punch?" They're listening, but I sense it's going over their heads, or maybe they just don't care. "So then, let us assume that we need x liters of the 40 percent punch. The total volume is 20 liters. So if we mix x liters of 40 percent punch, we have to mix 20 - x liters of 60 percent punch to make the total 20 liters." I grab the napkin from her and write as I continue to speak, "So the equation is $0.4x+0.6(20-x)=20*0.52$. Easy, right?" I push the napkin toward Katie. She picks it up, smiles, gives a little laugh.

"The hell with mixing that shit. Just drink the 60 percent and call it good. Or better yet, stick with beer. No percentages or formulas to worry about." I chug the remainder of my glass. Greg follows suit. "Another?" Katie grabs the glasses and steps over to the taps.

"Well, now," I continue, "formulas may still help with the beer. If we say that said party will have 25 guests plus the two hosts and one dog, say a black lab named Sparkie with a fondness for beer, and we also surmise that 20 percent of party attendees will drink only punch, 50 percent only beer, and the remaining 30 percent a mixture, how much beer will we need to satisfy the thirst of the party goers given that on average each beer drinker will drink 5.2 beers, with the exception of the dog, of course, who will drink only 1.5?"

"You crack me up. The dog drinks one and a half beers? How'd you calculate that? Next thing, you'll be making jokes about geometry."

"Geometry? Well, now..." She leans in to listen. Greg rolls his eyes. "After our party, the hosts line up all the beer and vodka bottles in a triangle with two equal sides and one side with seven more bottles than the other two. Not even they know why they do this given all the punch and beer consumed throughout the evening, but there it is, late night drunken bottle arranging. I think we've all done that. So then, if they use 400 bottles, as there were not a few unexpected guests, how many bottles are on the longer side? The sober among us might not care, but such things do in fact take on great cosmic significance in the wee drunken hours."

She grabs her coffee cup, clinks my beer glass with a laugh. "Cheers, but please tell me you're not that guy drinking and arranging bottles in the middle of the night."

"Me? Not at all. After the party, I'd be out at the bar hitting on a woman, trying to get a name and a number."

"No you wouldn't," Greg says. "He's heartbroken."

"Are you?"

"In a way. I lost someone last year, about eight months ago I guess, and I do still think about her sometimes."

"Aww."

"Ha, more like *all* the time."

"No, I wouldn't say that. It's mostly when I'm alone and not doing anything. When you lose someone, you eventually get to a point where you're ready for something new, but in the absence of it, the head and the heart will keep going back. The tricky point, though, is not to obsess."

"Yeah." She nods. "I'd agree with that."

I don't know if she's just being nice or if she really does agree, but to me it sounds like a load of crap. Maybe I am bordering on obsession, or wallowing somewhere well past it. I tell myself daily that I'm not, but the true answer won't reveal itself until I see her, until I run into lost love in some random location like a grocery store or some music club. Katie excuses herself to go clean the table of some customers who just left. Greg watches her for a couple seconds, then we sit there quietly looking into our pint glasses doing that thing all drinkers do. If we had bottles, we'd probably be peeling the labels off. I have old love on my mind, but that's okay. I probably still will when I find someone new. If it were love, *real* love, I'll still go back there sometimes, not to the actual but to the idea, and not because I haven't found something new, but because that old love moved me, changed my life, made a permanent mark. That's what love does, but there's more to it, so when Katie comes back, I feel the need to explain myself.

"The thing is, it's the same with music. I can put on a CD of an old band of mine and feel a pang, and it's a kind of loss that tugs at me every bit as much as the loss of a woman, sometimes more to be honest. Maybe it's just the loss of possibility, and no matter what comes after, we're always left to wonder about the good times and to imagine what would have happened in our lives if things had worked out differently."

"You played in bands?" she asks.

"Yeah, is that so surprising?"

"I don't know. I've only seen you drink beer."

"You got me there, but yes, I played in bands for years. I wish I still did, but now I just write about music."

"No, he writes about himself."

"What do you mean?"

"I was a musician for years." That thought gives me pause. "… But I write stories and other things too, and so last year in the absence of a band or a girlfriend, I started writing about local shows."

"Why?"

"Music is just so much a part of our lives, more so than any other art form. Hell, it's even part of other art forms, but it's more than that. There's music playing almost everywhere you go, even Muzak, and I've always felt that music is a prop for us, a comfort. We sing to our babies. We sing at weddings and religious ceremonies, funerals. We sing when we're cleaning or just walking down the street. There are commercial jingles and Christmas jingles and TV show intro music, mood music in movies, music to get you in the mood. Even if you go get a massage, they play that kind of soft Zen music mixed with sounds of nature. And it isn't something like food. It isn't a physical necessity. If we don't eat, we'll die. People can indeed live without music, but the life would be somewhat less fulfilling."

"Perhaps it would," Greg says, "but it'd still be life."

"Yeah, I love music, but I'd wager that plenty of people do just fine without it."

"What I mean," I say, "is that, uh, a world without music is a world without sound. Nobody wants that." I know that many deaf people lead fulfilling lives, happy lives, but it's a foreign thing to me. How could I possibly imagine such a world? How could I exist in one without going mad? "I mean, nothing captures a moment quite like a song. Nothing. That's why it's so entrenched in our lives, in every culture in one form or another."

"It is everywhere. I'll give you that." I appreciate Greg's willingness to concede that point at least.

"And here too, of course," I say, and we all pause to listen. The song playing over the bar's sound system is "Cold Desert" by Kings of Leon. It's a good tune, mellow groove, cool bass line, but the thing I never understood about this song is the fade out and fade in toward the end. It kills the momentum and the vibe, a cheap studio gimmick that interrupts the music to remind us that it's a recording, that there's an engineer turning knobs. It pulls the listener out just when the music should take hold and scream and envelope the head and the heart. I actually had to rip the song from CD and edit that pause out.

"I never liked these guys much," Greg says.

"They have some good songs." I decide not to elaborate about the pause since I want to continue on about music. "But anyway, I got to wondering about the desire to play music, to create it, and what that means, what it adds up to, and then I thought I'd write about it, the music of others that is, but not in the context of famous bands. It's easy to keep doing music when you're making millions, but I want to write about the local bands and music and the dreams people have while they age and still play for only forty or fifty or even a hundred people in a little hole in the wall selling only a few odd CDs along the way."

"It's decent stuff, but he writes about himself and his"—he makes quotes with his fingers—"lost possibility as much as the music."

"I still don't get it. What do you mean? You do or don't write about the music?"

"I found that the only way I could do it was to insert myself into the story. Otherwise, it'd be torture. I couldn't do it. I couldn't play critic. You could say I write about my experience seeing a band and how their songs affect me and my evening and my mood because we relate everything we do to our own lives. That's the only context any of us ever has. What experience is there that exists outside your head? So that's how I write about music."

"There's plenty," Greg says, "going on outside your head."

"Yeah, but when I see it, it goes though my filters and gets distorted in one way or another."

"Interesting. Who do you write for? I'd like to read some."

"Mostly a website called Seattle Subsonic." I take the pen again and write the website address for her on a napkin.

"Thanks. You don't play in bands anymore?"

"I do when I can, but my last band broke up about eight months ago."

"Oh. The same time as…?"

"Yeah."

"I'm sorry."

"I sang in a cover band in my early college days," Greg chimes in. It seems an effort to change the subject, or perhaps to impress, but that's okay. I'm done talking for the moment. At the reminder of lost band and lost love, it feels more time to drink and listen to the sounds of the bar and the music. I've heard Greg sing a few times at a karaoke bar, and he's pretty good, does a respectable job of Radiohead's "Creep," Led Zeppelin's "When the Levee Breaks," Pink Floyd's "Nobody Home."

"I love singing. We should do karaoke sometime." It makes me wonder what she sings. She has a slight roughness to her voice. I bet she'd do a good Janis Joplin, maybe something like "Move Over."

"Yeah, definitely."

They get to talking about their singing preferences, their karaoke preferences, and I zone out of the conversation for a moment. I think about the line near the end of "Nobody Home," the one that needs force and conviction and volume. I know the feeling. Picking up the phone, looking at a picture, driving by an apartment. Nobody home. Borderline obsession, I suppose, but I was being honest when I said I'm ready for something new. The heart is a strong thing. It wants to heal itself. It wants new love. Who knows? It could be Katie here. Or maybe some random woman I meet at a bus stop. Or nobody. I look around the bar and notice it's empty now. There are some glasses on a few tables, a book on another with a few crumpled napkins, but no people. It's one of those moments where everything else falls away. We could be the only three humans on the planet, and the sun shines in the window as if to say it is so. Radiohead comes over the speakers: "Videotape." Katie puts the napkin in her apron and heads in back, perhaps to do some stocking up. Greg goes to the bathroom, and I just sit rooted in the slow, mournful pulse of the piano in a song about an old man dying and saying his goodbyes via videotape in reds and blues and greens. I sip my beer, the pulse goes on, steady but tense, seeming to drag a little at times like it might end at any moment, just like the old man's heart. The voice of the song goes on to say that he shouldn't be afraid, but I am. A few chords on a piano have made me so, made me afraid of many things, or rather so quickly reminded me of fears I already had, and though I know there's no answer to anything in my glass, I drain it in one big gulp thinking that maybe one will be there in the refill. The song fades into the ringing silence of my tinnitus, and I grab a napkin and the pen Katie left on the bar and write one line, "This just isn't working," and then I stare at my glass until the world and its sounds come back. First, it's Greg.

"Christ, I know that look."

Then Katie.

"Another round?"

"We're moving on to shots, tequila, Aha Toro."

Katie smiles, looks around, and in the absence of more customers says, "I think I'll do one too."

And so we do a few shots, get a couple refills of beer. Greg and Katie talk, flirt, exchange phone numbers, and although the shots and beers do their thing, although I do get a little drunk, although we do laugh some, I have only one thought in my head, the written thought. It's under my beer now since I don't want them to see it, and it sticks to the bottom of my glass when I drink so it's safe, safe but there, repeating, drowning me more than the booze.

This just isn't working.

CHAPTER 2

"I DIDN'T KNOW YOU were writing tonight."

"I am."

"Cool, but the Young Evils hardly need another review right now." She laughs a little, pours me a Manny's. It's Jessie, the owner of the Skylark Café in West Seattle. I settle in at the end of the bar, my usual seat in what has become my preferred pub when out alone because of its proximity to my apartment, but also for the Sunday brunch, the mix of live bands, the local artists on the walls. The staff knows me, and I like the benefits of being a regular. I don't have to actually order, just catch an eye, and I don't have to leave my card to run a tab. They know I'm good for it.

"Mackenzie put me on the list."

"You know you don't need to do that here. Any time you want, just show up and you're in."

"I know, and I do appreciate that, but I like to okay things with bands ahead of time if possible."

"Well, this won't be their usual show, but I think you'll like it." She walks off, disappears into the kitchen. I turn toward the stage, drink. I can feel the chill of the liquid running down my throat and relaxing everything as it goes. It's a marvelous thing, that first sip of the night, the look around the bar, the wonder of how we end up where we end up. I played music for years back in Ohio and Michigan, even some overseas, but now I'm here in Seattle at the end of the bar while my bass is nestled in the corner at home wondering whether it will ever see an audience again.

The Skylark is a dark, L-shaped place with the stage at the long end of the L. My seat is where the L makes its turn and a little farther from the taps than I'd like, but it's the perfect spot to listen to the music and take notes on the shapes of chords and flag down bartenders when the need arises. And I need this spot because I'm writing about the show tonight, and that thought always makes me smile, for I've done it. I've ended up in a most unexpected place. At forty-two, I've turned into that thing I thought I never would be, the thing I mentioned to Katie the other day, a critic.

I've been doing this for a few months, but I still ponder the same questions when I get to a bar for a show. How does a musician, a writer, make the switch to critic? And what does that mean? Can the act of writing about the music of others be as artful, as meaningful, as personal, as the music itself? And the larger question, of course, is why even bother? Why do I spend my hours writing, writing, writing? Why did Third Stone spend all those hours jamming, gigging, playing every weekend for a few souls who would graduate college and move on with their lives forgetting those unknown bands in the small campus bars, forgetting us? And what about the Young Evils? I know from all my years playing in bands that often the best music is the local stuff, the bands that can only be heard in the small clubs, the bands desperately trying to make it as I had been with Third Stone, the bands that most likely will soon never be heard again, and so here I am contacting musicians, managers and clubs. They put me on the guest lists, sometimes even give me a permanent spot on such, and with a pen and a notebook I push forward into the unknown, into something I'd never imagined doing, just listening, just being in the audience, taking notes on the sounds of the E chords played by others and passing a kind of judgment on them. It's an unforeseen turn in this life, but one thing I've always known is that the greatest things often come from such, and I wonder in these moments, first beer half finished, if the word that truly applies is *serendipity*, and if so, what will I find?

"Are you here to see the show?" It's a woman dressed in blue genie attire. She has a stack of index cards and a few pens in her hand.

"Uh, yeah."

"I'm Sasha, an usher. Do you know how the show works?"

"Nope. All I know is that it's called Radio8Ball, and that it's kind of like that old Magic 8 Ball thingy."

"That is correct. Radio8Ball is the Pop Oracle. You see, audience members write questions on these cards. If your card is chosen by our host, then you'll go on stage and the band will play a song to answer your question. Do you have a question?"

"Uh, too many."

She hands me a card.

"Just wave to me when you're done, and I'll take it up to the stage and put it in the basket." Sasha walks off. Mackenzie, who is also a bartender here, comes over.

"Glad you could make it." She's a short woman, easy with a smile, straight shoulder-length brown hair. She's wearing an Iron Maiden tee shirt, the "Run to the Hills" drawing, got to like a woman who wears such. My very first band played "Run to the Hills," and the guitar player and I would push the tempo of an already fast song so that by the end the drummer felt as if he'd sprinted a quarter mile. He'd throw his sticks at us—"you fuckers"—but we'd all be laughing, and the singer would invariably say, "Let's do that again." And most often we would.

"Thanks for having me. How'd you get hooked up with this Radio8Ball thing? It's an interesting idea."

"They heard us on KEXP and contacted Troy. We thought it'd be fun." That seems reasonable.

Radio play is a large part of the reason Jessie had said they didn't really need any more reviews at the moment. KEXP is regularly spinning their CD, and that kind of thing will lead to shows and reviews and reviews and more shows and better shows and whimsical shows for fun. I have my doubts though because the other singer, Troy, is a DJ for KEXP, and it seems too convenient. I've seen and heard so many great local bands that deserve airplay but are never given so much as a courtesy spin in the dedicated local hour on Sunday nights when only parents and girlfriends, and boyfriends, are listening, bands that faded into nothing, bands that would have killed to have their singer be a DJ. And KEXP is not a student-run college station that gives its fifty listeners a chance to hear the local stuff that won't be heard anywhere else. It is a juggernaut of independent radio, a force, a stepping stone. They take chances. They play things, and so I have to wonder as I wait for the show to start where the Young Evils fall in that equation. Are they just getting air time because of an inside connection or are they worthy of the chance?

"That's cool. I want to make some preliminary notes, but let's catch up after the show and chat about music for a bit."

"Will do. Put a few drinks on our tab if you want."

"Thanks."

When the show starts, host Andras Jones steps up to the microphone. "Welcome to Radio8Ball." He spreads his arms. "We are experimental theater, part rock-and-roll cabaret, part mystic mind-expansion." There are a few claps in the crowd. "The idea here is that there will inevitably be some kind of answer buried in the song that the Great Spinning Wheel demands the band play, some kind of connection that will relate to the question at hand, because you, the questioner, will spin the wheel and thereby direct the band through your own energy." He has a table and chair on the right side of the stage in front of the wheel that has numbers one through ten on it. The band is on the left side of the stage, but there are no drums. Troy is in the center with an acoustic guitar and Mackenzie next to him with a microphone. There is another guitar player and a percussionist with an assortment of shakers and a tambourine, no bass player. As I gathered from Mackenzie a few nights ago, they are currently searching for one, and seeing them bassless up there makes me wonder about playing again, stepping up on stage, strapping on the bass, launching into the opening groove of Jane's Addiction's "Up the Beach." Maybe if I like their music, I'll inquire.

Andras ruffles his hand through the basket and draws a card. "John S., John S., please come up to the stage and ask the band what you will." John walks up to the stage. He's a thin guy, short hair, tall, maybe six-five. He leans down into the guest microphone with no greetings, no jokes, no hesitation. "How do we fix the economy?" Then he spins the wheel. It goes around four times with a whirring buzz that slows and stops on three. Some people clap. There's a list of ten songs on the wall behind the band with titles big enough to see even from my corner of the bar, and we all do the mental count down the list. One, Two, Three. Troy smiles. " 'Crazy People' it is."

He counts off, and the Young Evils play and sing of looking toward the past and trying to discern the meaning, the need to hang in there and the money made never being spent and staying on one's path. Afterward Troy says, "OK, that's creepy." It kind of was. Question answered. Economy fixed.

A few questions later, a guy named Carek steps up to the stage. He's got an athletic build but a beer gut too, the inevitability of middle age creeping up. I know the feeling. "Have you ever really hummed it in there?" he asks the band. I write in my notebook, "Hummed it in there?" I have no idea what he's asking, but it seems Andras and the band do as there is some debate on it being an appropriate question since it doesn't really apply to him or his life specifically. Andras muses that it applies to all of us when its sexual meaning is divulged for those in the crowd who may not know. Humming it in there. Okay. I get it now, though I suppose a woman would have it hummed in there. The discussion continues about the point of the question.

"Yeah, but shouldn't it be more *how* you hum it in there rather than simply have you?" Mackenzie asks. This brings laughter.

"Uh," the percussionist chimes in, "isn't that a question for Troy, Mackenzie?"

More laughter. Apparently, they're a couple. I hadn't known.

"No, Faustine, I'm just saying that I think the how of the question is where the meaning lies, or rather how well. I mean, we've all done it." She looks out to the audience. "There aren't any nuns here, are there?" Even more laughter, some clapping.

"Yeah, I think the how is where it is," Carek says.

"Let's spin the wheel." Andras gets the show back on track. Seven. "Get Over It." More laughter.

"Mackenzie, about last night…"

"Get over it, Troy." There are shouts and claps, and they exchange a brief kiss on stage to whistling and applause. Faustine counts in, and they play the song. Afterward Troy, still grinning, says, "That's pretty much a song about asking, 'Am I good enough?' "

"See? It's the how, not the if."

"Yeah, yeah," Andras says, "the eternal quest to hum it in there and to hum it well."

There is a lull, and those in attendance who, like me, are alone look around and wonder whether we'll get lucky, and when, and yes, how well we'll do it. It has been almost nine months for me so the odds of quality probably aren't on my side. These days I guess it's just a matter of the if. I'll worry about the how later. "Get over it," I sing to myself before glancing around to see if anyone heard. I have to admit that after a few songs, I like the band. The music is catchy, poppy, simple rock with jangly, unclean guitar. The kicker, though, is the vocals. Troy and Mackenzie do not harmonize. They simply double the melody in octaves, and that gives them an almost artificial sound, not unpleasant though. It takes some of the musicality away but in doing so opens it up like we're all just sitting in a living room singing together for the simple joy of it, trying to make it sound good but not too worried because it's fun. And there's me, the non-singer, the guy scribbling at the end of the bar who, in spite of himself, sings along to every song.

"Rob. Rob M. Your turn. Come on up and see what the Young Evils have to say."

That's me, my question picked from the basket, and the nerves come, and the fears, for if I do it, I will be divulging a secret few people know. I want to ignore it, but Andras is calling my name, "Rob M.? Rob M.?" Mackenzie squints. "He's over there at the end of the bar." Heads turn, so what can I do? I walk to the stage and take my card. Andras points to the microphone. I'd thought of many questions earlier. Should I quit my job and just write? What's the best cure for a hangover? Is it possible for elephants to vanish? Or this slightly more complicated one: The length of the second side of a triangle is four less than three times the length of the first side. The length of the third side is one more than the length of the first side. If the perimeter of the triangle is thirty-seven feet, what is the length of the first side?

They're all important questions, but not what I really need answers to at the moment. I look out at the audience. The place is silent. The jitters come for I hate speaking. That's why I write. That's why I play bass and hide in the groove. The ringing in my ears creeps up in volume for a few seconds and then subsides at the pop of a wine bottle being uncorked. I have a bottle of red at home, William Hill cabernet, think I'll have a glass or two later. Faustine drops a shaker, picks it up. I eye my question once more, brace myself and think, *Fuck it.* "Uh," I look over at the band. "when will my novel be published?"

"Whoa, you wrote a novel?" Andras asks.

"He's a writer," Mackenzie says. "He writes for Seattle Subsonic."

"Thanks for the plug, and yeah, I did."

"Okay then, so what's it about?"

I pause. It's about various things, and many short summaries come to mind, but I still have all that humming on my brain, the memory of that last time with the woman who still dominates my thoughts on some late evenings. I wonder if she thought I did it well. She *seemed* to think so. "Uh, it's about orgasms that change lives." I had orgasms back then, but did she? Or did she pretend? I'm sweating and turned sideways as if I'm thin enough to hide behind the microphone stand. *Did she?* So many doubts. A lifetime full. My face is flushed, and I just want to get off the stage.

But there's laughter.

"Don't they all?"

"Not all of them."

"Get over it."

"It's all in the how," someone shouts from the audience. Yes, I think, but there's also the luck of the opportunity, and sometimes that's all that matters. Good, bad, or otherwise, that's all there is, the if, the touch of another, hopefully a loved one, the desire, and when that's gone, one is left to linger with memories, maybe battle with them.

"Okay then, let's spin the wheel." He's a stickler for that spinner so I do. Four. "This Rock and Roll City is Done." I sit down next to Andras as the Young Evils play. It's a fun tune. All of theirs are, especially in the acoustic format. They're deceptive in some ways. The name isn't a happy one. The titles are not happy, but the vibe is. The tone is. I make a mental note to see them with the full lineup but not to inquire about playing bass. I'm more given to something musically that has a bit of melancholy.

"So, Rob, what'd you think? Did it answer your question?"

I step up to the mic again a little more at ease from the song. "Well, I used to play in bands. My last gig was on this stage even, last year. Now, I just write so in a way it is true. This rock and roll city is done. Maybe that means soon."

"Yeah, I hope so, Rob, but you have to promise me something," Troy says. "If… no, when you do publish your book, please do an audio recording because I love that deep baritone of your voice."

I lean into the microphone, and in the deepest, the baritoniest tone I can muster, I say, "Indeed, I will." It makes me think about Elvis. There are more laughs and claps and a couple shouts, and I'm no longer on the verge of sadness or doubt or fright. It's impossible to be so when on stage with people clapping and smiling, so I lean forward and say in my best Elvis voice, "Thank you, thank you very much."

There are more questions, more songs, more talk of humming it in there. Everything seems to wind its way back to that. We're human. We have needs. An Asian woman steps up to the stage for the last song and squeaks out, "Have I become a sad robot?" There's the spin of the wheel, the stop, the glance at the song list. "The Devil's Barricade."

Faustine counts, "One, two, three, four."

It's their most rocking number with a lengthy guitar solo at the end. I can't catch the lyrics, so I'm not sure if it answers the question in any way, but afterward there is a shout from a woman in the audience, maybe the same woman who asked the question since she vacated the stage when the song began. "You guys nailed that one!"

Troy smiles, scratches his chin. "Yeah… we hummed it in there."

There is more laughter, but I look around and being off the stage and back at the corner of the bar, a little sadness does come back, and then a lot, because I know that for me, there will be no humming anytime soon, and so I do what I always do. I close my notebook, put my pen in my pocket, pay my bar tab, and leave alone.

Chapter 3

WE'RE BACK AT THE BEVERIDGE PLACE with a couple of Manny's, no shots this time. It's pretty crowded for a Saturday afternoon, but Katie still spends a lot of time talking to us, to Greg. They went to karaoke last night. While I was on stage asking about my book, they were singing. She did Fleetwood Mac's "Gypsy," the Doors "Love Me Two Times," and something from Patsy Cline. No Joplin. Greg did "Creep," and Katie was impressed. "You should have been there. He was awesome." He's smiling.

"You were good too."

"He also did 'No Surprises,' but I thought 'Creep' was better."

"Yeah, I've heard him do that one before."

"He says you love Radiohead. What's your favorite song of theirs?"

"Lately, it's '2 + 2 = 5.' "

"Really? I thought you dug 'Myxomatosis.' Or was it 'Morning Bell'?"

"Both, but I'm stuck on the equation these days. 2 + 2 = 5."

"I don't know that one," Katie says. "Which album is it on?"

"*Hail to the Thief.* I've just been thinking about that idea that something somehow adds up to more than the sum of its parts, something that defies logic but is still true."

"Such as?" Greg asks.

"Well, to go with more equations like last time, let's say $2 + 2 + H = 4$. What would the value of H be?"

"What's H?" She writes H on a napkin, circles it.

"Heart. Or I guess it could be spirit. Some people might just call it 'it' in the sense of having something extra because, well… let's say we're talking about music. Many people can play guitar well, some very well, but only a precious few can play it magically."

"What does that mean, magically?"

"I'll get to that, but for now, let's say H is heart, and for most people H is zero. It's a constant. It's always zero. The heart beats. It does its job. They live, but they don't… create. I don't mean that to sound bad, though. We all give to the world in our own way, but many people don't give a damn about the meaning of life, the why of it all. They're content just to breathe, and for them that's fine. I do not judge. We need plumbers and cashiers and shoe salesmen and customer service reps and all the mundane things in order to sustain this way of living, and you could argue that simply breathing and procreating is one way to have a successful life, maybe the most successful way. $2 + 2 + H = 4$, so H can only be zero. It can only ever be zero. It *has* to be zero. It's the only logical solution."

"Another?"

I look at my glass. "Yeah."

"Me too."

"But what of the artist?" I continue, "And I don't mean any random Joe who can play a couple chords or maybe paint a picture of a tree like kids do in elementary school, you know, the tree that always has a hole for a family of squirrels. I mean the person who can play a G chord in the proper way, the way that makes it sing, makes it resonate in the deep recesses of our souls. That's the magic part. Art changes things. Music changes things. It's like Wallace Stevens wrote, 'Things as they are are changed upon the blue guitar.' "

"Wallace who?"

"Stevens. He was a modernist poet, died in the fifties I think, and that line was just a way of saying that art can alter perception, and that, really, is one way of altering reality. If your perception changes, so does your life. Someone hitting a home run at a baseball game might be a joyous moment. You might feel good, but it won't change anything. It doesn't make you a different person. It doesn't shine a light on anything. There's no understanding."

"Well, not unless you had a lot of money riding on the game." Greg gives a slight laugh, sips his drink.

"Okay. There's that. I know it's imperfect, but in trying to think about it in a provable way, or at least, in a somewhat demonstrable way, I came upon the idea of 2 + 2 = 4 but sometimes 5, and I know that serious mathematicians would laugh at it, but I do hold there's something extra there, and when I write about music, it's part of what I'm looking for, the idea that H can be something other than zero, that it can have mass and energy in the right conditions, that a constant can change, that sometimes you have to throw out everything you know and take for granted because you find something so wonderful and joyous that it changes things."

"But you could say that of anything that makes you feel good," Katie says. " 'Oh, now this thing is more.' "

"Yeah, and Radiohead referred to it in the *1984* sense in that it had nothing to do with something adding up to more than the sum of its parts." I didn't know he'd read *1984*. "It was more about the reality of the past, accepting alternate truths in the face of logic only because the party demanded it or you'd be tortured and killed."

"I know, but this is different. The past isn't mutable. It's there in all its pain and happiness and whatever. This is more about the present, the future even."

"How so?"

"Art, music in this case, offers the possibility to change or reaffirm people's lives, not in the past or because of some kind of penalty or because something is forced upon them. It's… it's the moments of people's lives where everything seems possible, where we step into another place and hold it and carry it with us through the years. I mean, what do we really live for?" Katie shrugs her shoulders. Greg twists his beer glass a half-turn and then drinks. "We eat, drink, sleep, fuck. We go to the grocery store. We pay electric bills. We work. But why? For most people, the point of it all is about having kids and maybe a little fun along the way, but think about it. What do you do when you're depressed?"

"Drink," Katie says without hesitation.

"I'll second that." They clink glasses and smile at each other, and I have to wonder whether I'm convincing anyone of anything.

"Well, yes, there's the desire to deaden the pain, but people listen to music. They play sad songs or angry songs or happy songs to try to lift them up. Do they look at paintings? Do they take the time to read novels in those moments of pain? No. It's music. We play songs again and again. We sing songs again and again. It's a life-sustaining force. $2 + 2 + H = 5$ even though H is literally zero. It's why sometimes a G chord is just a collection of notes and why sometimes it shakes the foundations of the universe."

"The foundations of the universe?"

"Yeah," I shrug my shoulders, "or at least one person's universe, the player, the listener, somebody."

"I don't know. It still seems like you could say that about anything." I'm certainly not convincing Katie. It makes me wonder what music she likes and if it really moves her or if she just thinks it sounds good, if it's just a reason to sing and dance before going on to other things when the music's over.

"Uh, do you remember Yngwie Malmsteen?" I ask. "He could play the guitar well, very well, one of those guys that can play a million notes a minute and all the music theory that goes with it, but his music fell flat. There was no heart in it, no life. It always added up to 4, never 5. He didn't have it."

"Who's Yngwie Malmsteen?"

"Exactly." But in the face of their less than enthusiastic response, I can't help feeling I'm missing something in there, that she's right, that I could say this about anything. It makes me feel good, makes me feel like things transcend, so it must add up to 5 and not 4. It works out too easily, too conveniently, and yet, I know that I'm right. I *know* it, but I feel like a scientist with a hypothesis that is nearly impossible to prove, that must almost be taken on faith. There is a heart inside the artist, inside the musician, buried in those E chords and noticeable to those who really listen, and that heart beats stronger, it soars, it makes us soar. I look at Katie, and she's writing something on a napkin. She gives it to Greg. He reads it, puts it in his wallet, and they smile at each other with the focus of their concerns worlds away from my theories.

I pick up my beer and turn around to look out over the bar. Nirvana comes on the speakers, "All Apologies," and I get to wondering whether there's a Seattle sound out there now. The closest, I suppose, is the alt-country-indie-folksy thing that seems to have more than its share of adherents in this city. One such local band filled the Moore Theater (almost 1,800 capacity) two nights in a row recently, and I don't think many bands in this town could do that even for one night. They also played the Jimmy Fallon Show, and after seeing them at the Moore, I'd give them a fair shot to be the next big Seattle thing. They are called The Head and the Heart, and my favorite song when I saw them was "Rivers and Roads," a quiet number, one of those mellow tunes that has an undeniable power, a song that lifts things as much as it settles them. The audience sang along about missing faces and cheered a little extra when female singer, Charity Rose, sang her solo bits about reaching that elusive "you" that populates so many songs, and she sang with her characteristic lilt, almost like a teenage male voice breaking. The tune ended a cappella with everyone in the theater, yes, everyone, popcorn makers, ushers, ticket takers, people sitting on the crapper, roadies, sound people, *everyone*, hell, even the bums outside who could hear the music bleeding through the walls, singing about those rivers and roads and those missed faces. It was beautiful. It deserved more than 1,800 people. The music indeed had heart, or more like Heart.

There it is, Heart with a capital H. They were the first band that struck me like that when I started writing about music, and to see their popularity in this city, and seemingly others, it was easy to think they might be the next big thing with audience and six band members all singing together, with the acoustics quiet, the shakers quiet, the drums and keyboards quiet, nary a distortion pedal in sight. They seemed to be on the verge of something big, something vocal and loud in its own way. I sang too. It was very real in the moment, but as "All Apologies" comes to a close, I can't help wondering if the moment is over for them, if they'll sustain or fade, if there is something else coming.

CHAPTER 4

AT HOME, I HAVE the Young Evils CD in hand and their set from last night still fresh in my mind, but I place the disc on my desk without even opening it. I rather have the idea running through my brain that memory is like a poem. It isn't a story with the whole plot and all the subplots and minutia. It's just moments, expressions, only some details, a few of them exaggerated and embellished, maybe even made up, others perhaps forgotten. It's free from rhyme and the constraints of form but a poem nonetheless, and here nearing four in the morning, I am reminded of a night a couple weeks ago on which I went to a bar called the Little Red Hen up by Greenlake. I'm not much given for country music, but a co-worker had told me that it's easy to meet women there. "All you have to do is ask one to dance. They're just waiting for it. Ask a few women and you're bound to meet someone you can talk to, and then, well, it's just a matter of talking." I went there on a Friday night seeking something, someone, no one in particular, just someone, but sitting here now alone, it seems a fragmentary experience. It happened, but all I can remember is being

out for a night of country music
at a countrybardrinking and reading
and watching the pre-band dance instruction
at the suggestion of a friend.
The learners step, twirl, slip side to side
as the instructor instructs. Their movement is

a distraction from bookand even beer,
and I realize I like women
too much for depression
to come over one.
There is the blackhairedwoman with legs
and upper body of equal lengths
and hair so straight as mine and hanging,
settling, snaking its way almost down
to her ass as she circles the dance floor.
There is the woman with hair
both blackand blondand withangels
tattooed on her right bicep.
She's wearing a maroon dress
which drops down
just below the knees and lifts
up slightly every time she smiles.

There is the nondancingvoluptuous blond
in an overly tight Lynard Skynard tee shirt
and brown leather boots, middle-aged,
looking from guy to guy for some shred
of hope for the outcomeofthe evening.
She stops to offer me
a smile and I smile too and raise
my glass meaning to ask, "Drink?"
but it comes out like a command,
"Drink!"
or perhaps a statement of the obvious,
the thing I have in my hand,
"Drink."
So she moves over to a tancowboyhat
at the end of the bar
and places a hand on his shoulder.
He doesn't speak. His hand goes up
and the bartender comes over.

There is the brunette, largebreasts
largehips, large lipscoloredscarlet

and leaving remnants
of themselves on her cans
of Rainierbeer as she walks
past our eye contact and out
to the dance floor.

The dancing goes on, the drinks go on and on
and then the night is over, and I sit
in the Jetta in the dark of the wee
hours as the beer still swirls
in my brain, and I contemplate
the swervingquiet of the drive
home where the only woman who matters
is not. She is at her place, alone I imagine,
I hope,
where I have in times
passeddrunk,
slept, and other things,
but where I have not been invited
for far too long, and where her last words
sustain in the deeper parts of me,
"This
just
isn't
working."

And then it does come...
and like a motherfucker

SoIbegin to make drunken promises
in the silence of the car while waving arms
about and speaking to the steering wheel
in the hope that it will relay
one simple message,
"I'm here."
I stop then and wait
for the phone to ring
so I can answer to

that belovedalmostforgotten
voice, "Rob?"
"I'm here."

But there is nosound, nolights
lighting up on my phone,
and my heart stammers, explodes
in the absence and continues
to do so weekly, daily, every hour
of every second,
and will not heal
itselfjustyet,
if ever,
as I still hope
for the hope of the miracle,
still whisper into the dark
of the mornings, days, nights
and latenightdrives home,

"I'm here."

CHAPTER 5

THE FRIDAY AFTER THE YOUNG EVILS' SHOW, I stop at a copy shop before work a little before seven in the morning. I need to have them print and bind a few copies of the book that I'll then send to agents and publishers back east, and perhaps with a little luck, someone somewhere will pick it up and put it out there into the world, and that is the point, or at least part of it. I needed to write it, to get those thousands and thousands of words down, but I didn't do it just to have it sit on my own bookshelf or just to have it reside within the zeroes and ones on my laptop. There's that other part of doing art that is the sharing, the look-at-what-I-did, the hear-what-I-have-to-say bit, the feel-what-I-feel bit. Music is the same way. We don't form bands just to play in the basement while drinking beers after work. We don't record just to listen to ourselves when we're eighty and think, *Man, we rocked!* Maybe that day will come, but we hope a few others along the way will listen, and remember, and say. "Man, you guys rocked!" both in the moment and also those many years later at the pub when two old guys at a corner table can ignore the young beauties and think about all that's been and remember a night many years prior when the music was more than good. "That night was pretty cool, man, pretty cool. Hell, I still put those tunes on from time to time."

Don't misunderstand. It isn't about making millions, though no one would mind that. It's about being heard, even if only by a precious few people, and understood, and remembered for what we had to say during our brief time on stage, and my words come back to me from the other night, "It's about orgasms that change lives." Maybe it is.

I hand the guy at the copy shop a thumb drive and tell him the name of the file, "I need to print and bind five copies of it, that spiral bind you guys do."

"Sure thing, sir." He pulls the file into Word, scrolls down and then back up, pauses, reads the opening sentence, "'It is a simple collection of bones.' Hmm, interesting." He smiles waiting for some kind of response. What can I say? They are old bones, old words, old thoughts, but they are there. I got them down, and they will never get older.

During my lunch break, I pick up the bound copies and walk to the post office in lower Queen Anne where I get in line. There's only one worker behind the counter, and he's asking a woman whether her packages contain any hazardous materials or firearms. I always wonder about that question and just can't believe that anyone would ever answer, "Oh, shit! That's right. You got me. This box has a bunch of guns in it." And yet, the woman at the counter seems to be considering the question or not understanding it. "Could you repeat that, please?" I shake my head knowing I'm going to be here for a while as there are seven people ahead of me, and we all have multiple packages. I should have brought a sandwich. I consider leaving, but I have five copies of the book to send. "I'm sorry, ma'am, your card was declined. Do you have another?" The woman looks in her purse, back at the postal worker, "Could you repeat that, please?" Everyone in line sighs, but we wait, and wait, and wait. No one leaves. It takes about thirty minutes of my life leaking away into nothing before I get to the clerk. I hand him the envelopes I'd filled out in line. He weighs them. "All of them to New York?"

"Yep." He stamps each one. I pay. He drops them in a cart behind him, and it feels as if I've sent five copies of myself out into the world, and old self or not, that's a good feeling, something akin to staring death in the face and saying, "I know you're coming, but you'll never get all of me." It's like being on stage in the brief lull between the end of a song and the audience reaction. It often isn't clear which way it's going to go. Sometimes they clap, sometimes laugh, or nothing, but it doesn't matter. The joy of it is out there. The song is out there, or the story. I open the door to leave the post office.

"Oh, hi."

"Uh, hi." There's an awkward pause as we stare at each other. "You… look… great." She does. She shrugs.

"Thanks."

She's the woman I used to love, the one I thought about during all that talk of humming it in there at the Skylark, a woman I still love for each love gives us something permanent before it fades. And all love fades. It's a thought that saddens me instantly. *All love fades.* I used to know this woman. I used to sleep with her. She inspired the book. We talked naked in bed until all hours, and these days I write and write and am at no loss for words, but meeting her here at the post office and feeling the sadness take hold, I have no idea what to say. I have no apologies to win her sympathy, no declarations of love to win back her heart, no jokes to make her smile. Nothing. I'm empty. I've wondered about this moment so often over the past eight months, thought about the conversation we would have, wondered whether we'd share a coffee or a beer to catch up, maybe hugs and tears and promises to try again, but here, now, there is just this silence hanging from the hinges of the open door.

"…"

I notice she has an envelope in her hand. "Uh, mailing a letter?" I ask. Nothing like stating the obvious. I just want to disappear.

"Yeah."

I step out of her way holding the door open, "The line is long." Again with the obvious, and she's probably wondering why she ever spent any time at all with me. She starts to enter. "Nice to see you."

She nods and steps forward, and then she's in. I'm out. The door closes. It's glass so I can still see her there, envelope in hand, blue jeans on, green coat, black hair hanging halfway down her back. I can't leave just yet. I want to reach out and open the door and do something, say something, anything. The line moves. She steps forward without looking back. There will be no coffee or beer, no tender hugs, no forgiveness. That book is finished. It's on its way to New York.

There's no going back to work after that, so I head over to Alki beach in West Seattle after texting my boss that lunch left a disagreeable feeling in my stomach. He doesn't need to know the truth as bosses tend not to understand the debilitating nature of an empty heart, and besides, my job is utterly dull. I do data entry, document scanning, some editing and reentering of data. Not a day goes by that didn't go by the preceding day, but with the book out there, I want this day to be different. I want to be as far away from a cubicle as I can. I park in front of Starbucks at Alki and then walk up and down the beach where I come across a little kid, maybe ten years old and with no parents in sight. He has a bowl cut of blond hair much as I did at his age. He runs up to me, "Hey, mister!" and flips his middle finger. I say nothing as he runs off laughing. He's got wild arms and an awkward stride, but he's fast and is soon gone. It's one of those odd things that makes me doubt it even happened, and after a few moments, I sit on a bench and disappear as the people and the couples and the dogs go by and by, back and forth, up and down, and the waves swoosh in and roll out. The little boy never comes back, and as the daylight wanes, I wonder what to do with my evening. Sit here? Go to a movie? Home? The girly clubs?

When I get to the Skylark, I park next to a rusting, white minivan, a Ford Windstar. Its engine is running. Inside are Greg, Katie and a woman I don't know. Greg waves and motions for me to get in so I open the door and sit next to him in back. Katie's in the front passenger seat fiddling with CDs. She takes one out of the player and drops it in the cup holder while shuffling through a stack of others, all of them without their cases, some of them probably getting scratched in the process. It always makes me cringe a little to see people treat their CDs as if they aren't the fragile things they are, the fragile things they contain. The other woman is smoking a joint.

"You're late," Greg says.

"Apologies, but I couldn't pry myself away from the beach."

Katie puts a CD in, a mix, someone's idea of the best of Pearl Jam, and the beginning notes of "Who You Are" drift about. It's a song that always makes me feel like I'm at a campfire. Katie turns around.

"This is Lindsay." We nod at each other. Katie takes the joint, puffs, starts to hand it to Greg but then offers it to me.

"Have a hit?"

"He doesn't smoke."

"Not cigarettes," I say taking it, "but I will on rare occasions smoke pot." This is true. I've never understood cigarettes, but over the years, I've known so many musicians who smoked pot and spoke well of its effects that I have been inclined to try it sometimes. It usually just makes me tired, but then I've typically been drunk on those occasions. Maybe since I'm sober now, it'll do its thing. I inhale and cough.

"Easy there," Lindsay says.

"Yeah, man."

"Here." I hand it to Greg, and we all pass it around for a few minutes while the music continues. A car pulls up on the other side of the minivan, and a guy gets out carrying a guitar, walks into the Skylark. A police car drives by but thankfully doesn't turn into the lot. "Indifference" comes on.

"I love this tune," I say. "It's one of Pearl Jam's best."

"Indeed." Katie exhales a cloud of smoke, and we all sing under our breath with the first chorus and wonder how much of a difference anything makes. Greg takes the joint, inhales, hands it to me. "If you knew you were going to die tomorrow, what would you want to do tonight?" The question makes me wonder how much he's already smoked.

"Fuck," Lindsay says.

"Okay. That's obvious. How about other than fucking?"

"I'd work at the bar and give everyone free drinks all night and let the good times roll. Maybe it doesn't seem like much, but it'd be a good way to make a lot of people happy and maybe be remembered."

"I like that," I say. It's the best answer I've ever heard to such a question. Most people go on about sex and the extraordinary bucket-list type stuff, but here she's just saying she'd go to work and ease the pain of others, make their lives easier even as hers was dwindling.

"I'd come for the free drinks." Greg touches Katie's shoulder briefly and then retracts his arm.

"As would I."

Lindsay lights another joint. "I think I'd go out with Larry, probably for pizza. I mean, what better comfort food is there? Hell, maybe
even McDonald's. Why not? Nothing to worry about health-wise.
Then maybe up the Space Needle to look down on it all one last
time. Sex would be unavoidable. How could you not? Maybe even
sex on the Space Needle."

"I don't know what I'd do. It's something that..."

"Something that what?"

"Well, I guess something that scares me."

"What? Sex?" Katie asks.

"Death."

"I always thought that silly. It's unavoidable so why fear it?"

"The finality. The total darkness. The not knowing what comes
next, if anything comes next."

"Nothing comes next," Lindsay assures me. "Here."

"I agree, but that's exactly the fear. There's also the bit about losing
everything in this life, all these years just gone in a breath. To think
about tonight, we're all just sitting here smoking pot. In a hundred
years, we'll all be dead, and who will give a damn that this night
ever happened?" I take a hit, cough. There's a bit of smoke in the
car even though the two front windows are cracked open. I take a
deep breath and look out across the street. There's an old, one-story
brick building nearly overgrown with grass and trees. "I'll lie in bed
and almost shake sometimes for fear and try to wonder if anything
means anything." I realize that I'm speaking slowly, that I'm stoned,
swirling a little, floating a little as Pearl Jam keeps doing its thing,
"Oceans" now. "I mean, look at us here," I continue, "We feel good,
but we all want a little something more, kids or love or money or...
whatever, but even getting all those things, what... what have you
really got? Our hearts will stop one day."

Katie hands the joint to Lindsay. "All the more reason not to
worry," Lindsay says after taking a hit and passing the joint back.

"I fear it sometimes too, who doesn't?" Greg says. "But you're not
answering the question. What would you do?"

Katie holds the joint back while looking straight ahead. I take it
and speak. "Well, a big last act would be meaningless so I guess on
my last night I'd drive out to the beach, not Alki, but the ocean, the
coast, maybe down to Long Beach or on into Oregon and just stare

at the water." I take a hit imagining the scene, the waves on the sand in the sunset, beer in hand as I watch my time slip away. I wonder which songs I'd listen to. "Or maybe I'd stay home and get drunk and write a poem. Maybe solitude is the answer to it all, a certain level of comfort with oneself so that the end can be faced head on without fear."

"For someone who wants solitude, you spend a lot of time out at the pub or seeing bands."

"Yeah, I do. Doubts and fears are hard to face alone. Maybe I would end up at a bar and just play out the night like any other."

"I believe in living in the moment," Lindsay says. "The pleasure principle. Life will have its ups and downs, but so as long as you're happy now, who gives a fuck what happened or what's to come or when you'll die." She snuffs out the joint in the ashtray. "Who's up for pizza?"

"Me."

"Hell yeah. Talarico's?" Greg loves Talarico's. It's one of those places that have the New York style monster-size slices that are the equivalent of a whole pizza at some places.

"I'd love to, but I need to get in and get settled at the bar. I decided to write about the show tonight so I think I'll just eat here."

"Sure? We can bring you back some pizza." Katie smiles when she offers this, and for half a second I almost think it's what she wants, to come back here to see me after food, but that must be the pot speaking. She isn't in my cards. She and Greg are on the verge of something. I'm just taking notes.

"No thanks."

"Okay. We'll see you in a bit."

CHAPTER 6

"YOU'RE GOOD, MAN," says the guy working the door at the Skylark before stamping my hand. This isn't the most popular club in town, but I still feel quite privileged to have a place where I can get in free for any show I want, and though they aren't exactly my friends, I know the bartenders, the owner, the door guy, the sound guy. I'm on the edge of their community, welcome but still left to my own devices. When I get to the bar, Jessie has a Manny's waiting for me at the usual spot. She smiles and goes on about her business, and I see Faustine from the Young Evils sitting next to an open seat. She has her hair pulled back into a ponytail, a few tattoos down her arms, a red and blue dress over black pants, brown boots. She looks almost as if she's ready for a gig.

"Hi. Good show the other night."

"Hey, yeah, you're that writer guy, right?"

"That's me. Rob." We shake hands. "Sorry I had to duck out after the show before I got the chance to say hello. I had to collect my thoughts and write a little bit."

"No problem. Did you get a CD from Mackenzie?"

"Yeah, I did. So how'd you get into music anyway? Sorry, I know it's the obvious question, but I'm always intrigued at such. There are a million different paths in life so I'm curious about the why, and why people stick with it."

Faustine thinks for a moment before speaking. "My first crack at playing music was when I was mimicking playing guitar with a broom at the age of three, even got pictures to prove it."

"Nice. Yeah, I remember the broomstick days too, and the days when the vacuum cleaner was just tall enough to be a mic stand. I'd pretend to be Robin Zander and sing 'Surrender' and 'Ain't That a Shame' while holding onto the handle for dear life before my mother would knock on my bedroom door and ask me to vacuum the living room. That tended to kill the spirit of it."

"First rock moments interrupted by mom, funny. Anyway, I guess the real answer is that my dad played. He and a few buddies started a Friday jam night in this big warehouse space in Redmond when I was eight or nine. I would run around the whole place getting into my own debauchery and playing pretend while these four or five dudes would play their favorite covers, things like Pink Floyd, the Allman Brothers, the Rolling Stones, basically the classic rock stuff. I would always hassle them to let me sit in, and I remember those nights being really, uh, vivid, like there was a little more color to everything." 2 + 2 = 5. *It's true.* "Hearing those songs over and over again at home and then those guys playing them at the warehouse, I was pretty stoked. I just kind of took to it. It sunk in. I'd sit down behind my dad's drum kit and bang for a while, and my dad would tell me, 'Don't play them if you can't feel it.' But I did feel it. I still do, so here I am twenty years later sitting behind the kit."

"Or dancing on the stage with a tambourine and a shaker like the other night."

"Yeah, that was an unusual show."

"Fun, though."

"Congrats on finishing a book."

"Thanks. So what exactly do you mean when you say you 'feel it'?"

"I suppose I mean an outlet of emotions, or something for me to do where I can just be me and share what I feel through the drums. It's hard to explain. I suppose it's been the best therapist. Every gig, every practice I walk away feeling some sort of relief and release of emotions or things that I have perhaps kept to myself. I spend a lot of time listening to music and thinking about it. There are times where I am not playing enough, and I don't realize it until I step fully back into it and walk away feeling that release. It's like having great sex. You feel confident, beautiful, in love and humbled. You are swept away in a moment of passion. It just happens to be music that you are making love with."

"You're right about the sex bit." She is. Sex. Music. There's a definite release, *orgasms that change lives,* vibrations deep within all present, even in rehearsal, but the live show is the thing. The Gig. I love recording. I love playing at home alone or at practice when I have a band, but even with all my doubts, live is where the biggest fires happen, the good and the bad, the performance, the give and take with the audience, the exchange. Writing is a one-way street.

Her phone buzzes with a text message so I drink and watch the night's first band set up for their sound check. She types a response to someone, then stands up. "Sorry, but I gotta go. Meeting a friend for pizza. I'll catch you around." We shake hands again, and she's off.

The band that did the sound check earlier is called Like Lightning. They are the first of three acts tonight, and when they go on, they take the stage quickly and get right to it without a word. There is a woman playing a keyboard and singing. The guitar and bass come in simply, and the vocals, "Every day felt like a dark horse..." Indeed, many of them do, sometimes the months as well, and the song ends soon enough, and I have a few more beers and Jessie smiles. "Thanks for all the writing you do about the bands here. It helps get the word out. Next one's on me." Live music. Beers, some of them complimentary, smiling bartenders and bar owners. In such moments, it's easy to forget that feeling I had on the beach earlier, or the fears mentioned in the car. I can feel almost happy. The music of the next song goes on with a building repeated chord progression, just A to F#, A to F#, and the vocals over and over. "I'll never be the same." A to F#. "I'll never be the same." I never fail to be amazed when musicians can take only a couple simple chords and one phrase and through the act of repetition build it into something so much more than the sum of its parts. It's only two simple chords and a phrase, but it is *music.* The more it repeats, the less repetitive it gets. "I'll never be the same." Neither will I. Art will do that. A painting. A poem. A D chord pumped through an overdriven tube amplifier. They all change the heart and mind and soul when done right, and I think of the woman I saw at the post office. We never are the same from art or love. A touch, a shiver of the spine, an orgasm and an opening of the heart, a changed person. A melody, a few chords, a new perspective.

The singer's voice reminds me of someone, and it bothers me through the set. It is a good reminder, a compliment, but I can't place it, and the music and the beers go on until there comes a tune that starts with a quiet piano, the snare more keeping time than a beat, some bass, some guitar fading in and out. The vocals come in softly, and then there is a drop and the snare rolls and there is build and the voice: "I don't want to disappear." It comes to me. Her voice reminds me of Markéta Irglová from *Once*. I love that movie and its music. Like Lightning has the exact same kind of deeply honest pop feel but with a little more edge, a little distortion on the guitar, a solo, and then into the last verse.

> *This is where we go wrong*
> *We are here and in a blink*
> *We are gone…*

It drops then. There is only snare and vocal, that same line, "I don't want to disappear… I don't want to disappear…" The line moves, the line gives strength as it repeats. *I don't want to disappear.* A song like this with a voice like that makes me almost hopeful, almost strong enough to believe in the now, and maybe even the future. The audience applauds.

"Thanks. We're Like Lightning. We'll see you next time."

With the music ended, the feeling subsides, a little at first, a little with each breath, a tiny gas leak, a hiss, and then the inevitable explosion. Maybe that's why we listen to songs again and again, and again, the junkie's quick fix for what music does to the brain. The singer makes her way to the other end of the bar so I walk over, pen and notebook in hand, meaning to introduce myself, but I skip right to the song. "Loved that last tune. What was it called?" She's thin, long brown hair, good piano hands, long fingers with a wide reach. She adjusts her glasses.

"Disappear."

"I should have guessed. I'm here writing about tonight. Could I get a set list?"

"And you are?"

"Rob. Rob from Seattle Subsonic. I'm writing about tonight."

"Yeah, you said. I'm Stephanie."

"You mind if I get the lyrics to that last tune, and maybe a set list too?"

"No problem."

She writes in my notebook, and I interrupt with questions. "I'm curious. How would you describe your sound?"

"Well, keyboard and guitar driven pop, I guess. I like to think people might compare it to a little Cocteau Twins or Aimee Mann. Ha, maybe you can tell my age by my references. And maybe a little Golden Palominos or perhaps some of Sia's stuff. Those popped into my mind just now, though I have no objectivity to say that's what we sound like. I mean, do any musicians really describe themselves well? I heard a band once describe themselves as cosmic punk. What the hell does that even mean?"

"Not a clue."

"I guess by mentioning certain bands, I'm telling you more of what I'm into rather than what we actually sound like. People compare based on what they know and like, so if you're writing about us, I'll leave the comparisons up to you. I'd like to know what you think."

"Fair enough." She gets back to writing the lyrics for "Disappear," something I seem unable to let her finish. "I remember an interview with Eric Clapton in which he said that when he was learning how to play guitar, he'd play along with old records he had and that he knew his playing was awful, nothing near what was coming out of the speakers, but he kept at it and eventually there was a day when he realized he was playing every bit as good as those old records and probably even better, and in that moment he knew he had something magical."

"Interesting."

"You ever have a similar experience?"

"Ha! I'm still waiting for that moment, which I guess means I'm still unsure of whatever talent I may have. We've all had those times where we've played something magical as you say, either alone or with a band, but I think that just makes us realize how much more there is to learn. Those moments are what keep us going actually. Why keep playing if it never happens? For me, I simply feel driven by curiosity toward new musical experiences and have been compelled by my own ambitions and ego, sad to admit. As I get older, the former seems to be the dominating motivator, but when I was younger, I was very much the egoist."

"Yeah, when I first started playing, I developed a bit of an ego, but I quickly got over it."

"How so?"

"I started to play guitar when I was in seventh grade, and after I learned a few chords and a few songs, I started to think I did it better than I really did, thought I was pretty damn good actually, and pretty cool. So one day a friend of mine came over, and we were in my room just hanging out, and he pointed to the guitar suggesting that I play something. I grabbed a pick and sat on the bed with the guitar in my lap and then banged out the first few chords of Quiet Riot's 'Metal Health'."

"Now, there's one I haven't heard in a while."

"Yeah, me too, but on that day, I had the song blaring in my head and barely listened to what I was actually playing, and so I felt like quite the rocker until I saw the look on my friend's face, and he was just like, 'What the hell is that?' and I had no idea what to say because I knew instantly that I'd fucked it up, that I wasn't close at all to making actual music."

"Wrong chords?"

"Tuning. I'd just never bothered much to learn that all-important tuning bit, but I vowed to myself right then and there that I would. And I did, but I never played for that guy again. Hell, to this day he probably still thinks that I absolutely suck." I wonder about that and remember the Third Stone gig long ago with its bad notes, *my* bad notes, and the doubts come back as they so often do. Maybe I do suck. Maybe that's why I hit those bad notes sometimes. Not fear, not doubt, but lack of ability, lack of courage.

"Some people wilt in those moments and run away. Nice that you kept with it."

"I know what you're saying about ego though. It does take a certain amount of ego to step on a stage, and that has nothing to do with whatever doubts or talent one may I have."

"True, true. Here are the lyrics and set list for you. I have to go help load the van. Nice meeting you."

Stephanie and the rest of Like Lightning leave, and I'm alone again and wondering what to do with the rest of the night but knowing I should probably just go home. I've filled up on music and talk and beer and even pot. My phone vibrates. It's Greg so I step outside to take it.

"Hey, man, we're on our way back. Lindsay wants to meet up with her boyfriend so she's going to drop us off there."

"That's cool. I'm pretty much done here though. Maybe we can just go back to my place."

"Works for me. We'll be there soon."

I go back in and wait, but feel myself starting to drift off to sleep, so I settle up my tab and head back out thinking I shouldn't have smoked that much. They arrive in ten minutes. Greg and Katie get out of the car. Lindsay waves as she drives off.

"Man, you look tired."

"Drunk. High."

"I'll drive," Katie says.

"Sure." I hand my keys to her and wonder how much pot she's smoked, how much alcohol she drank during dinner. I don't have the answers for this, and I don't ask, but she seems fine. We get in my car and drive with the windows down. Greg directs Katie to my apartment while I just take in the fresh air. Near my place there's a 7-Eleven, and seeing its sign shine beacon-like in the night, I ask, "You guys want to get some beer?"

"Yeah, man, you got any money?"

"Sure." I hand Greg a twenty as we pull into the parking lot. While they're in the store, I stare out the window at the Red Box DVD rental machine out front. There's a young black couple there tapping away in search of a movie. They're laughing. The woman points to the screen to suggest something. I miss what she says, but the guy's response is loud and clear.

"Hell, no. I ain't watching that shit." She doesn't take offense at his honesty. They just keep looking for a movie, and now he has his arm around her. I wonder how their night will go. Will the movie be good? Will it lead to other things? He reaches down and grabs her ass. She playfully swats his hand away without taking her eyes off the screen. "How about this one?"

"Did you miss us?" Greg and Katie are back with the beer.

"Of course."

We get to my place with a twelve pack of Blue Moon, which is my go-to for bottled beer. It's lighter than Manny's, much less hoppy, a little citrusy. It's a Belgian white and is possibly the most refreshing beer I've ever had. "I also have some soju if you guys are interested," I say as I put the beer in the fridge.

"I suppose as a bartender I should know, but what's soju?"

"It's a Korean rice-based alcohol somewhat like vodka. It's good, and it's relatively cheap."

"It's also a good way to get a hangover, but what the hell. Fire it up."

"Hey, this is awesome," Katie says touching the little statue of a bass-playing dragon on my desk. She doesn't mention the picture of the woman next to it. "Can I have it?"

"Uh, no."

"I'll buy it. How much you want for it?"

"Not for sale."

"Yeah, man, it is cool. When did you get that? I don't remember it."

"I've had it for a while, but it was back in the other room. This is a shoeless house by the way." It's a habit I picked up in Korea.

"No problem," Katie says. I bring three bottles of soju and three shot glasses to the coffee table. She picks up one bottle. "These aren't very big."

"Hence the need for three. Don't worry. I have more."

She reads the label slowly. "*Chami... sul*. What's that mean?"

"Morning dew."

"More like morning hangover. Last time we had this stuff, I was just done the next day, wiped out," Greg says as I pour out three shots. He takes his without hesitation. "Cheers." We drink. Greg motions for another shot. "Put some music on, man."

Katie pours the second round, and I forage through my CDs, all in their cases, all on the shelf, all except for one, Radiohead's *I Might Be Wrong*, which is a collection of live recordings from *Kid A* and *Amnesiac* and one previously unreleased track that is just Thom Yorke singing and playing acoustic guitar. I never really understood Radiohead until I saw a live performance of theirs on TV of a show they did somewhere in France, maybe Paris, not sure, and the set list, like *I Might Be Wrong*, included only songs from *Kid A* and *Amnesiac*, and it was the live essence that drew me in, was something I'd missed in their studio recordings. When *I Might Be Wrong* was released in November of 2001, I bought it the first day, rushed home, put it on. I turned it louder and louder with each song, and with my eyes closed and the speakers nearly full blast, I felt as if I were at the show. I did the same for the next few days and often enough ever since. Unfortunately though, I've misplaced the CD. It isn't in its case. It isn't in any case I've looked in for the past few weeks, and I've looked in almost all of them. It isn't in my car or laptop. It isn't anywhere, but I know it's here, somewhere. With company, I don't have time to look for it now, so I opt for something else. "Check this out." I put a CD in and click forward to track three. There's an acoustic guitar, then a voice, a deeply beautiful female voice singing of a place in Mexico. We listen and drink.

"This is pretty cool. Who is it?" Greg asks.

"Kristen Ward with a guy named Gary Westlake on guitar. It's local stuff." I hate qualifying things like that, but it's true. They've never heard this before. Few have, but millions should.

"It's kind of sad," Katie says, and she's right. I know this might not be the best music for a late-night drinking party, but I can't help it. I wallow in this sometimes. "How'd you find this?"

"I saw her back in January and wrote about the show."

"I remember that article."

"I'd like to check it out."

"I'll send you a link."

We sit and drink and listen to the CD. Katie and Greg talk some, but I don't pay much attention to the conversation. I just sit with the CD cover in my hands. There's a human-sized heart resting on the back of a bird with blue wings that are extended up cradling their burden, a rose on either side of the bird. It's very cool and fits perfectly with the content of the CD, acoustic tunes, songs of broken love and loss and longing. Good stuff, mellow, melancholy. It doesn't feel contrived at all. Her voice is low, the heartache palpable.

When the CD gets back around to the first track, Greg gets three more bottles from the fridge and we let the aching voice do its thing. And it does. The song ends wondering how love ends up the way it does, over, and that's it, a line of lament without any resolve. It's a perfect way to capture the feeling. The broken heart wants the last goodbye, the last moment, something, anything, but so often it isn't there. It just ends, nothing tied off, nothing resolved, just lives going in different directions, one glad for it, one left wondering where it all went wrong.

The tunes go on, and there comes one called "Die of a broken heart" that is about just that. It reminds me of the feeling I had on the beach, after leaving the post office. When I saw Kristen play this song, the audience was transfixed by the quiet intimacy of the moment. There was no other sound in the world but those acoustic guitars, that aching voice singing of a broken heart and the knowledge of the death it would cause. The place was silent, and then there was me. I felt the same as the words, and I wanted to scream with what was going through my mind. There was the song with its minor chords and its longing and loss and despair, and there was the other sound in my head. I couldn't help it. My brain just went the way of imagining my ex-love having sex and sex and sex. It was loud, much louder than I had experienced, and she was passive in my imaginings, spoke only things like, "Where do you want me?" or "Like this?" but mostly she just moved and moaned to the imaginary man's requests, verbal and otherwise. "Turn around… get on your knees… bend this way…" It was every position in every place. Up, down, front, back, kitchen counter, kitchen floor, shower, balcony, not giving pleasure, just receiving it in every possible way, and enjoying it, relishing in it, getting lost in it, so much so that memory of those who came before was lessened if not completely forgotten. I can't hear this song and not think about that, and maybe it's unhealthy, but I come back to it again and again and again even though I imagine her getting it again and again and again.

"Where do you want me?"

"Bend over…"

There are the chords of the verse, A minor, C, G. The progression goes a few times over, then an F, and then the broken heart.

This just isn't working.

I drain my glass.

"She sounds so sincere," Katie says. The song ends with an acoustic solo over those simple chords. It's tasteful. Beautiful. Mournful. The longing bleeds from each note, and I feel like crying. "You ever had your heart broken?" It's a silly question, but then it isn't, and anyway I'm not sure whether she's speaking to Greg or me or both of us.

"Everybody's has," I say.

"He still has one."

"Is it true?"

"Yeah." And I wallow in it, but I don't want to disappear.

"Oh, that's right. I remember. I'm sorry."

I wake up later on the floor. Greg and Katie are asleep on the couch. He has his arm around her. There is a bottle of soju next to me, tipped over but empty. We killed it, number seven I think. Looking at them on the couch, I notice her feet for the first time, and her crunched-up toes, the big ones seeming a little too big and the others a little too small and scrunched, and there's a smell. Is it her feet? Did someone vomit somewhere? I struggle up and walk to the refrigerator and grab a couple beers. I open one and drop the cap on the counter then walk over to the window and raise the blind, and there it is. A fence. My apartment is on the first floor of a corner house with a six-foot fence around it so that I have no view. That's okay, though. When I'm home, I keep the windows closed and the blinds drawn, and music becomes my connection to the outside world.

Leaving the blind up, I open the door, step outside, and feel the pavement of the stoop cool on my feet. It makes me look at my toes. I set the unopened beer down in front of the door and open the gate, step out to the sidewalk, look up the street and down. I love this, the quiet wee hours out of doors, the occasional car or dog barking, the cats and the raccoons spying from the bushes, the late-night arguments from the place across the street. They're at it now. I can't make out their words, just the tone, the unmistakable sound of anger and resentment, maybe even regret. There's the shadow of a man in the window. He raises his hand but not in a manner of violence.

I imagine his words, "How can you be so stupid?" or "What the hell is wrong with you?" He moves away from the window, and there's a pause. Maybe it's over for the night, and then a blue Honda drives past and parks on the street a half block up. A couple gets out laughing. They pause near the car, and I think they might kiss, but the woman takes off running toward the third house up from mine with the guy close behind. There's a shriek of joy. Then there's quiet. It's a beautiful thing to witness, but I wonder if they fight too.

I look back toward downtown and there's the Space Needle in the distance. I remember a night up there with, well, with her. Or maybe Her with a capital beginning. I like that better than her actual name. It feels like an important step toward the abstract, toward getting over it. A name might give power, but a pronoun only gender.

An old man took our picture up on the observation deck, but I resist the urge in this moment to pull out my phone and look at it. Instead I turn to go back inside, but I hear sounds and through the window see Greg and Katie in the beginning movements of passion. He's behind her but has his hand down her pants, her arm up over her head, fingers running through his hair, so I don't go in. I just stand outside and hope it ends soon. I give in then. I look at the picture of us on the Space Needle. It was a June day last year. The sun was out. The clouds were gone, the magic with us for a moment.

All sound stops then, well, except for that ringing, my old friend tinnitus. At times it blocks all else while its own volume goes up. I shake my head a little in an attempt to make it lessen, but it doesn't, so I try to hone in on the note, a C# I think. Or a D. Sometimes those semitones are difficult to decipher. The sound goes up a bit more, and my ears hurt a little in the absence of all other sounds. They strain for something, anything, the clink of a bottle set on cement, the *ting ting ting* of a beer cap flicked out to the street, the hushed moans of passion from within my apartment, but there's nothing. There are headlights a few blocks up, but they turn soundlessly onto a side street, and I begin to wonder if this is it, the end of sound, alone in the early morning hours and in all the days to come, broken and deaf. My fingers make the imagined chord, a D. My right hand makes a strumming motion hoping to get it right. There is each imagined individual note. D. A. D. F#. And it's there, a breeze, a slight rustle of the trees, a couple of cats fighting somewhere.

I look back at the city, across the street, up the street, back to my place. There's love everywhere even if it's shattering at times, even if it's broken and lost. What was once there will always be in one form or another. Maybe it's a fool's thought, but I cling to it. I sip my beer, and the light across the street goes off. I'm the last one here, the last one up. I always am because I'm afraid to fall asleep. I don't want to disappear. I don't want to die alone in silence. I look up at the trees, the houses, the parked cars and sing a little, "I don't want to disappear." My voice is flat and wavering, but I continue in a whispered way, "I don't want to disappear."

No, I do not, but in the silences of such moments, and the now very audible sounds coming from my apartment, I do very much doubt my strength in the matter.

Chapter 7

She once asked over tacos,
"So what did you have going
on last night?"
I'd fiddled on the acoustic
playing and singing the Scorpions
"Holiday," a favorite of hers,
I'd written a poem about my family's
first dog, Buttons, nearly bit
in half by a large neighborhood
canine, my first experience
with death.
I'd stared at the stars with beer
in hand far into the wee hours.
All miraculous
things, and I told her such,
but the real answer was that
without her that night I had
nothing.

Now, there is
only the sound of the keys
clicking
clicking
clicking
as I type

and
type and
type
to drown out
the questionless
silence.

The beer bottles
fill the counter
the floor
the table
the nightstand
the soul
so that only
the emptiness
remains.

One night can last a thousand
years, and we had a whole year
of those nights atop the Space Needle,
the pinnacle, a moment that dripped
with goodness.

An old timer up there
offered to take our picture,
to capture the millennium with the press
of a wrinkly finger to the screen
of my phone.
And the finger
pressed, the finger captured,
and a night turned into a lifetime
to be gazed at, longed for years
from now when wrinkly myself
I pull past lives from a box
and say to anyone
who will listen,

"She was the one!"

She slept next to me
that night, and I thought
my life complete,
and it was,
to watch her sleep soundly naked
under no covers, to see her breathe,
exhale,
breathe again
as my body got ready for one more
time, one more
millennium,
with everything,
if only for a while,
in its right place.

CHAPTER 8

I HAVE A PRINTED copy of the book with me at the Beveridge Place. It's changed since I last sent it out to New York, so I need to go over it one more time before I visit the post office again, and well, it's easier to read on paper. There's no glare from the screen, no eye fatigue. The words in my hands are solid things to grab and hold up in the light as if examining a hundred dollar bill to see whether it's counterfeit. Typos and grammar errors are more easily caught as well, and there's the feel of it. Turning page after actual page gives the illusion that it's close, that it's already a book. Unpublished, I know it's just a story, a simple mass of words, but the illusion takes hold, and I imagine wandering in the fiction section of Barnes & Noble, pausing at such names as McCarthy and Murakami, and then doing a full stop at my own.

Katie and Greg are out somewhere on a date, dinner and karaoke, so I'm here alone reading and editing and looking around at the patrons in their groups of two and three and four all smiling and drinking and making whatever they can of this moment in their own lives, and in their absence, I'm happy for my friends in their newfound coupleness. It's only been a week, but I wonder how they get along when alone, if they fight. I finish reading the first hundred pages and then pay up and head out to the Jewelbox Theater in Belltown where a band called the Jesus Rehab is playing. I love that name. When I came across it—on a flyer stapled to a telephone pole—I knew I wanted to see them. After an easy drive in from West Seattle, I park on 2nd Avenue only a block down from the club and before getting out of the car, I notice the pages there on the passenger seat and decide to bring them into the show. Maybe there'll be more time to read before the music starts or when the music's over.

The Jewelbox is a small theater in the back of the Rendezvous Restaurant and Lounge and dates back to 1927. In fact, the theater used to show talkies, which is pretty damn cool, and to get to it, one has to walk in and turn right past the Rendezvous bar, which I do, pausing of course to get a drink, and then back to a couple of closed doors that give the illusion of entering a movie house. There's a sign on the left door with the band's name and picture. The cover charge is written in bold black marker: "$5.00." The girl working the door sees me looking at the sign and speaks when I step forward.

"I think the first band just finished their set. The Jesus Rehab should go on in about fifteen minutes or so."

"Okay."

"You can go in now if you want or maybe wait at the bar." The doors open then and about thirty people come slowly out to have drinks or go outside for a smoke. Among the crowd is a tall pale woman, thin with blond hair and wearing a Cheap Trick tee shirt, who seems to be alone. She makes her way to the bar, takes a seat, orders something, starts tapping on her phone. I turn back to the woman at the door.

"I'm on the list." I give her my name, and she grabs the stamper, dabs it on a red ink pad, and marks the inside of my left wrist, "PAID." I go in, and it's dark, movie theater dark, but thankfully there is a candle on each table and some light from the stage. Both members of TJR, it's only a guitar and drum duo, are up there plugging in amplifiers and arranging drums while the sound guy places microphones for the snare and kick. The room is too small to need anything else on the kit. After tapping the vocal mic a couple times, he walks up the center aisle and out of the theater, and watching him, I look to the back corners of the room. I'm surprised to see no mixing board but notice a light coming from an opening in the top left corner of the back wall. Ah, the old projection room. I wonder what this place was like back in 1927 as I'm pretty sure there was a speakeasy here during prohibition. What must have gone on in this very room, the drinking, the dancing, the music. I order another beer from a waitress, five dollars plus a buck tip. There's a shadow in the projection room, and then a face in the hole, the sound guy peeking through it. Up there? The mixing board is up there? That gives me a bad feeling about how the mix might turn out. That room is too high, too removed from the actual sound.

I place my things on a table about halfway back and sit down to read a little more by candlelight before the band begins but promptly knock over my beer, which promptly soaks the pages. So much for reading. The waitress isn't around so I walk out to the bar and grab a stack of cocktail napkins that are in front of the woman in the Cheap Trick tee shirt. When she looks up, there's an awkward moment of eye contact, so I speak. "Hi."

"Hi."

She looks back down to her phone and starts typing what I assume is a text message, so I head back into the theater and get to cleaning. When I'm done, the waitress appears. "Oh, I'm sorry. Need another?" I answer in the affirmative, and she's off quickly leaving the soiled napkins and the empty glass on the table. I push them to the edge and touch my printed pages wondering if I should have left them in the car, but think not. They are just pages. They can be reprinted if more beer comes their way, and it doesn't really matter because beer and the written word go well together. Maybe the combination will give me some sort of insight.

When TJR hits the stage, they open with a song called "Carry You." It starts with a couple big chords, some pauses. It's heavy with crunch and tone, much more tone than other local guitar and drum duos that I've heard. There is a band called My Goodness that's getting some airplay on KEXP and had an in-studio performance there, but the one time I saw them, there was a huge hole in the sound, a bass-shaped hole. There was guitar. There were drums. But there was nothing in between, and it quickly got old and repetitive, sounded like the bass player forgot to show up that day as they did little to account for the absence of lower frequencies. Maybe it was because I play bass, but I just couldn't get into the music. There's also a woman named Betsy Olson who does a similar thing, just guitar and drums. She's also had an in-studio at KEXP. Someone recommended her to me so I watched the video of the in-studio on YouTube and then, uncharacteristically, listened to some of her studio recordings before seeing her live. It was the studio recordings that surprised me because there was bass. It filled out the sound and gave it life. It was cool, but at her live show the bass was not there. It vanished, perhaps spontaneously combusted like the Spinal Tap drummer, and left just guitar and drums in its wake. I had the same reaction as I did to My Goodness. There was, again, a huge hole in the sound that someone needed to fill. Alas, no one did. The music fell flat. I asked Betsy after the show about not having a bass player live. "Sara—she's the drummer—and I feel like we have enough energy without it." I had to disagree, but I didn't say so. Rather I asked her that if they had enough energy live, why had they added bass in the studio. "We thought it filled up the sound." She was smiling, apparently unaware of the contradiction, unaware that without the bass her music suffered, especially live.

When I wrote about that, I thought again that it might just have been because I play bass. Maybe I was biased, was just looking for something to criticize, playing the role of the music critic in too ordinary a fashion. Maybe I was falling away from music, losing some perspective on what's good, new, interesting, on what pushes envelopes into new territory. I wondered late into some nights while listening to My Goodness and Betsy Olson with a growler of Manny's if I was missing something. But after a few growlers, I knew the answer. I wasn't missing anything. They were.

I smile in the moment to remember that because hearing The Jesus Rehab rip through "Carry You" right now confirms that I was correct. There's no bass, but the sound is full. It tilts and swells. It's filling, like a hearty helping of lasagna. Jared Cortese runs his Les Paul through both a guitar amp and a bass amp, adds different eq to each, a few effects, and voila, a rich full sound. It's the drummer, too, though. His younger brother, Dominic, plays rhythms and grooves, but he also fills out spaces where they need to be. They're aware that there is no bass, and though they don't fill the space in the same way a bass player would, they fill it nonetheless. And there's Jared singing over a G, an E, a D, "I want to carry you. I want to CAR-RY you." He is. They are. People move to the front to dance and shake their bodies. By the last chorus, the audience is singing along. "I want to carry you. I want to CAR-RY you." And they are. Band lifts audience. Audience lifts band.

And it's beautiful, tone enough to eat. It feels like it's dripping from my notebook and being absorbed in the moisture from the bottom of my pint glass. TJR eventually closes with a number called "Spaceships" that has a slight kind of Queen feel in the bounciness of the chords in the verse, something like "Killer Queen." The song builds, heavy at times, until an instrumental bit that qualifies as nothing short of BIG, heavy chords, chunking, throbbing, C to G, A to E, E minor to B, resolving on G, and then the music comes down. Jared switches his sound so that it's only going through the bass amp. The tone descends, as does the volume, but the energy is there. We know it's coming back. It's just a dynamic shift, one more way TJR is a master of their sound, and then the guitars, yes, seemingly plural, but still undistorted, still building, pausing, singing, "All those spaceships in her head, all those spaceships in her head." The crowd up front swells. The guitars swell. The drums swell. All movement in the room becomes circular. "All those spaceships in her head, spinning round and round and round and round and round and round." Jared steps on his distortion pedal, and the crowd moves in the same pattern as the chords and the vocals and the sound waves, "and round and round and round and round and round…"

After the show, I head back out to the bar and see the woman in the Cheap Trick tee shirt sitting in the same spot, and empowered by the good vibe of the music, I sit next to her. "Hi. You were sitting out here before. Did you miss the show?" Only good music can do this to me.

"No, I saw it."

"What'd you think?"

"It was my first time, but I liked them."

"First time? What made you come?"

"I frequent a coffee shop where Dominic works, and he pestered me to come check it out. What about you?"

"I'm here to write about them."

"Oh, that's you, the writer guy. Dominic said someone was going to come out to write about the show. He wrote the name of your website on the back of a flyer."

"Which website?"

"Seattle Subsonic."

Seattle Subsonic isn't mine actually, but I'm the only writer still posting there. The guy who runs it recently had a kid and has been too busy to do much. He even stopped sending suggested writing assignments, so now I just contact bands directly or work out deals with bars like the one I have with the Skylark. The other Subsonic writers were people who thought it'd be cool to write about music and get into shows for free, but they came and went quickly after realizing that it's work with little reward and even less pay. It wasn't the writing that held meaning for them. To look at the site now, the front page is a collection of only my reviews, Like Lightning, the Young Evils, Sightseer, Witchburn, In Cahoots, Bone Cave Ballet, and given the personal nature of the writing, it's probably easy for someone to think the whole site is mine, my story of sorts through music, and really it is in a way. I have taken over. "Yep, that's it."

"So I checked it out and liked that review you wrote about Sightseer. The song you linked to was cool. What was it called again?"

"Biggest Storms."

"Yeah, that's right. Think I'll check them out sometime. It actually got me thinking I should get out to see more bands which is partially why I made a point to come out tonight."

"Glad I could help."

"I was actually supposed to meet someone here for a first date, Match.com. Don't ask. Anyway, he didn't show up, but that's fine. I enjoyed the show. How'd you find the band?"

"I liked the name when I saw a flyer posted for this show."

"Yeah, the name thing is cool. Time for Jesus to get a little rehab."

"I like that. Maybe I'll use it when I write about them."

"If you do, you'd better give me credit."

"Indeed, I will." She sips her drink. I order one. I want to ask about Cheap Trick because I love that band, but it seems an obvious route, the tee shirt connection. She seems comfortable coming to a show alone, even if that wasn't exactly the plan. Many women might not. I wonder if she's a musician. "So, do you play an instrument?"

"Me? No, I paint."

"I'm no good with visual art. That's why I write and play music. How'd you get into painting?"

"I think I needed my own way of coloring the world. I tend to paint things from my life, but I don't want to say it's a way of capturing a memory because that's impossible. The details of memory are too fleeting. I guess it's like trying to describe a dream to your lover in the moment you wake up. You shake them and start to speak, but it's impossible. I guess we feel the need to try because we feel like we know something even if we don't know what that is."

"I agree." It dawns on me that the past might indeed be a changeable thing. Like describing a dream, it's never the same. We invariably alter and embellish either intentionally or because we can't quite remember, and once we've started the story, we don't want to stop, and then this new version becomes reality, reality the dream, at least in the moment of telling, but if you write it down, or paint it, the moment hardens, the fictional solidifies, the actual withers. "I've recently been thinking about how two plus two can equal five in the sense that art can alter perception."

"It can. I painted a picture once of a bench in Central Park in New York. I went there about four years ago with my then boy-friend and afterward wanted to capture the moment of walking in the park on a beautiful day, so I painted a picture with sun and trees. It was a simple scene, and there was a bench next to the path but no people around. It was a wood bench for two people, and it was old and scratched, weather beaten, but there was no graffiti on it. A bird was sitting on the handrail looking away, maybe just about to take flight, but it hadn't yet, and everything was blended together, sun with sky, trees with grass, bird with bench. Things were clear but the lines of distinction were blurred in the oranges, browns, blues and greens. When I showed it to my boyfriend, he said he remembered us sitting on the bench, but the thing is, we didn't. I made it up. It was just a symbol, but in seeing the picture he got it into his head that it was real, that we'd seen it and paused in front of it before sitting down, and the funny thing is that I have a hard time now remembering that. Sometimes even I think it was real."

"Did you tell him it wasn't?"

"Nope, never did. He seemed to like the idea so why bother?"

"I know the feeling from similar moments with my writing. I'd love to see that painting sometime."

"Sure. If you look me up on Facebook, there's a photo of it there I think. I'm Elena." We shake hands. "I'm in the list of Dominic's friends." I smile to think that's the modern day equivalent of saying you're in the book.

"Can I buy you a drink?"

"Sorry, but I've got to get going. Maybe some other time. Nice meeting you though."

"Sure." We shake hands, she goes, and I don't even mind. For a brief moment, I almost feel famous as I look around the bar, notebook in one hand, beer in the other. She knew who I was by my writing, a recognition of sorts, the first ever one, and the phrase goes through my head, *the writer guy*, and that's what I am in this moment. That's all I am, not a musician, not a lover, and that makes me think of another name I have, Ex. There's a cliff somewhere on the edge of heartbreak, maybe just off the curb in front of my apartment on those late nights where one slip can turn Ex into any number of bad things. Obsessive Ex. Suicidal Ex. Asshole Ex. Stalker Ex. I haven't stepped off that cliff yet, but I know it's there beckoning for a bit of lunacy that reaches for the impossible. Maybe it is time to make peace, to make whatever of the past that I can in my writing and let history take a turn, create a sound of thunder and blast the world into the smithereens of a deliberately fragmented memory. *This just isn't working*. Sometimes, we must take a bullet. Sometimes, we must die, or kill.

It's just before one, and I'm still at the bar. My ears are ringing as always, especially after a show, and thinking about the exact sounds of music, remembering them, I'm certain the note is a G, the first note of "Metal Health," well, the first chord anyway, but the ringing gets louder for a few seconds drowning out all else, even itself, and then quickly subsides. I see Jared and Dominic over at a table having post-gig drinks with a few people, but I don't walk over. I take a pen out of my pocket and open my notebook, write out the formula, "2 + 2 + H = 4." Maybe the up and down of the volume of the ringing in my ears is getting to me, making me a bit crazy, pushing me to reach for something that is not there. I motion to the bartender for another beer. There are instruments at home, a bass, an acoustic guitar, an electric, and though I reach for them often, there is no music, and, as I sip my beer, sometimes not even any sound.

Chapter 9

"**LET'S GO TO THE ZOO,**" Katie suggests. It's Saturday morning at nine, and we're sitting at my table drinking the cheap champagne they brought over, Cook's, we're a classy bunch, one bottle down already, one more to go as we try to decide what to do for the day. I want to write, and then go see a band later, but they arrived unannounced, even walked in all Kramer-like, "We're here!" Greg shouted holding up the bottles. I was asleep on the couch, fully dressed in the clothes I wore to the Jesus Rehab show last night. "What the...?" But I got up and grabbed a few glasses from the kitchen, so I'm stuck with them for the moment, maybe even the day. "I like the zoo on cool days," Katie continues trying to win us over. "It isn't crowded, and it's more romantic. We can bring some Baileys and drink coffee as we walk around."

"I'm game."

"Me too, I suppose."

"Put some music on but not that stuff from last time. It was good but too mellow. That won't work for Saturday morning champagne."

"Uh, Pink Floyd?"

"Too depressing. I don't want to shoot myself." She walks over to the shelves where I have books to the left, CDs to the right. The books are arranged by topic, some textbooks from college, some poetry, some fiction, other random stuff. A few authors have their own sections. Charles Bukowski, Graham Swift, Haruki Murakami. "I love Murakami," she says. The music is alphabetical, all in its cases, so she finds one very quickly, "Put this on."

She hands me Filter's *Short Bus*. "Crank it. I love that first tune."
I smile and wonder whether she knows what the song is about.
She looks at Greg, "Let's leave by ten and..." but then there's that
opening bass line of "Hey Man Nice Shot" and she starts to bob
her head. We all do, and we just drink and listen and sing. It's
a rousing tune, and she's right. The non-mellowness of it works
very well for a Saturday morning as Greg plays air guitar and
Katie bounces in front of the desk. We finish the champagne and
then head out to the zoo.

I meet them at the entrance. They came in Greg's car, stopping on
the way for the Baileys and a flask. I showered quickly and put
on some fresh clothes since I'm heading downtown later to see a
band called Alabaster at the King Cat Theater. When I mentioned
it to them earlier, Katie asked, "What kind of stuff do they play?"
and I had to admit I didn't know. "I like to experience the bands
live and let the music do whatever it will because live is when the
magic really happens. That's where things take hold." I was already
a little buzzed.

"Yeah, but wouldn't it be easier to just listen to their CD and then
write?" She didn't quite understand, or maybe I just wasn't very
good at explaining it.

"It would be easier in one way of thinking, but there'd be no experience. I can't write about it with just a CD in my hand. I want the
beer, the crowd, the feedback during the guitar solo." I mimicked a
little solo with my hands.

"Yeah, but if you don't like them, it's just a waste of an evening."
I had to admit that sometimes it was.

"He doesn't write about those," Greg says.

"No?"

"Nope. Just the good ones."

"Why so?"

"Two reasons. First, I don't want to waste time on a band I don't
like. If I go out to see a band and they're awful, why should I waste
a second night of my life thinking and writing about them?"

"Understandable."

"The second thing is that I try more to point where to go than where not to go. And, well, sometimes bands redeem themselves. Sometimes they get better, and if so I'll tell people to check them out, but if not, I'll probably never mention them."

In front of the zoo, Greg asks, "So what time you need to go?"

"I should leave by two. I want to chill downtown for a while before the show and sober up a little since I wasn't anticipating a champagne breakfast."

"Nobody expects a champagne breakfast," Katie says in her best impression of the old Monty Python skit. She smiles and holds up the flask of Baileys, and we all laugh a bit. I motion to the gate.

"Let's go in. First round of coffee is on me."

We get our coffees and wander around the zoo. They're holding hands. I'm holding a notebook, and when we stop by the hippos, I get the urge for a new tattoo. We have sandwiches at this point, and while we stroll past those large beasts, I pause with the sudden desire to add some fresh ink on my arm or maybe my chest. I'm not sure why it happens with the hippos, but there it is, an idea lodged in my brain in much the same way as my first tattoos. The desire came and grew into a need and finally an idea for which I paid cash to have someone repeatedly jam a needle in my arm, chest, or back, wipe the blood, repeat with needle, wince in pain. After the last one back in 1995, I wasn't sure if I'd ever get another, but here by the hippos, it is decided, my brain wants a new tattoo. There's a hippo staring at me. I do the same, but there's no moment of clarity, no understanding of anything, no mind meld with the animal. It's just a hippo.

We walk over to the elephants, and Greg says, "I have to go to the bathroom. Be right back."

"Pachyderm. I always liked that word," Katie says when he's gone.

"Elephants were my favorite when I was little. I thought they said, 'Boo wheat.' "

"What?"

"That's what I thought their sound was."

"Boo wheat?"

"Yeah, boo wheat."

"That's hilarious. How the hell you come up with that?"

"No idea, but my parents and grandparents loved it. They always asked, 'Rob, what does an elephant say?' and would laugh when I said the words. They got me a stuffed one that quickly became my favorite thing."

"I have an elephant tattoo."

"Where?"

"Here." She points to a spot just above her right breast. "It's just a small one, upside down like on the cover of *The Elephant Vanishes*."

"Murakami."

"Yeah, I loved that book. I noticed it on your shelf."

"Me, too." It makes me want to see the elephant, but I know that won't ever happen. She's with Greg. I look around. He's taking a long time in the bathroom. "Why on your chest?"

"It's somewhere where people won't see unless I really want them to." The elephants are milling about. Like most people, they seem unsure what to do with themselves. "What's your favorite Murakami?"

"*Hard-boiled Wonderland and the End of the World*."

"Interesting. Why so?"

"I like the oddness of it all, the alternate realities of the conscious and unconscious mind. I love what he does on his last day. It's so understated but perfect."

"Ah, that's where you got that bit about driving out to the water the other night."

"Yeah, I must admit. I also like the insight the narrator gives into *The Brothers Karamazov*."

"What's that? I don't remember."

"That unhappiness can be a future thing, that you can be happy now even if you have an overall miserable life. I think I was too dumb to get that when I read *Karamozov*. Or it just floated past me. I've meant to re-read it since but just haven't. Instead I end up reading Murakami over and over."

"Me, too."

"I also think I love *Wonderland* because it was the first Murakami I read. I liked the title when I saw it on a bookshelf so I bought it not knowing anything about him or his writing. Oftentimes, the first thing you discover is the one you like best because it opens up a whole new world. I like a lot of his books, but that's the only one I've read more than once."

"I've read *Elephant* a number of times, and *Norwegian Wood* too."

"I hated *Norwegian Wood*." It's Greg finally back from the bathroom. He's more of a sci-fi/fantasy reader, loves Tolkien of course, and also something else he mentions that I should read called *A Song of Fire and Ice*, but I've never heard of that apart from his recommendation. He's holding three more coffees. "Let's head this way."

We move on from the elephants with our new Baileys-supplemented drinks, but now I'm thinking of something animal for the tattoo, maybe the elephant and his phrase from my childhood, maybe a wolf, a bear perhaps. Something powerful and significant. Not a tiger, though, they've been overdone. As we walk past the monkeys, I am struck by the image of King Kong, and while not thinking of that for a tattoo, it does make me think of the mythical, which brings dragons to mind. I do have the little dragon statue in my apartment, but dragon isn't me. Those who know me will attest to the fact that its combination of danger and elegance isn't representative of my character. A dragon tattoo for me would be more like the clumsy dragon, slightly overweight, the one who flies too low and hits his head on a tree branch while ogling beautiful women and drinking a beer.

Continuing around the zoo, we come upon the elk, and I hear some people speaking Chinese. There is a family, father, mother, son. The boy says something unintelligible to me, and his parents look up and smile. They all nod and move off while I think about something in a foreign tongue, a symbol of some sort or a phrase. I've seen people with Chinese characters tattooed on their bodies, and they're always people who have no knowledge of the language. They've just seen a design they like either for its look or whatever meaning they think it has, but I do often wonder if they have the meaning wrong. Those symbols are complicated. One small stroke can make a huge difference, can generate things unintended. I know a fair amount of Korean from my time overseas so the idea pops into my head. It's simpler than Chinese, but still, drawn well it could look cool trailing around my arm. I could write out a phrase that is significant to me, something I wouldn't mind having on my body for the rest of my life, something significant in my life as it is now.

사라지고 싶지 않 (I don't want to disappear)

Or not. Writing is for the page, not the flesh. I want an image with colors, a symbol, something that says something about me without coming right out and saying it. I always liked Flea's tattoo of elephants circling his left bicep. Very cool. The strength and bass of those large beasts and the fun childishness of the rainbow colors, blue, orange, green, purple, seems to describe the man. The worst I've seen was a guy in Ann Arbor, Michigan who'd come to see my band play a gig years ago. He was middle-aged then, had long scraggly hair, and wore only jeans and a black leather vest, no shirt. On his right arm there were five letters tattooed in blue ink: M E T A L. That said something about him too.

It's a strange thing this desire for a tattoo, the urge to mark a body with designs or phrases that have some sort of meaning to a particular point in a life or that just look cool, the unrequired tattoo, the one not for initiation into a gang or to mark the body for passage into the afterlife but simply to express something, to decorate the skin, the soul, to declare something however meaningful or mundane. But it's important to make such declarations, to say something permanent. The tattoo is one form of such, and it's a form I like. And now with the seed once again planted, I need the idea, the design, so that I may once again hand over cash for the pleasure and grimace of the needle, and of course the inevitable question from some, "You got *that* tattooed on your body?"

A little after four, I'm downtown watching the men of Pike Place fish market throw dead fish about. They have a particular one they toss back and forth when there aren't any orders to fill. I think it's a salmon. It's been gutted, deboned, and by the limpness of it, it seems they've tossed it about quite a bit. They use a motion as if they were bowling with both hands swinging back to the side and then tossing the ball so that it lands halfway down the lane and bounces two or three times before rolling into a pin or two. This gets it to the guys behind the counter, and they repeat the same motion to lob it back to the guys out front. There are shouts when they do this, both from them and those watching. There are tourists taking pictures, kids smiling and pointing. An elderly couple steps up and nods to the premade shrimp cocktails on sale for four dollars. There are more shouts, "Shrimp cocktail… shrimp cocktail!" The old couple pays, walks away. There's a group of high school girls, maybe sopho-mores, snapping photos a few feet away with Rachel, the 550-pound bronze pig, the oversized piggy bank, at the entrance to the market at the corner of Pike Street and Pike Place. Two of them climb on it after depositing some coins while the third girl takes a picture. There's a guy with an acoustic guitar busking a little off behind me next to a pole. He's playing some blues and tapping on the body of his guitar with his fingers and sometimes his palm for a little rhythm in the pauses. He's good. He plays with an ease I wish I had, seems to have no debilitating fears of performance. The high-school girls walk past me and past him, and the one who took the picture drops a few coins into his guitar case. "Thanks," he says without missing a note, even adds a little flourish followed by a big E chord, tilts his head. "Have a nice day, ladies." They walk off giggling as the busker starts playing and singing, "My girl, my girl, don't lie to me, tell me, where did you sleep last night?" There's a shout over by the fish market, "Snow crab... snow crab!" I look back and there's a guy about my height with long straight hair. He has a hand raised holding a bag of crab legs for a picture after which he turns to hand the bag over the counter to be weighed and properly wrapped. And then I see it, her. She has on the black leather jacket that she wore on the one Valentine's Day we spent together. That was last year, and as she took it out of the closet that night, she said, "You haven't seen this yet, have you?" I hadn't. It fit her form, was a little too tight even, but that made it all the better. We had sex right there on the floor before dinner, and she even meowed as she playfully reached between my legs and coaxed me into a second time. Plans for the evening dissolved in the pile of clothes. We ordered pizza, stayed in. But now, she's here this afternoon with someone else, maybe the man from my visions. "Where do you want me?" She steps in, laughing, and puts her arms around the guy. They hug, and she closes her eyes when he kisses the top of her head. They get the crab, pay, walk off in the other direction. I turn and drop a ten into the busker's case. He nods his head while singing, "My girl, my girl, where will you go?" There's a crowd gathering around him for this song. Some people start to sing along. I make my way to the nearest pub followed by the guitar, the singing, the shouts of the fish guys.

"Snow crab... snow crab!"

CHAPTER 10

I DON'T WANT TO FEEL anything tonight, and I'm actually pretty well there. As drunk as I am, I know I should go home, but I still end up at the King Cat Theater by eight because I've turned into a critic and said I'd write about this band. I want to be elsewhere though, home where I can venture out into the quiet wee hours and keep a detached eye on the world as it sleeps and fights and makes love. I guess I just want to drink tonight, not listen to music, not write, not stand on the sidewalk listening to lovers fight. I don't want to think. I don't want to play bass. I just want to let it all go, all feeling, all memory and new experience. Taking notes as a band plays is one of the last things I want to do, but I'm here, and something deep inside me keeps me rooted at the bar. I had to come. I have to stay. I gave my word, and for someone who writes as much as I do, someone who has so little else, that's about all I have. My word. My words.

Alabaster is second on a three-band bill, and the only contact I've had with them has been with the guitar player, Joe Bosslet. He put me on the guest list and emailed, "Looking forward to hanging with you after the show." From my seat at the bar, I can hear the first band. They're called Can't Complain, but really I can. The only word that comes to mind is ordinary. I motion to the bartender for another beer three more times during their set. I take no notes and do not feel anything. Success so far.

When Alabaster steps on stage to sound check, there are drum hits, guitar chords on both sides, bass thumps, and of course the vocals. "Check... check... check..." lead singer Shaina Rae says into her microphone. Guitarist Kate Orlowski speaks next, "Check... check... ch—son of a bitch! This thing shocked me, man. You're gonna have to fix that." The sound man makes his way down and twiddles a few cables, taps the mic in question, "Check, check... seems OK now," and so the show starts.

Drums and bass come in, then guitars left and right, and then a full stop as the vocals soar. I don't catch the line, but it's a great way to start, a great way to deliver the first bit of melody. There is no hello, no how are you, no welcome or thanks for coming. There is just the music and that one line. They cut straight to it. I like that. They go through a few songs, all an upbeat kind of pop punk that leans a little less toward the punk element. They don't introduce songs either, they just play. There is no banter, no "Let's put our hands together," just music for them, beers for me. And they move. They jump and scream. It is enough to draw one in. Kate steps up to the mic again, opens her mouth, twitches in pain and screams, "Son of a bitch!" One of the sound technicians runs down to the stage.

Six songs into the set, there are three big chords, F, G, E, that fade into a bass riff over a steady beat. The bass does a descending run, accents on the beat, repeats. I lean forward, sip my beer and say aloud to myself, "That's cool." And then Shaina comes in with the vocals. "Beauty rests underneath my chin tonight..." I sip again and mutter to myself, "I wish..." The guitars come in noodling at first, then small chords, then big into the chorus.

> and I'm dying to know what love feels like
> to find infinity in the heart of another...
> death is upon us love, I don't have much time.

No, we never do have much time, for love or for anything else. Katie's friend, Lindsay, doesn't worry about such things, but I always question people who don't. How can we not be worried? The end will come. That should make us strive to be better people, to love more, fight less, live, create, but we don't. People get caught up in the everyday. They live lives without living them. They don't see. They don't read. They don't hear. There is another verse, another chorus, a breakdown. The bass does triplets accented by the kick drum, very heartbeat-like, three on G, three on A, then E and F.

I can't see my breath in here.
I can't feel my heart beating.

Rae's voice is earnest, a plea, one of the most heartfelt I've ever heard.

I can't feel my chest rising.
I can't feel anything anymore.

The music builds. The line repeats.

I can't feel anything anymore.

There is crescendo, fall off, diminishment, but still the line repeats as Shaina bends over totally lost in the music, sprawling on the stage, crawling into the words.

I can't feel anything anymore.
I can't feel anything anymore.
I can't feel anything anymore.

It fades.

There is applause, a lot of it, but I want the show to end right here. I don't want anything to follow that. It is too good, and yet it makes me think I should have skipped the show and gone home earlier. Maybe I'd be better off never having heard that line for it's a sinker to anyone like me. I am susceptible to such lyrics and moods. With a bag of crabs in hand, she laughed. He kissed the top of her head, and though the tune was good, I'll never know if it really moved me, if it really did alter something deep down, or if I'm just latching onto it in a moment of pain because I don't want to feel anything, because I'm starting to think that maybe disappearing isn't so bad.

So I stand up after making a note to try to meet the band some other time for a drink. As I walk through the lobby, Alabaster starts a U2ish song that has a groove reminiscent of "40." I'd normally be caught by such, but not now. For me, the show is done. *I can't feel*

anything anymore. The night is done. So many things are done that I
have to wonder if anything will ever start again.

When I step out of the theater, I am filled with that line as I walk
to my car. The beers are swishing to and fro inside me, and I sing
to myself, "I can't feel anything anymore." I get to 7th Avenue and
Blanchard. I parked a half block to my left, but looking right, I notice
the Dream Girls strip club just down the street. The bright, flashing
sign seems a mirage, a desert oasis for a man dying of thirst, which,
of course, is what strip clubs are, an illusion, a trick for the gullible
and desperate, but still, there are nights I would make a beeline for
that place while lost in a moment thinking about her. The illusion
of intimacy and desire can be a powerful thing. I think about the
woman, the strippers, the music. Yes, the music. Nothing moves the
soul like music, like the repeated line. Maybe not even love. There is
nothing that gives more power than the musical phrase that builds,
repeats, pulls in, and then withdraws into a body flailing about a
stage plaintively calling to someone somewhere in the ether.

"I can't feel anything anymore…"

No, I can't either. I have let go of everything for the moment.
When I get to my car, I unlock it and place the keys underneath
next to the back passenger-side tire. It's a safety thing. I crawl into
the back seat then and lie down. I've had a bit much to drink for
driving, but I can still let the music do its thing as I drift into sleep
and dream.

"I can't feel anything anymore… I can't feel anything anymore…"

I realize I'm singing and also that I'm lost. I am as lost as a person
can be, and it's pretty sad. Pathetic might be a better word. I know
people are starving in the world and have to sleep in huts with mud
floors and no running water, no clean drinking water, and no beer,
but this is all I know, this life, this emptiness, the knowledge that
she is probably getting fucked right now by the guy with the crabs
and that I'm nowhere in her brain except for that place called the
past. I'm out, out like Pluto, once a planet, now nothing, and so I
repeat the line and repeat the line and repeat the line.

"I can't feel anything anymore… I can't feel anything anymore…"

I wake to a tapping sound and notice red and blue lights spinning about, and for a moment I think I might have made my way down the street only to pass out in the strip club, but the thought is gone in a second as I realize what is happening, so I say it in a whisper, "Shit." There's a police officer tapping at my window, and he probably wants to get me for DUI, probably thinks he has me on one. "Shit." I sit up thinking I might as well face it. I might as well just get it over with.

There's a squad car behind mine with its lights ablaze. The officer is waiting patiently and looking in at me through the passenger-side back window. He's smiling and kind enough to point his flashlight down at the sidewalk rather than into my eyes. I'd roll the window down if I could, but they're powered, and the keys are under the car, so I shout through the glass.

"Is there a problem, Officer?"

He says something I can't make out.

"I'm sorry. Could you repeat that?" I say louder.

"Are you okay, sir?"

"Oh, uh, yeah. I'm just sleeping rather than driving." I feel like I'm having one of those conversations with someone who doesn't speak English, so being the English speaker, I compensate with volume as if it will bring understanding. He turns his head to the side to better listen. "My... keys... are... there... under... the... car... by... the... tire." He bends down, shines his light.

"Would you mind... ing... the car, sir... license and...?" I don't catch it all, but the meaning is clear enough so I open the door. As I do this, he stands up and steps back to allow me space to exit the car but loses his balance and falls backward. The flashlight rolls a foot or so. His hat falls off. "Damn!" He has a bit of a gut, short legs, pants that don't quite reach his shoes, no hair. He winces a little while twisting his body.

"Are you okay, sir?"

"Yeah, thanks, I'm fine." He reaches out with his right hand, so I take it and help him up and then I get his flashlight while he dusts himself off. He seems to forget his hat for the moment. It's upside down on the sidewalk. "Damn back," he says to himself. He works his neck around a couple times and is in a genuine amount of pain.

"Your hat." I pick up it. "Here you go." He puts it under his left arm rather than on his head, and we stand there for a moment looking at each other. The Dream Girls sign beckons from down the street. He looks at it and then back at me. I try to seem confident, friendly, sober.

"Thanks, again. Uh, listen. I just wanted to make sure you were okay, but you seem to have your faculties about you so why don't you head home?"

I consider briefly asking how he found me and why he knocked on my window, but decide against it. He seems willing to let me go, and I have no desire to tempt fate otherwise. "Uh, thanks."

"Just be careful out there."

"I will." I get in my car and watch him walk slowly back to his. He shuts off the flashing lights and drives by with a wave, turns left a block up and is gone, and once again, I'm left with the Dream Girls sign. There's no such thing. Dream Girls. Dream Girl. Life doesn't work that way, and I wonder if I've passed the happy part of my life, if I'm in the miserable future part, and this makes me think about Katie. She's probably lying naked in bed next to Greg, her elephant tattoo exposed. Interesting that she likes Murakami. I guess there is, all things considered, the possibility that she'll come around, that she'll show me the tattoo, give me a chance, but then, that thought is an illusion just like the Dream Girls. She's with Greg, and I'm just mentally grasping at anyone who is near. Best to hold out for something different, someone completely new, someone not taken. Either that or pack it all in. Disappear. Maybe disappearing isn't so bad. Maybe I already have. I start the car and notice the time. 4:32 a.m. Another day gone, another hundred thousand or so beats of my heart, and I wonder how many more of them I'll have alone before music comes, before love, before the time of my last breath. I'm forty-two. I should probably be married by now with a family and a house and a dog, maybe a cat, but here I am sleeping in the back of a car before driving home to a little one-bedroom apartment where the only things waiting for me are beer and soju and a laptop. There used to be a girlfriend, a band, a life beyond my apartment in which I participated rather than just sitting in the corner taking notes. All that is gone now. I know I got lucky with the not-so-nimble cop, that I should take pause and consider the course of my actions, that I should be more careful, that more taxis should be in my future, my present, but I just keep driving. I put Radiohead in the CD player and click forward to "Myxomatosis." I revel in its excellent fuzz, repeating it the entire time it takes me to get home. I sing along about mongrel cats and the need to be put down and swerve a few times along the way. I bang on the dash to the rhythm and check the rearview for flashing lights, but there's nothing.

PART 2

CHAPTER 11

ÓLÖF ARNALDS. She's a singer/songwriter from Iceland, and I've noted her in my notebook for two reasons. First, and most obvious, is that she's coming to Seattle so I'll go to the show and write about it, hopefully talk to her about music and other things, maybe buy her a drink. More important, though, is her song "Surrender" with Björk on background vocals and the fact that it is hauntingly beautiful, something akin to a ghost that whispers in your ear, breathy, warm, soft, telling you to relax and that the haunting isn't really a haunting; it's simply a connection to another world, another plane of existence. It's terrifying, yes, but also exhilarating, even lovely. The song is played on a charango, which is a small acoustic Andean instrument with ten strings and a tight plucky sound, and in the moment I'm trying to transpose the music to guitar. It's slow work stopping and starting the song and figuring out the notes. I get one phrase and work at it until I play it well and then move on to the next, back and forth and back and forth, and the song starts to take shape outside of my head. It's in my hands now, a physical thing that I toss about the apartment. It bounces around in a delicate way, landing on the couch and rolling on the floor, but then I get a little more confidence with the music and dig into the fret board to grab hold of the notes. I use a pick rather than my fingers and the sounds harden a little and jump about with more force. They shoot around the kitchen, crawl across the ceiling and hover above me until I stop playing. Then they splash down like a waterfall, and I kick my left foot out and knock over a few empty beer bottles and one nearly full one. I should clean it up, but spills can be cleaned any time. Musical moments like these don't always come, and they never last too long, so I let the beer soak into the carpet. I play the song again and feel glad that I'm home alone on a Friday night, and this time when I get to the chorus, I sing about choosing now, about claiming my power.

I stop playing after that line and sit in the quiet. There's still a sense of the music in the air, and it makes the apartment seem full, crowded even. It makes me feel like a complainer for as much as I go on endlessly about lost love, lost touches, about tender moments remembered and thinking that I can't let them go. Is my experience so unique? We've all had broken hearts, and this isn't the first time in my life that I've experienced this, this thing at times when my heart feels like an old paper bag trying desperately to contain some kind of liquid but failing as it seeps through at the seams and turns dark in the middle ready to burst. And it probably won't be the last time. The heart is a strong thing, though. The bag never truly breaks through. It wants to heal itself so we get over lost love, we put things in the past to remember them but not to feel. We move on. She moved on. "This just isn't working."

This just isn't working.

I put the guitar down. I know I need to move on. Maybe I already have. Or maybe I'm deliberately lingering, refusing to admit it, obsessing. She would probably say I am. There's a birthday card from her on the bookshelf, a picture of her on the desk, one in my wallet. *Am I?* If so, it's a dangerous place to be. It makes people do stupid things. I walk over to the kitchen and grab a beer, walk back to the desk and place the picture face down. It's the first time in a long time that her face hasn't been visible in this place, and it actually feels good. It's scary too. What does it mean to declare your love to someone only to have it fade, to move on, to get over it? What does that say about anything if it's all so temporary? If I ever tell a woman again that I love her, I'll remember this moment, this feeling that it all ends, that something new always begins, that we move on to other places, other lives, other planets. And I'll doubt myself in the moment. I'll hesitate. I'll pause, and maybe that as yet unknown woman will doubt me too. But even so, when the time is right, when the woman is right, I'll say it. Hell, maybe I'll even sing it, shout it, wake the neighborhood at three in the morning. "I…"

CHAPTER 12

I FINISH LUNCH ON SUNDAY at one and think that after a weekend here alone, I need a little interaction; I need to get out for a while. I want to hear the questions of an unrecorded voice; I want to see an eye blink and a head tilt as it considers my opinions; I want to see a woman and think about possibility. Not being quite in the mood for a bar just yet, I decide to see a movie. I know that means recorded voices and images, but there are interactions too. I have to buy a ticket. I have to get some nachos. There'll be beer somewhere afterward, which means bartenders, waitresses, patrons. And maybe there'll be friends. I call Greg, "Hey, man, you want to catch a movie?"

"Uh, maybe. Let me ask Katie." There's a pause as he covers the phone to speak to her. I imagine them in bed together, naked under the blankets, even in the afternoon, the upside down elephant that I want to touch, a lazy Sunday of sex interrupted by the single friend. Greg comes back on, "Yeah, man, but I need to shower. See what's playing and call me back in fifteen minutes."

I check the listings online but can find only two that seem interesting, *True Grit* and *Black Swan*. I've heard that in the latter Natalie Portman masturbates and gets it on with another woman, but that doesn't entice me in the moment, or rather it does, but then what does one do afterward when coming home alone with those images in the brain? Only one thing really. I opt instead for Jeff Bridges doing the role made famous by John Wayne. It's a remake but one of the few that is purported to equal or better the original, so I'm game. I text Greg, " True Grit. 4:30. Pacific Place. Meet you there."

That gives me three hours so I pick up my acoustic, but rather than play, I just look it over. It's an acoustic/electric actually, an unknown brand in these parts, Tornado. I bought it in Korea back in 1999 for four hundred dollars, a sum of money that on my then ESL teacher's salary set me back quite a bit, but I needed a guitar. That was all that mattered. I needed to play those songs going through my head. "Fluff." "Is there Anybody Out There?" "Then She Did." "Fire." And the other "Fire." And so many more, and some from my own bands. I had all the music, the CDs and cassettes, but listening isn't the same. It needed to be played. D chords are better when they're fretted and strummed. It's the difference between active and passive, and even to a point, between right and wrong. Everyone should play music or write stories or make movies, even bad ones, the voice should sing, the heartbeat should be heard.

I play a B minor chord and let it fade. My guitar is in sad shape. There are numerous scratches and nicks, and the pickup came loose and rattles around on the inside when picked up, when played, when knocked over, but I'm used to it and can always make my cheap little guitar sing and even scream, and yet there are those days when something more is needed, and this is one, this rainy Seattle Sunday afternoon, and with time and hours before the movie, I want to play some music that does not rattle. I want notes and riffs and darkly bright chords that ring with undisturbed clarity, so I go to the Guitar Center downtown where they keep the really nice, and really expensive, acoustic guitars in their own separate room. It's quiet and removed from the noise of the rest of the store where all the amateurs try out the cheap electrics and play all the popular songs badly as they try to impress parents and girlfriends and salespeople and other musicians. When I get there, one guy is testing a Les Paul through a Marshall 2x12 combo. It's loud and he's running repeatedly over the opening of Lenny Kravitz's "Are You Gonna Go My Way," but he keeps missing the bend of the first A note each time through. It's brutal to hear. The salesman next to him has to pretend for the sake of the sale that he's nailing it—"That's awesome, man!"—but I imagine him cringing under his Guitar Center tee shirt and silently apologizing to the guitar gods for such blasphemy. He'll probably laugh about it later with the other employees.

I head back to the acoustic room and find what I'm looking for, my absolute favorite, the Martin D-35 which lists for $2,299, just a little more expensive than the Tornado, and simply standing in front of it as it hangs on the wall I can hear it sing, can hear chords yearning to be played, and my fingers make the movements, D to G to E minor, of some imaginary song. There is a woman in the room playing a few soft things on a rather nice Gibson, a J-35, same price range as my beloved Martin but a little too bright in the sound for me. The woman has long black hair, so I can't see her face, and though she seems almost too small for the guitar, she holds it well, plays the notes with ease. They ring clear. She looks up at me, nods. "Hi."

"Hi."

I carefully grab the Martin from the wall and sit on a stool, play a few soft notes of my own. The woman and I make eye contact again and have an understanding. We'll each play softly so as not to bother the other, and that done, we each get to it, strumming and plucking various things. I play the intro for the Red Hot Chili Peppers' "Under the Bridge" and morph into Black Sabbath's "Laguna Sunrise" and then into the Doors' "Spanish Caravan." The Martin feels like air in my hands, like cradling an armful of that which sustains life. I play a few of my own things and drift into parts of Zepplin's "Babe, I'm Gonna Leave You," and the vibrations of the guitar work their way into my chest and there continue to resonate within my veins, and the music is so easy and so beautiful that I have to pause for a moment and relish in the fading sounds, and the woman starts something soft then. I look at her, and she keeps playing. I smile.

"Ólöf Arnalds?"

"Yeah, 'Surrender.' You know it?"

"Yeah."

She starts playing again from the beginning. I join in, and the combined joy of the two guitars on those melancholy notes nearly brings me to tears. Then she starts singing, and when it's done we let the notes fade into complete silence. It seems there can be no other sound in the world. How to describe that to the non-musician? That feeling of absolute power while playing, while letting the final notes fade off into the cosmos. Sex is the only comparison, sex with true love, sex that ends finishing inside a woman. There's no more intimate moment two lovers can have than when the woman says, "I want you to come inside me," and the man complies and two bodies quiver for a time as one.

"Nice."

"Yeah, that was cool," I reply, and then I speak as that man would, that lover, who after a brief spell of post-coital spooning trails his hands down the length of his lover's body, her neck, her back, and says, "One more time?"

"Yeah, all right."

We start again, but then someone comes into the room before we can get through the first verse. It's the guy who had been slaughtering Lenny Kravitz. "We need to go now or we'll be late."

"Okay, hon." She stands up, places the Gibson back on the wall, takes his hand. She looks back at me as they are leaving. "Nice playing with you."

Then she is gone. *Him? She's with him.* Even the guitar gods play their little jokes on mankind. The woman had taste. She could play well, and sing, and do them both at the same time. And yet, he has her. No matter, I guess. I had her too for a few moments, and maybe in a much more intimate way than he ever will. I decide to try the Gibson, so I get it and then play the first thing that comes to mind. I chunk out a few chords and start to sing "Back Door Man," and I realize I've only ever heard the Doors' version of the song. I stop playing and make a mental note to look up Howlin' Wolf's rendition, and then before I can get back to playing, my phone buzzes, a text from Greg.

"Hey, man, it's nice out. Let's do Space Needle instead. Same time."

I don't respond. I just put the guitar back on the wall and head out since it's getting pretty close to the time anyway. When I get to the Space Needle, it's surprisingly crowd free for a Sunday, but then it was raining earlier, and only in the last hour or so has the sun come out. I get my ticket and walk through the souvenir store on the ground floor, where I catch the elevator up to the observation deck. It's the south-facing elevator, and I can see Mt. Rainier, which always surprises me for how big it looks even from this far away. It seems almost photoshopped there, out of proportion, bigger than it ought to be, bigger than anything ought to be. When I exit the elevator, I see Katie tapping away at her phone. She looks up and smiles to see me. "There you are."

My phone buzzes, a text from her to Greg and me: "Where are you?"

"Here I am," I say.

"Greg's late, and he's not answering his phone. Can you call him?"

I try. No answer. I don't leave a message.

"Let's get a drink. I'm sure he'll be here soon."

We go to the snack bar and get a couple beers, find an empty table with a westward view. It looks pretty windy out this high up.

"You don't know where Greg is?"

"He said he wanted to work out and then run a couple errands so we should just meet up here."

"Why here?"

"I don't know." She sips her beer a few times while I look at the view. There's an airplane, United, I think, a ways out over the Puget Sound making the westward turn to head out over the Olympic Mountains and the Pacific. "Part of me thinks he might be lying, but whatever. He can do what he wants." She doesn't seem too concerned. Or else that's what she wants me to think.

She gets up to go to the bathroom, and while she's gone, I get a text from Greg. "I can't make it today. Sorry, just need some time to myself to figure out how to end it with Katie. She's too clingy. Will make it up to you with beers next time we meet up." I delete the message and decide not to tell Katie for now. She'll get the idea that something's up with him soon enough. I know it's difficult, the decision to end things, to wrench your own life free from the entanglements of relationship and head off in a different direction when you realize the sexual attraction has worn off and that you can't just go out and get drunk and screw every night, that personalities and ideas matter, but he should have cancelled and told her himself. I guess that's how it is, though. Some people send their friends in. Some do it via email.

The last time I was here I was in love. That old man took a picture that I'd hoped to show grandkids someday. Now, I'm just a single guy out with my friend's soon-to-be-ex girlfriend, two people without love. I think about the phrase from the email. *This just isn't working.* No, it wasn't. Maybe it's just the right moment, facing a ghost up here. Maybe it's knowing Greg and Katie are done, but I know that if I saw her walking on the other side of the street I wouldn't cross to say hi, and I wouldn't run away either. I'd just keep walking my own way. I think about the picture, the way she smiled with her head tilted slightly to the right and showing no teeth. I had my arm around her and was saying to myself, *Never forget this moment.* I wonder if I will. I lift my beer and make a silent toast to her. *Goodbye.* I haven't disappeared.

I'm here.

Katie comes back singing the chorus of a song called "Spinning My Wheels" from Star Anna and the Laughing Dogs' *The Only Thing That Matters* CD. I loaned it to Katie last time she and Greg were at my place, told her I thought she'd like it, and she'd texted a few days later to say that she did. Everyone should like it actually. Star's voice is passion embodied, similar to Kristen Ward's in that respect, but she has a little more grit, an edge that slices into lives. There's a repeated line at the end of the song that I love: "Too many lifetimes and not enough years." It echoes a sentiment right out of my book, the book that is currently making its rounds on the desks of certain editors and agents in New York, or in their trash bins. So many lifetimes in the course of one, but in this one there is never enough time. Plenty of beer, though, and Star sang that night. And I drank. And my heart ached for the lifetimes and the lack of years and all the beers consumed to somehow even that equation.

A few weeks ago, the thought of that song would have crushed me. It certainly did when I heard it live, and though I'm past that point now, I will always remember letting that melody and those lyrics consume my emotion. I'll always remember that picture too, the picture of us up here, but any grandkids I have will never see it. They'll see other pictures of some possible future lover, and I'll tell them about different songs.

"So you've been listening to Star Anna." I notice her eyes are a little bloodshot. She was in the bathroom for about ten minutes.

"Yeah, I love that CD."

"Any word from Greg?" I ask.

"Yeah, he texted that he won't be coming and that he wants to meet up tomorrow to talk about things."

"I'm sorry," I say, but I'm glad he told her. "You okay?"

"Whatever, it's not like I was in love with him."

But she looks away, and we sit quietly staring out at the view, she suppressing more tears while I just sip the rest of my beer not having any idea what to say. After a few moments, she looks back at me. "Listen, can we just go back to your place? I don't want to be out in public right now. I just want to have a few drinks and listen to some music. I don't give a damn about the Space Needle."

"Okay." I know I should suggest that she just go home and try to get some rest, maybe pop in a movie, a comedy, and try to forget today or what will happen tomorrow, but then she's unhappy now, she doesn't want to be alone, so how can I possibly send her home? What kind of friend would that make me? I'm getting what I wanted, though. I'm only out because I wanted some interaction after a weekend alone. Another Star Anna song pops into my head, "Alone in This Together." The song hasn't been released yet, so Katie hasn't heard it, but after I wrote about Star's show, I asked her if I could have an advance copy of her next album. She was nice enough to agree, so I have an unmarked burned CD of stuff few others have heard. It isn't even mastered, but the magic is there, the shards of that voice doing their work. I only had to promise not to share it with anyone, but I'll probably break that tonight in an effort to ease Katie's mind and let the music consume her emotion. Star's music helped me. Music always helps me. Without it, I'd probably be a suicide. What would there possibly be to console a lost soul in a world without music? There are words, of course. We'd depend doubly so on them, but I don't think I'm wrong in saying it'd be easier to live without literature than without music. So, I'm sorry, Star, but the circumstances are warranted, and I hope you'll be happy to help in the consoling of a friend of mine, a fan of yours.

She follows me home, where I twist open a couple beers and put on the unreleased CD and crank it. We just listen and let the music take us somewhere else, and she looks forward with her eyes fixed on the dragon that she'd once offered to buy. I look up at the ceiling and float away on an F chord as Star sings.

> ...we sit alone in a crowded room
> 'til there's nothing left, and your heart is bruised
> and the water shines over your eyes.
> And we're all alone in this together.

"I just can't help but feel as if I'll always be alone."

"There are worse things," I say knowing full well that I go on at length about being alone, about having trouble sometimes with the solitude. I should take my own advice. There probably are worse things than being alone.

"Are there?"

It strikes me that Katie is someone for whom things have never really worked out. Clingy people often desperately latch onto something, someone, but I do have to wonder whether it's true what Greg said about her, and if so what was so terrible about it. She obviously cares about him, so I understand her feelings. It's rejection, rejection in the present tense, and unlike the past, the present doesn't diminish. It isn't like a poem. It can't be forgotten or manipulated. It must be endured.

> *Does it make you weak?*
> *Is it something new*
> *to admit you failed*
> *that you can't get through*
> *and all of this is real?*
> *And we're all alone in this together.*

When it ends, I play it again, and during the solo I get us each another beer and sit down next to her. The song is a variation on the same three chords between the verse and the chorus. It's a simple thing to play, but it's the dynamics that give it lift. There are mellow acoustic parts and big chunky distorted sections. It's open and full of air and yet tight, punchy at times, and hell, now I feel like crying, but not for any lost love or the possibility of such or for Katie's sadness. It's all my old doubts. I'm not getting any younger, and though I do have a certain talent with the bass, I'm far from the best one around, and that makes me feel like a failure. I tried the music thing for years, for the whole of my adult life, but here I am sitting with Katie on a Sunday night getting drunk and just listening to music, the music of others in which we hope to find strength enough to continue as neither of us has anything else at all going on. I realized earlier that I am finally over lost love, but I don't know where that leaves me, or rather it seems it leaves me nowhere.

When the song ends a second time, she says, "Thanks for playing that," with a tear running down her cheek so I put my arms around her, and she leans into me in such a way that she can't put her arms around me but she takes hold of my right forearm and squeezes with a strength I wouldn't have guessed she had. I don't say anything. I just let her squeeze, seems she needs to, and hell, not too long ago it could have been me crying on the edge of a song. I don't know whether she loved Greg or the idea of him or just the idea of someone to wake up next to. In the moment, I guess it doesn't matter, but it has to be something more. She must be damaged in some other way. She just hasn't known him that long. But then, how long does it take? She sits back up.

"I like that song. I'm not sure what it means, but it has a sadness that's comforting."

"What I gather after speaking with her is that she's leaving it open to interpretation. It means whatever it means to you." It strikes me as a very Radio8Ball kind of thing. The song will answer the question. I don't know what Katie's asked of the music, but it seems to console in some way. "There is a line, though, that I don't agree with when she says that time isn't anything at all. Time is all we have. It's everything."

"Maybe she means only the moment matters."

"She might. I've lately been thinking about how the past matters, or I guess I believe these days that how we remember the past matters more than the actual past since the past is really only what you make of it."

"Is that why you write?"

"Partially."

She tilts her as if just struck by a thought. "Can I see your book?"

"Sorry, but no. Only when it's published and out there."

"Why, does it suck?"

"It might. I mean, I believe in it, but will anyone else? I don't know."

"Isn't that why you wrote it, to show people?"

"Yes and no. I want to show people, but not until it's ready, and I wrote it because I couldn't not write it. All those thoughts were weighing me down so I had to get them out. They would have crushed me otherwise. In some ways, art is just an outlet for people who have deep flaws."

"What flaws do you have?"

"Well, I don't know. I guess I..."

"No, never mind. I don't want to know, or at least I don't want you to tell me. It'd take the mystery away of getting to know you better. Or maybe I'd just start looking for them. That's one of my own faults." I grab a couple more drinks for us, sit back down. "You mind if I crash here tonight?" she asks.

"Not at all."

"Can you do me a favor? When we sleep, can you hold me? I'm not coming on to you, and I don't want sex. I just want to be held for once without any expectations."

"Uh, okay," but I'm not sure what she means. Does she really just want to be held or does she want something a little more? I've never been able to discern the motive for that question. Most guys hear that and probably think sex is imminent, that holding will lead to rubbing shoulders, that caresses will follow, that clothes will come off. I don't sense that from Katie, but my mind briefly goes there which makes me imagine the tattoo, the upside down elephant. The cover of the Murakami book is red with a splash of white in the center in which the elephant floats. Whenever I look at it, I keep waiting for it to fall and drift off the edge, but it doesn't. The elephant is only about a half inch square, a tiny thing. I wonder how big it is on her chest. I still have an arm around her, she her head on my shoulder, and though I really would like to see the elephant, tonight isn't the right night to make an effort at that. It isn't worth the cost of two friends, so I decide then to get her drunk in the hopes that she passes out and sleeps on her own without my arms around her. Do I not trust myself? Maybe not. It's been awhile for me, better if I didn't hold her. "I have some soju. You want a shot?"

"Okay."

When she finally does lie down and close her eyes, I cover her with a blanket. I know I should get to sleep myself, but I open one more beer and step outside. I walk to the edge of the curb. The light is on across the street, but it's quiet in there. I know that if I turn left toward the city, I'll be able to see the Space Needle, but I don't do it. I don't want to. I just keep looking at the window wondering when the light will go out.

Chapter 13

I WAKE UP TO the smell of coffee and a pain on the left side of my neck, stiff shoulders, the price of sleeping on the floor. Katie is in the kitchen filling two cups. She walks over and hands me a mug, "Cheers."

"How you doing?" I ask.

"Good. I'm sorry about last night." She sits back down on the couch.

"No worries." We drink, she with both hands. I set mine down and go to the bathroom where I splash water on my face a couple times before relieving myself. I put the lid down, wash my hands, and then go back and sit down on the floor next to the sofa. "So what are you going to do about Greg?" She looks into her coffee cup in the same way drinkers look into their beers and whiskeys and vodkas.

"I was thinking about that while you were sleeping. You were snoring by the way, loudly. That's why I woke up."

"Was I?"

"Greg snores too, but his is softer, more like heavy breathing. It's a little scary because there are times when he seems to stop breathing for a few seconds, and I'm not sure if I should wake him up or not." I imagine them in bed as she watches him sleep. Perhaps she strokes his hair, pulls the blanket up a little, maybe whispers a few words, "I love you," because she can't quite come out and say them yet. I wonder if she watched me before getting up to make coffee.

"You want me to put some music on?"

"Nah." She sighs. We're quiet for a few moments.

"So what were you thinking before I woke up?"

"I… I had the idea that some people are in a perpetual state of heartbreak. Do you think that's true?"

"I've had similar thoughts."

"And I mean even happy people, maybe especially them. When you're happy there's the constant fear of losing it, and when you lose it, it's bad in the moment, but then it's done, and you move on, maybe sad, but the fear is gone."

"Or a new kind of fear sets in. I suppose, then, the trick is not to fear."

"Impossible, well, at least for me. Maybe I should get some help with that. Anyway, I was thinking, too, that I've listened to a lot of the music you've written about, and so much of it has a touch of sadness that I wonder if the musicians aren't afraid too. I'd always thought the opposite."

"To be sure, that says something more about the critic, but I would say that artists are the most afraid. That's one of the reasons for writing or playing or whatever. It helps to silence the doubts and fears."

"Does it work?"

"Most of the time, but I still have a whole number of fears when I step on a stage or show someone a bit of writing. I force myself to do it, but sometimes it's downright agonizing, even just to read the comments on a blog post."

"Doesn't sound like it works."

"But you have to remember that if I didn't have that outlet, I'd probably end up killing someone, maybe even myself. Maybe it doesn't cure everything, but it does enough."

"How so?"

"It's hard to explain if you don't do it."

"Try me."

"Okay." I sip my coffee. It's in a white mug that has a blue guitar on it, a birthday gift from the woman I used to love. I have seven mugs in my cupboard, and Katie happens to give me this one. I did mention the blue guitar to her once, though, so maybe she's paying attention to my theories. "What's the single greatest feeling you've ever had, the moment in which your body and mind and soul were... were so happy it almost hurt?"

"Sex, I suppose, but not all sex. I mean sometimes it really isn't that great." She laughs a little, "Honestly, sometimes sex is like those times when you end up watching a bad movie on cable, and you know it's bad, but you just keep watching because, though it's awful, there's still some kind of thrill."

"And that's the greatest feeling you've ever had?"

Another laugh. "No, that's just most of it. A lot of sex isn't really the act but rather the closeness, the intimacy, even if it's one, two, three boom, and over. Greg is like that, actually, but don't tell him I told you. There was this one guy, though, who just knew what he was doing. I mean he just knew how to work it. He was good."

"That's it then. If you take that feeling and multiply it a thousand-fold you'll come close to how the musician feels when stepping on stage, even if the playing on a particular evening isn't technically brilliant, even if there are some fuckups. In an odd way, a looseness can help the flow because you can really see when it comes together. And then for the individual musicians, you get this sense of frenzied excitement on the inside, here" — I tap my chest — "and there's release, and everything washes away."

"Sounds kind of like masturbation."

"Not really, it's more making love." Faustine was right. "Masturbation is a solo thing. Writing and painting are too. There's no audience, no give and take, none of that dynamic that can take the music and the audience to new places. We don't watch writers write or painters paint. How dull would that be?" She gets up to grab the coffee, pours us both a refill, sets the pot on a coaster on the coffee table. "But with music we do. We watch. We participate. And we cover. That's another thing. Someone writes a song, but anyone can play it, and it'll be different. The musicians covering it will make it their own if they're good enough. Do you have a favorite cover song?"

"I always loved Cheap Trick's version of 'Ain't That a Shame.' Wasn't that originally a Chuck Berry song?"

"Fats Domino, but you see what I mean. There's that song and the Jimi Hendrix version of "All Along the Watchtower," the Doors' "Back Door Man," and one you might not know is "Diamonds and Rust" by

Judas Priest, which was originally done by Joan Baez. All covers, but they made it their own. Music can adapt to the artist, to the moment. Writing can't. A painting can't. Can you imagine someone saying they were going to rewrite *Ulysses* and just change a few words, maybe a few characters' names, maybe draw the ending out a little more? No, that person would be laughed at."

"Hollywood does that kind of thing."

"Well, Hollywood is stupid."

"No arguments there. So why do you write about music? Your writing is so imbued with the drive and the need to get back to playing that after reading a bunch of it I'm left to wonder."

"You're right. I do want to play, but I think in this moment I just need to figure out a little more of what it means to me in my life."

"After everything you just said you don't know?"

"It'd be easy to simply say music means everything, but then that's a cop-out since it isn't really saying anything in detail. It's why I started to think about 2 + 2 = 5. I wanted to somehow try to figure out why music means so much to me, why it moves me to extremities the way it does, and then one late night I was listening to Radiohead, and there it was, the equation. So I picked up my guitar and worked out the chords and played it a few times through and even sang it."

"Play it for me."

"Uh, okay." I normally wouldn't as I don't sing so well, but the moment seems right, and in light of going on about music, about needing music, about being a suicide or a murderer without it, it'd be disingenuous of me not to do it, to fear it. I grab my acoustic and pluck it a little to make sure it's in tune. It isn't quite. I take a few moments to make it so while Katie refills our coffee cups. She hands me mine. I sip and set it in front of the dragon and then sit facing the wall so that I don't have to look at her directly. I finger the first chord, F minor, exhale, begin to pluck the notes. I sing. It's a more subdued version of the song, my version, the only one she's ever heard, and I surprise myself toward the end when I bump up the energy a bit, not quite to the frantic pace of the original, but some, and it feels good, and I never once think about which chord is coming next. Maybe it's the singing. Maybe I should sing more often. This notion pumps me a little more, and I get a little bold, lean forward as if to crawl into the guitar and swirl around with the sounds. I sing a little louder, shake my head, hit a few chords. And then it's done. There's a tail of reverb in the studio recording, but this being my apartment, there's just quiet. I wonder for a moment if I'm having another deaf spell, but no, my chair squeaks when I lean back and look at her. She smiles, nods, but otherwise does not respond. I finger an F minor chord, "So what did you think?"

"I liked it," she says slowly in a calm voice. "That was easier to understand than talking about it."

"That's the point. Music needs to be heard and experienced. I try to capture as much as I can when I write about music, but I probably end up woefully short. You just... you have to be there."

"You do okay in writing about it." She says okay in a way that means more than okay. It's the tilt of her head slightly to the left, the squint of her eyes, the measured pace of her voice. More than okay.

"Thanks. Should I play it again?"

"I'd like that."

CHAPTER 14

I GET TO THE TRACTOR just before ten when Ólöf Arnalds is supposed to go on. I order a Manny's and settle at the corner of the bar where there's a small lamp next to the lemons and limes and oranges, and I jot down a few preliminary notes and glance about the room wondering whether the woman from Guitar Center will show up. Over near the entrance, there's someone who looks very much to be Ms. Arnalds. I've only seen pictures of her on Facebook and in the video for "Surrender," so I'm hesitant to think it's her, that the woman over there is the woman whose video I've watched about a hundred times being so captivated by the song's dark beauty. She comes over to the bar to order a drink.

"Ólöf?"

"Yes?" she says, looking over.

"Hi. I'm Rob. I'm here writing about the show tonight for a website called Seattle Subsonic."

"For who?"

"Seattle Subsonic. It's, uh, just a local website you've never heard of, and anyway, I was hoping I could get a set list from you after the show."

"Oh, I don't use a set list," she says with an Icelandic accent, "but I will take care of this. Just a moment." She goes over to where the merchandise is, speaks to a guy there, motions for me to come over. "This is George. He will write down the songs for you as I play them."

"Thanks." We all shake hands. "I must say that I loved the video for 'Surrender.' What a great song. I saw someone post a link to it on Facebook and just fell in love with it and decided to come out to the show, and also get this"—I realize I'm speaking quickly, that I'm excited like a fan—"I met someone in a guitar store last week who knew the song, so we played it together and she sang." I mimic playing guitar and speak the lyrics as I'm not foolish enough to sing them to her with my voice. There's a pause when I'm done. And then she smiles.

"Wow, that sounds like a nice moment!"

"Indeed, it was. The kind only possible with music."

"Ólöf?" George taps her shoulder and points to his watch.

"Oh. I have to get ready now so maybe we can catch up after the show."

"I'll be here."

She goes up on stage. Those in attendance clap. "Give me two minutes please while I, uh, do some tuning. I didn't have a chance to earlier. Thank you." The audience is quiet then, respectful of her wish. It isn't always the case for single and/or acoustic acts. I've seen shows where there was a constant chatter throughout that could be heard above the music. It made me wonder why people didn't just stay home and listen to the CD if they couldn't shut up for a few minutes to listen. During quiet sets, there was laughter at times. There were cell phone rings and beeps. There was a droning buzz of activity that marginalized the music and those playing it. Ólöf finishes tuning and speaks, "This is a song about girlfriends. Each verse is about a past girlfriend." It is "Vinkonur" from her *Innundir Skinni* CD. As she plays the song, I see the woman from Guitar Center over in a corner with a group of people, all of them female, and make a note to speak to her after the show so as not to interrupt the music.

Before the second song Ólöf says, "This one is about a simple place and a simple state of mind… and a good time." She then plays a few notes and chords on the guitar, stops, leans into the microphone. I think she is going to sing about that simple place, but she says, "That's it." There are laughs. The song was twenty seconds tops. Nice. She goes on to play songs from her CDs, a few covers, covers unknown to me but that she makes her own. Before one song, she takes out her charango and begins to fuss with the tuning. "This is a beautiful instrument, but it's such a bitch to tune." More laughs from the audience. She is easy up there, like it's a rehearsal, and as the show continues it feels as if she's sharing things with us, divulging little secrets, rather than simply playing a show. For each song she is saying, "See this cool thing I found? Come here and check it out."

Her set has only a few songs with English lyrics, but that doesn't matter. It makes her voice more of an instrument. We listen to the melody, the tone, the blending of voice and guitar or charango. It's wonderful. All the while the audience sits quietly listening, floating, singing when Arnalds bids them to. They're here to see and hear the music, not talk, and it's noted, "You seem like a receptive audience, so I decided to trust you." She plays a new song then, one with no lyrics. She simply hums the melody. After a few measures, she stops and speaks, "What do you think? Should I keep working on that one?" The response is an overwhelming "Yeah!"

After the set, she leaves the stage, and I keep thinking she has to come back to play "Surrender." She *has* to. No one in the audience makes to leave or even stand up. We all stay there in the diminishment hoping for one more song, one more note. I look around the room and wonder how these people ever found out about this show. Icelandic folk singer comes to Seattle. It isn't exactly a top item in the news. But it should be. And she does come back. She steps up to the microphone for the encore but is without an instrument. Instead she sings an Irish folk song called "The Tree That Grows Too High." She just sings. Just her voice. And it's beautiful, a perfect ending for the show followed by some lively applause.

She finds me at the bar afterward. "I'm sorry, but I forgot to play 'Surrender.'" Who would ever have thought that Ólöf Arnalds would apologize to me? But it happens. I feel a little starstruck so the apology almost makes her not playing the song worthwhile, almost.

"You have time to talk awhile?" I ask. "I'll buy you a drink."

"Uh, sure. Okay."

I get the drinks. "So how did the whole Björk thing come about? How was that recorded?"

"Ah, that's great isn't it? We sent her the tracks, and she recorded her parts on her own and sent them back to us. At first, we attempted to do some edits but then we realized that you don't edit Björk."

Thinking about the blend of Arnalds and Björk on "Surrender," it's impossible to argue with that.

We finish the beers, and before ordering more I ask, "What are you guys doing now? Maybe we can continue to talk about music and have a few more drinks?"

"You mean like party?"

"Yeah, sure."

"Uh, let me ask George. We're staying in an apartment near here, and I'm not sure if we can do that there." She goes off and comes back a few minutes later. "I'm sorry, but we can't. There's a baby there who would be asleep by now, and we don't want to be rude."

"Understandable."

"It was nice to meet you, though. I'll play 'Surrender' next time."

"I'll be here."

After she goes, I look in the crowd, but the woman from Guitar Center is gone. Just as well, I suppose. I leave and get a cream cheese and jalapeño bratwurst from a guy working a cart a block up from the Tractor. I eat it in the car and it's awesome. I don't mind that I drip cheese and grease on my pants while listening to "Surrender" and wondering if Katie will show up at my place. It's Friday night, and we've been texting regularly since she slept over on Sunday. Greg broke up with her when they met up Monday, and she says she's okay, but one can never really trust the rejected lover. They always say they're fine, but they never are. We've emailed a couple times as well, and she texted today asking if I wanted her to come over tonight after the show. I said she shouldn't bother, that we'd catch up next week, that I'd come see her at work. She said that was okay, and anyway I want to see Greg before I go down that road. We've made plans to meet up Sunday evening at the Skylark, so until then I'd prefer not to see Katie because her emails are good and the tattoo grows in my mind. I can't remember whether she said it was over her left breast or her right, and the not knowing is all the more enticing.

On my way home, I switch the music to Radiohead. I always seem to on the late night drives after shows and beers. I sing along thinking that the chords from the blue guitar do not play things as they are, but as they are perceived, remembered, forgotten, embellished. When things slip into the past, they never stay the same.

There are no eyewitness accounts, no videotape, only poems, only that which we think happened, that which we reshape. When I get home, Katie's new car is there, her certified pre-owned car, a green Toyota Camry. I wonder if she ever got that formula right before heading to the dealer. She gets out with a growler of beer in each hand and walks over to me.

"Hi. I thought you might be thirsty."

"I am." We go inside, and though I wonder how long she's been waiting, I don't ask. I put "Surrender" on again as I just can't get enough of it.

"I'll pour a couple beers," Katie says. She goes into the kitchen, and I turn up the volume a little. I wonder whether I would have made a complete ass of myself if I had gone out for more drinks with Ólöf and George. Maybe there was no kid in the apartment. Maybe she just didn't feel like hanging out with me. I can't blame her. Who the hell am I to her? Just another lonely writer in a random town at a random show. I turn around, and there's Katie with the growler trying to twist its cap off. Her effort makes her body shake a little. "Uh, can you give me a hand with this? Seems it's stuck." I walk to the kitchen and find I have to squeeze with all my might to finally get it open. "Damn." I set the growler and cap on the counter, but before I can pour a couple glasses, Katie steps in and puts her arms around me. She leans up, kisses my neck, my left ear, my lips, and I think that maybe this is it. A little crazy or clingy or whatever Greg thinks, she's here, which must mean that she wants me. We sink to the kitchen floor where there's an elephant waiting for me.

Afterward, when we've made our way to the couch, I lie awake as Katie snores. It's her turn now. It's possible that we might find some love in all of this, but all I can think about is the Kristen Ward lyric, so I sing it in a whisper. Katie stops snoring briefly. There's a pause in her breathing that lasts longer than seems safe, and I understand how she feels when watching Greg sleep and snore and stop breathing, her hesitation to wake him. I know it's temporary, but it feels like watching someone die, perhaps a test run, and watching her sleep with suspended breath, I remember comparing the loss of hearing to death, but what do I know? What is the loss of sound compared to one's last breath? Everything and nothing. She begins to breathe. It's regular, quiet, and I sing the Kristen Ward lyric again, again in a whisper. Maybe I will die that way, all alone, broken, miserable, maybe Katie too when this is over. Many people will. But it's heartache in the future in exchange for some happiness now. Her eyes open.

"What're you thinking about?"

"I'm going to jail tomorrow," I say.

"You're what?"

"I'm driving down to the Oregon State Penitentiary to see a band called The Slants. They bring in bands sometimes to play for the inmates. When I found out it was happening, I asked if I could tag along."

"Why didn't you mention it before?"

"I haven't told anyone. I just wanted it to come out in my writing. Band plays in prison. Writer writes about it."

"You're pretty secretive, aren't you?"

"Private would be a better word."

"Until you write about things, though."

"Yeah, I guess so."

"It makes me think of Johnny Cash with you going to prison. That's pretty cool. Do many places do it?"

"No idea. I'm only doing it for my own experience. The band's happy to have a writer tag along, and I suppose the prison is too if it makes them look good. For me though, it's the chance to go somewhere I'd otherwise never be able to. That's one of the great things about writing. Every experience is research, and everything can be written about."

"What time will you get back tomorrow?"

"No idea, but probably late."

"You want me to come over?"

"Maybe. I'll text you."

"Okay."

"For now, though, let's just sleep."

But sleep isn't what she has in mind as she rolls over and gets on top and works me inside her. I have no problem getting aroused and have to wonder how closely tied sex is to love. The heart and mind can be anywhere, but the body is ever ready. She works up a good frenzied pace, and when she senses me about to finish, she says, "I want you to come inside me." It brings me out of the moment. If I'm not careful, our lives could take a sharp turn in these next few seconds, so I pull out, but we're still in the motion and she comes down on me and nearly bends my penis in two.

"Ouch!"

"Oh, shit! I'm sorry. Are you okay?"

I cup myself in my hands and make sure everything is still as it should be. I don't want to go to the hospital and when asked what the problem is say, "Uh, I think I have, uh, well... I think I have a broken..." and point down hoping not to draw attention to myself until the nurse says, "What's that, sir? You have a broken PENIS?" Thankfully, everything is fine, sore but fine.

"Yeah, I'm okay. I just can't do that. I know maybe it's safe sometimes given a woman's cycle and all, but I refuse to until I'm ready for the possible consequences."

"I'm on the pill."

"We never talked about that."

"You didn't ask."

"I know, but even so, I can't finish that way. There's too much risk."

"It's okay." She looks down between my legs. "You want to try again?"

"I don't think I can tonight. Let's just go to bed."

We get up and go to the bedroom where she falls asleep quickly, and after about an hour of trying to sleep myself, I go back out to the couch and sit with a beer and listen to Beethoven on the headphones, the "Presto Agitato" of *Moonlight Sonata*. It's the third movement and one of my absolute favorite pieces of music, and something I've heard inspired Chopin's *Fantaisie-Impromptu*, which is itself awesome. I've chosen poorly with the music, though. I need to think about all of this, but one can't form thoughts when Beethoven is doing his thing. One can only listen, feel, so I decide to think tomorrow on the drive down to Salem, and being suddenly hungry, I quietly get dressed and make sure Katie is still asleep. Then I write a quick note saying where I'm going and that I'll be back soon and head out to a McDonald's near my place where the drive-through is open twenty-four hours. I pull in, and there's no line, so I drive right up and order a cheeseburger and an apple pie.

"That'll be a minute on the apple pie, sir, if you just want to pull ahead."

So I do that and park in front where they've promised to bring me said apple pie. I kill the engine, unwrap the cheeseburger, toss the pickles out the window. I don't like pickles. The guy in the next car is looking at me. It's the cop who tapped on my window downtown after the Alabaster show. He's either undercover or off duty as he's out of uniform and in a plain car, a gray Chrysler minivan, and since he's looking, it's too late. There's eye contact, recognition. He smiles, gets out of his car, and motions for me to do the same. He has two cheeseburgers, one half-eaten. He sets a large drink and large fries on the roof of his car and finishes chewing a bite.

"I remember you from downtown, the sleeper by Dream Girls."

"Yeah. I appreciated your advice that night. Thanks again, Officer…"

"Adams, Wilson Adams, and you're welcome. I hope you're being more careful."

"Trying."

"I saw you tonight at the Tractor, by the way."

"You were there?"

"Yep."

"How do you know about Ólöf?"

"How do you know about anything? You just find out here and there. For this show, though, I saw someone post a link to a video on a music blog I read sometimes."

"Seattle Subsonic?"

"Yeah."

"That's me, man. I write under the name of robertmusic on that site. Thanks for reading."

"I was thinking it might be you when I saw you talking to her."

"She was cool and very nice, but she didn't play 'Surrender.' "

"Yeah, I was a little disappointed at that, but it was still a good show."

"Were you there alone? You should have come up and talked to us."

He just shrugs his shoulders. "I didn't want to interrupt. That would have been rude." We both eat for a moment. I take a few bites at once thinking I should leave soon. I mean, what am I supposed to talk about over late-night cheeseburgers with the cop who could have arrested me last time we met? He starts in on his second just as I'm finishing mine.

"Here, you are," says the McDonald's woman. She hands me my apple pie.

"Thanks." She goes off smiling, and I decide to eat it quickly so I open the box and take a bite, but it's burning hot so I spit it out. "Shit!"

"Careful there, pal." He steps closer, and I wish I'd ordered a drink to ease my burning tongue. "You smell a little like booze actually. You okay to drive?"

"I'm fine," I say, and taking a breath, I decide to go the somewhat honest route. "I had a few drinks earlier with a woman who just got dumped by a friend of mine, but I'm okay now."

"I'm not going to bust you, so don't worry. I just want you to be safe. I'm off duty anyways, and well, I have a cheeseburger to finish, and some fries. Fry?" He offers the container to me.

Saved by an order of fries. I take a couple. "Could I have a sip of that?"

"Sure."

I take a good long drink and get the idea that if Katie wasn't back at my place, I'd invite him over for a few beers and maybe a few more cheeseburgers while listening to "Surrender." He seems a good sort, but Katie's there. Why the hell am I here?

"I have to go. The woman's still back at my place."

"Your friend's girlfriend?"

"They just broke up. It's complicated."

"So, is she your girlfriend now?"

"I don't know. I need to talk to my friend first."

"Why? Didn't they break up?"

"Yeah, but…" I don't know. But what? They did break up, or more specifically, Greg broke up with her. He left us at the freaking Space Needle, didn't even show up. It doesn't matter what he thinks. I still have half an apple pie, but it's time to go. I should be at home with my arm around a naked woman, spooning, cradling, listening for breath. Instead I'm here eating fast food with an off-duty, over-weight police officer. And yet, he does read my blog. He came to a show because of it, and he seems more interested in my safety than in getting me on a DUI, so I get an idea.

"You want to catch a show sometime? There are a few cool things coming up."

"Yeah, sure, man. More fries?"

I take more fries. His ready response makes me think he's looking for a friend. Maybe I am too. We're both here alone in the middle of the night, and I don't think either of us came here at this hour simply to eat. We came to be out, to somehow interact. "I have to go home. You got a card or an email?"

He pulls a notebook out of his car and writes on it, gives me the paper. He wrote his name as "Officer Adams, Wilson" followed by an email address and phone number. "You can reach me here."

"Will do."

"Drive carefully."

"You too." We shake hands, and he drives off, his car not sounding too healthy, which is the way he looks in his chubbiness, the way he moves for his lack of grace, but here we are on the verge of possibly becoming friends, seeing bands together. A woman in a McDonald's uniform walks over to me. She's all smiles as she says, "Here you are, sir," and she hands me an apple pie. There must have been a mix-up inside, but I don't say anything. It would seem bad karma to refuse an apple pie at this hour. I take it, thank her, she goes back inside. I get in the car and head toward home. Are Katie and I on the verge of something? We did have sex twice, or rather one and a half times, but maybe that doesn't mean anything. Maybe it's just two lost people who simply don't know what else to do. And what about Greg, my friend? I don't know. All I know is that each day is a new cliff, a new chance to love, a new chance to get that present-tense happiness.

CHAPTER 15

I ARRIVE AT THE OREGON STATE PENITENTIARY. It's ten, and after an uneventful drive down from Seattle, I park in the visitors' parking lot but leave the engine and air conditioner running for a bit while my mind tries to figure how the day will go. This is prison after all, maximum security prison, and shit can go down at any time for any reason. I wait for a few more minutes in a mixture of excitement and fear as I'm about to willingly enter this facility and spend an afternoon in the company of two thousand felons milling about a courtyard, what they call the Big Yard, with but a handful of guards to keep them in check. I turn on the radio and switch it to classical, but finding nothing worthwhile, I turn it off. I pick up my notebook from the passenger seat and write on the first page, "Writer guy goes to prison."

The band playing here today is an all-Asian group with a sense of humor and an eye to turn what some see as a derogatory term into a positive. The Slants. They're having an uphill battle with the U.S. government, though, about trademarking their name as the powers that be insist "slant" is offensive in the context of Asian people. Application denied. But an appeal is under way. As for their music, they play what they describe as eighties Chinatown dance rock, think Depeche Mode with a little more guitar, a little more grit. It's fun stuff, so I'm curious to see how the inmates take to it.

The Slants' van pulls into the parking lot so I get out of my Jetta and head toward the prison. They see me and wave: "Writer guy!" one of them shouts as they continue to the restricted parking area where they need to check in their equipment item by item. When I get there, I shake hands with Thai Dao, one of the guitar players. "You made it. Good to see you." I reply in kind and nod to the rest of the band as five prison guards are going over the list of gear and trying to match it all up. One guard reads, "Uh, Vox 2x12 tube combo?" Thai points out the proper piece of equipment. It goes on, down to the extra clothing items, the guitar strings and picks, the condoms in one of the duffle bags. "These will have to stay in the van, guys." I half expect them to count the hair on our testicles, "Gentlemen, you'll have to forgive us, but now it's time to drop your pants." Thankfully, that does not happen, but they do turn to me. "And you, sir, what do you have there?"

"Just a notebook and a couple pens. I'm writing about today so I'll need to bring these with me."

A few guards load the music gear onto carts and take it into the prison while two others, one of them a slender female, lead us in through the guest entrance where they check IDs and take cell phones before giving us orange mesh vests to wear. The female guard gives us a warning, "Do not take these off at any time."

The singer, Aron Moxley, asks, "Can we take them off while playing? We run around and sweat a lot, and it's pretty damn hot today." He shimmies a little to his left when he speaks. The other guards in the room smile, and we laugh, but she's all business.

"Not even while you're playing. If anything should happen, the guards in the towers look for people in orange vests as those not to shoot." She pauses for dramatic effect. It registers, and we all make the mental note. *Hold on to orange vests above all else.* She continues, "Now, since you're playing in the Big Yard, things will be much different than if you were just visiting. I urge you to pay attention at all times. There will be some police tape separating you from the inmates, but remember, it's just tape. There will be two gates right behind the stage, so if there are any incidents follow me or the other officers through the nearest one."

Simon Young Tam, the bass player, asks, "How will we know if something's happening? I mean, the music will be loud."

"Well, screams, gunshots, general panic, that kind of thing. You'll know."

"Sounds like a rock show," Aron jokes, but again there is the sound of mental notes registering in the awkward laughs to his comment.

We go through a metal detector, and then the first set of bars shuts behind us. Oddly, this makes our group want to hasten farther in so that we may sooner step out into the yard. It's already an oppressive feeling to be in prison. We walk down a hall where another set of bars opens and then closes behind us. Two levels in. In this room, we exchange IDs for prison badges, and in the awkward moments of not knowing what the hell will happen, Aron says, "These vests make it seem like we're challenging the prisoners to a game of football." There are pokes and jabs and laughs to cover up the uncertainty, and he's right anyway. The vests do give a comical element to the whole affair. They're short with elastic around the bottom, so they keep riding up. After about fifteen minutes, we go through another gate. It closes behind us, and I try to imagine being here, being in a cell the first time those bars lock one in and everything else out. My imagination fails me, though. I'm here in an orange vest with a guest ID badge. My air-conditioned car in the parking lot is probably still cool. What do I know of forever? We walk down to the other end of the hall where our prison badge numbers are read to a man in a booth behind bulletproof glass. He controls the last gate, four to get in. Four. If shit does go down, I can't imagine we'll escape quickly.

We're among the inmates now. Some are doing odd jobs, one with a mop but no bucket, a few lingering by an unmarked brown door, and we all note that their blue uniforms make quite the contrast to our orange vests. Going through a door at the end of the hall, we step out of the building and get our first glimpse of the Big Yard, which is surrounded by a fence maybe fifteen feet high and topped with barbed wire, and the yard is indeed big, perhaps two football fields in size with a running track around the perimeter and benches at various places. The center is grassy and open, and the far corner is set up for baseball with an infield, a pitcher's mound, some bleachers. "Follow me," the lady guard says. We turn left and walk toward the gate. Even outside, everything in this place is behind bars with locked entry points. We look around and notice men with guns and sunglasses in towers along the walls, the sky a blue backdrop. It's the only thing of the outside world that can be seen in here. As we walk, I finger the edge of my vest and get the feeling that our first interaction with a prisoner will dictate the way of things, the amount or lack of shit that will go down. Near the gate, we are approached by a tall inmate, a thin bald guy who walks with a forward lean and a surety of self.

"All right, all right, all right. Here come the artists!" He shakes Aron's hand.

"How you doing, man, you making it?" Aron asks.

"Yeah, man, you got it, everyday, everyday. I'll be back out later with the second lot. Peace." He goes off on whatever prison business he's up to, but he has indeed set the tone. We aren't just seven individual guys—five band members, one drum tech, one writer—stepping into their village for a visit and a glimpse. We're more a collective piece of the outside world, a bit of everything normal and extraordinary that these guys have lost, that hopefully we can give them back for a few brief hours, and we come bearing guitars, drums, Vox 2x12 tube combo amps, a notebook and two pens. I watch him walk away and wonder what it must be like to be stuck in a place like this and carry the load with such ease. I scribble a picture of him in my notebook, write a few words, "tall guy, confidence, ease, everyday, the artists." Our anxiety diminishes a little.

"Sir, Mr. Writer Man, please don't linger behind."

"Oh, sorry."

I catch up with the group, but I'm smiling now with the thought that shit will indeed go down, but nothing bad. It will be good shit. It will be music. He was right. The artists have come.

We go through a gate that leads into some basketball courts and walk to the far end and stop in front of another gate, the entrance to the Big Yard. The female guard speaks into her radio. "Tower ten, gate nine, please." Silence as the gate remains locked. "Tower ten, gate nine, please." The gate clicks and opens, and finally being in, even though we're out, we sense the air of an outdoor music festival in the sunshine and openness of the yard where there is a stage set up just inside the gate and already many guys in prison blues, denim, the reason we were told not to wear jeans, busy at work setting up for the show. It's the prison roadie crew, which is the kind of work I'd volunteer for if incarcerated here.

There are two mixing boards, one by the stage for the monitor mix and one about fifty feet directly out front. The instruments are already here, so the Slants begin to tune guitars and instruct the inmates where to set the amps and keyboards. People are buzzing around me, running wires and cables and setting up speaker columns, mixers, amplifiers. There's a cluster of four guards lingering over by the fence behind the stage. The roadie crew is placing microphones around the drum kit and testing volume levels, and in the swirl of movement, I fall out of the scene then, have a moment of disappearance, a moment where life seems to move along without me, and I look at the walls, the prisoners, the guards with guns and can't believe where I am. *Fuck.* Everyone moves. Everyone is busy as I stand still. I take measured breaths as bodies go here and there, and the thought comes again, *I'm in fucking prison*. Everyone in this place must have experienced such a moment, the total disappearance, the disbelief. Radiohead's "How to Disappear Completely" pops into my head, so I sing a little under my breath about not being here, about this not happening as I imagine many of these guys must have thought when they first arrived. I see an old man over by the long fence that runs the length of the interior of the yard. He's sitting on a bench and leaning a little to his left. He's sweating in the heat of the sun but doesn't seem to notice or mind. He's a perfect cross between the skipper from *Gilligan's Island* and Ernest Borgnine and there on the bench seems a lost, lonely, left-out old man. I keep looking, and our eyes meet. He nods his head. We have an understanding. The old guy has indeed disappeared, but he's where he wants to be. I give him a slight nod back, and looking away, touch my left hand to my right forearm where I have a few bruises and a scratch, scars from a moment of passion.

I count the marks in the skin, five, and admire the purple blackness of each. They're from a good moment, but I get a little sad over it. The bruises will heal and disappear. The scratch will not scar. There is memory, of course, but one day that may fade, and it will be like it never happened, like those beautiful moments of life did not occur, like those nails did not dig in and leave marks, but they did, and in this moment, I can still feel her hand squeezing my arm, clawing into flesh, impregnating memory.

"Woman, huh?" I look up to see a middle-aged guy standing next to me. He's fifty at most, probably just under. "Anyone with a look like that in this place is thinking about a woman."

"Yeah," I reply. He's a little twitchy but seems friendly enough with a smile and wispy thinning hair. I suddenly get the idea, though, that I shouldn't have answered in the positive. When was the last time this guy had a woman? Why rub that into his wounds? But then, why lie? He already suspected anyway, and he was right. We haven't even been in the yard for thirty minutes, and I'm already missing the idea of a woman. Prison must indeed be a kind of hell.

He scratches his cheek, "I can hardly remember the last woman I had. And there weren't that many of those back then. Funny the shit you forget."

"How long you been in here?"

"Oh, almost thirty years. I'm up for parole again next year. I tell you, when I make it out I don't care if she's fat or ugly or whatever. Maybe fat's better. Why get my hopes up for anything else?" He has a gleam in his eyes as he says that. He truly will be happy with any woman if he ever gets out of this place. He won't care about looks so long as she offers herself to him. He won't care about her sense of humor, political leanings, reading habits, TV habits, musical tastes, so long as she offers herself to him. I've turned down or willingly let go people who have offered themselves to me. I've been the one turned down too. We all do this at the slightest whim, but this guy won't. It's perspective. The world looks very different from inside these walls. They do things to the brain.

"Sorry to hear it."

"Ah, well." The guy gives a mild grunt and leaves before I can ask him his name or why he's here, but I don't say anything. He must be thinking about women now, specifically that unknown future fat woman. What does one do in this place when the ladies enter the brain? I can't even imagine as I watch the band and the roadie crew still setting up for the show. Maybe I just don't want to know. I look at my arm again, put my hand on the bruises. The old guy over on the bench has his eyes closed and is smiling at the sun. Every prison I've ever been in has been of my own design, except for this one. I've escaped them all in the end just as I will leave here in a few hours, but that old timer and that guy thinking about fat women might never get out. They could very well die behind these thirty-foot walls and leave not a trace of themselves upon the world, and that makes me wonder what they've forgotten about their past lives or whether anyone out there still remembers them with any sense of fondness. There is so much lost in the course of a life, but maybe that's what life is, a kind of extended, even willful, forgetfulness as we go from one story to another. Sometimes we need to forget.

Sometimes we can't.

This just isn't working.

The Slants end their first set, and I speak to the inmate standing next to me. "So if you don't mind my asking, what are you in for?" His name is Charles, the head of the prison roadie crew, and he's trying to do out his time in earnest with good behavior while learning about live sound production.

"Murder."

What does one say to that? I'd come here prepared to ask the question and even to hear that very answer, but in the moment I'm stricken dumb. The word has such finality, and his tone is so matter of fact. Murder?

Murder.

"Look, it wasn't premeditated or anything. My woman was sleeping with another guy, and I just lost it in a moment and killed him. Never was in much trouble before, just a few parking tickets. The mind is a crazy thing. It just snaps sometimes."

"I know what you mean." It seems the right thing to say, but truth be told I don't know what he means. I only know the edge of it, that cliff in front of my apartment. I never fell off it. I never snapped. I could have. Perhaps on that day at Pike Place Market I could have followed them after a kiss on the head and done something worthy of being sent here, but I didn't. My desperation knows bounds, even as I feel at times that it's limitless. "It must be hard to be stuck in here for the actions of one moment."

"Yeah, when I woke up that day and went to work, I certainly didn't expect that to happen. My life and his gone for the sake of a fuck." It makes me curious to ask how he killed the guy, but I don't.

"What do you do in here to get by?"

"There's this sound stuff, and I play bass too. I don't know. I guess I just survive. People in here get through each day, day by day. It's all you can do, but the pain is still there... well, here." He taps his head and his heart. "The funny thing is that for the first couple of years I regretted losing my woman more than the loss of that dude's life." The rest of the roadie crew is busy making adjustments, nudging faders and eq knobs on the mixers, repositioning mics that have shifted during the first set.

"That's understandable in a way. People often do equate love with life, maybe even value it more, a willingness to die for love kind of thing." I have the further thought that people kill for love too.

"Word, man, they do. In this place, though, you realize that just to still be alive is all that matters. I'm giving at least twenty-five years, but I'll have a few on the back end. The view is limited here." He motions to the prison walls. "But we have our moments like today. A little sun and some rocking tunes. I bet some people on the outside actually have it worse."

"In some ways, you might be right. How much longer you got?"

"At least fifteen years."

The number is a punch to the gut. He has at least fifteen more years in here, mandatory minimum, twenty-five to life, and he's only ten in. I'd go nuts for sure, nuts and then some. He must certainly have a strength that I don't. Maybe it's these walls. Some people cower behind them. Some never lose focus of what lies beyond. I look over for the old man on the bench, but he's gone.

"What do you think you'll do when you get out?" I ask.

"Fuck if I know, man. That's too far away What about you?"

Again, I'm at a loss for words. What will I do when I leave here this afternoon? Drink a beer? Write a poem? Have Katie come over? He says just being alive is the thing. He has at least fifteen more years behind bars and fences topped with barbed wire and armed men in sunglasses, and he's happy just to be alive. Me? I have a car, a job, the freedom to come and go as I choose, sometimes a girlfriend and the requisite sex that goes with that, but the word "happy" just so often does not apply. Is it enough just to be alive?

"I'll write, or maybe play some guitar."

"You should find a woman. I suppose that's the obvious first thing I'll do."

"Perhaps, but not tonight." Katie comes to mind, her offer to come over this evening. I was planning to hang out with the band after the show, but it suddenly seems like a good idea just to head home, maybe drink a couple beers later and listen to music, or maybe I could drive out to the ocean and sit in the car listening to the waves. Being in Salem, the coast is only about an hour away. "There are more important things than finding a woman," I say.

"Spend any amount of time in here and you'll realize how dumb a statement that is."

"Maybe so."

A member of the roadie crew comes up to us. "Hey, Charles, that fifty-eight we had for the bass player's vocal mic fucking died, so we put in a fifty-seven. We'll tweak the eq a bit."

"Sounds good."

The other guy heads off to the mixing board. Simon and Tyler from The Slants walk up. "Thanks again for coming out today," Simon says to me, and then to Charles, "and thanks for the good sound." They shake hands.

"Sure thing, man."

"So," I say to Simon, "how'd you get into playing bass?"

"I first got into playing music at a pretty young age, I think around six, mainly because it was something that seemed fun and several of my cousins were getting into."

"So why bass?"

"There were too many guitar players. Well, that and my parents thought that the drums were too noisy. Otherwise, I'd have your job." He pokes Tyler in the shoulder.

"The hell you would."

"I loved your drumming, man. Been playing long?" Charles asks.

"Thanks, and yes. I remember my parents had signed me up for piano lessons in elementary school, but whenever they took me to music stores, I'd disappear only to be found in the drum room sitting in complete fascination trying to bang on crap. It just felt more natural to me. That's how you have to do it. You can't be forced into an instrument. You have to find it."

"Word, man."

"You play anything?"

"Yeah, bass. I did the same as him," Charles motions to Simon. "There were too many damn guitar players."

"You play bass too, right?" Simon asks me.

"Yeah."

"Christ. I'm surrounded by bass players."

"Who's your favorite player?" Charles asks. "For me these days it's Les Claypool for sure." He mimics playing the bass, slapping the bass, raps his thumb on his hip.

"Roger Waters and Geezer Butler," I say without hesitation. "I've never been much of a slapper. It's impressive to watch when done well, but it just isn't me, though I've always liked Flea and will occasionally thump out a little bit of 'Higher Ground.' "

"Ah, the Stevie Wonder version is where it's at," Simon says. "It's just so grooving, so authentic."

"It is, but I heard the Chili Peppers first. I know Wonder wrote it, but sometimes that first thing you hear just takes hold and seems the original even though it isn't. It speaks to the power of how well they did it. They made it theirs."

"Yeah, I love that album," Charles says. "What's that short little instrumental on there?"

"Pretty Little Ditty."

"Yeah, great fucking bass line."

"Agreed. Love that whole outro bit."

"What about you, Simon?"

"If you're talking about style of playing, I suppose I'm more a mix of Duff McKagan and Dee Dee Ramone."

"Yeah, thinking about your first set now, I can totally see it."

"You guys ever get stage fright?" I ask. This makes us all look up at the stage. The female officer who led us into the yard is up there now looking out. She's smiling. I wonder if she's imagining it, the concert, the music, the roar of the crowd. She exits stage left.

"I don't get stage fright," Simon says. "If you're passionate about it, you can completely lose yourself up there. Nothing to fear. When we take the stage, I just can't help but think that this is the most amazing thing I could do with my life, so I just let myself go and enjoy it."

I wish I could be like that. I do have those moments where I get completely lost in the music, where the playing flows and I don't worry about the next note or chord, where I "just let myself go and enjoy it," but then there are the other times like that Third Stone gig, those moments when the fear creeps in. It happens every show, every time I step on a stage. Am I a fool or am I brave to face such fears? I don't know. Maybe bits of both. I look again at the stage, long for it, for one more chance before my hearing goes for good, one more chance to make 2 + 2 = 5.

"Agreed, man, just let it fly. I remember in sixth grade a guitarist friend and I performed 'Wipe Out' at a school band recital, and I finished the song with a flashy Buddy Rich-style drum solo, and then afterward so many parents and classmates came up to me to tell me how good the performance was. From then on, no fear, no doubt."

"What about you?" Charles asks.

"I must admit I do on occasion."

"So then why even step on stage?"

"Because I love it as much as I fear it, because it adds up to five."

"What?"

I hadn't meant to say that, but it's out there now, my untested theory. So far, Katie and Greg are the only ones who have heard it, and they're not even musicians. Here goes, I guess.

"Five what?" Simon asks.

"I've been thinking lately about what music is, what it means, how it makes me feel like there's something more going on in the universe." Thai is up on stage now tuning his guitar. Aron is over talking to a group of inmates, one of them the bald guy we saw, the one who set the tone. The artists have come. An airplane flies far overhead unheard.

"Okay."

"And also that art isn't a direct representation of reality. It changes things, and so I got to thinking that maybe 2 + 2 can equal 5 sometimes, when the music is just so."

"Isn't that from *1984*?" Charles asks.

"Yeah, but this is different. In this way of thinking, I created a new constant called H, and H = 0, that is until the artist gets to doing his thing. 'Things as they are are changed upon the blue guitar.'"

"What?"

"It's a quote from a famous poem. So anyway, 2 + 2 + H = 4, and since H is a constant, it can never change, but through the miracle of art, it does, and the constant is reality. We get a new perspective, maybe even a new life. In *1984*, the main character is made to accept that 2 + 2 can equal 5 if no one else is willing to admit otherwise. If everyone agrees that 5 is the answer, then it's true. Anyone who wouldn't admit that would be tortured and perhaps killed, but this is different in the sense that I don't mean a forced denial of reality. It's an acknowledgement that reality can change through the magic of a G chord played in a certain way. And that reality changes things. It's hope and power."

"Fuck yeah, man. We used to have a recording studio in here too, and this one night I laid down a groove that just fucking made my world. It was kind of like 'Summertime Rolls' meets, uh, well, shit, 'Pretty Little Ditty,' a little slapping, some beautiful open passages. It was awesome."

"I'd love to hear it."

"Yeah, me too."

"As would I, but I don't have a copy since they dismantled the studio and got rid of all the equipment."

"Why'd they do that?" I ask.

"People fought over recording time. Eventually someone died right there, knifed while trying to mix a tune. They shut it down right away."

"Fuck man, that sucks."

"It does, but I still have it with me. I'll never forget that recording." He looks to me. "Maybe that's the first thing I'll do when I leave this place." The same guy who came over earlier taps Charles on the shoulder. He turns.

"Uh, can you give us a hand over here? I think Joey fucked up the reverb settings."

"Okay. Be right there." The other guy walks off. Charles turns to us. "I gotta go, but it was great talking with you guys."

"Indeed it was." We all shake hands. Tyler takes his leave as well to go fiddle with his drums so it's just Simon and I.

"I'd agree," he says, "that art isn't meant to reflect reality as it is, but rather what it should or could be."

"Or maybe what it was, or what was wanted."

"I've thought that the only thing constant in life is change and that all life experiences are distorted by the person experiencing life."

"I say the same. Everything I see is only the way I see it. That's why I write the way I do, not to show people what they should see, but what I see. I wonder about the truth of it, though, if truth really exists since we all see only what we can, what goes through our filters."

"I wouldn't say that truth doesn't exist, but perhaps it isn't as constant as we'd like to think it is."

"Maybe not at all. I've lately begun to think that the past is mutable, and it's art that does it, so H can change, or maybe I should change it to R, and, well, that makes me wonder if the present can change too, and so I sometimes question what is true. What is real if nothing is constant? I don't know. The only way I seem to be able to figure anything out is through music or writing, and even then I don't seem to figure out very much." I wish we were sitting at a bar now with a couple cold pints in front of us, a few already in us, some music coming over the sound system, a pretty woman sitting by the window alone, two more at the other end of the bar, and all the possibility in the world for the outcome of the evening. But we're here. We're in prison. The only woman here is that officer, and every man in this place must think about her from time to time. I would. I wonder if I will when I leave this place.

"I'd say that often times the kind of truth you're talking about is revealed through art: an epiphany, a fresh look at the past, a crooked twist where straight lines once stood. Other times, the numbers might not change at all, four being the only answer, but rather *we* change, whoever is experiencing something, and in doing so, the truth of what we experience changes. I think the change within ourselves rather than that which is around us is the most honest one of all, maybe that's what it is."

"I think you might be on to something."

"You ever heard of Karl Germain?"

"Nope."

"He was a magician who once said 'Magic is the only honest profession. A magician promises to deceive you… and he does.' Perhaps, it's the same with art. Art promises to change you, and so it does sometimes, and with it truth and reality might change as well."

"In that way of thinking, maybe I have it wrong. The constant is not reality but rather the self, as you say, and yet the self can change."

"Yeah, maybe so." Tyler and Aron motion to Simon from the stage for the start of the second set. "I have to go tune. We'll catch up after the show."

The Slants finish their second set with a rocking and very dance-able version of the Stones' "Paint It Black," a version all their own. If I didn't know it was a Stones' tune, I'd leave here singing the lyrics and thinking, "Wow!" Their version is raw and played from the gut, which is perfect in this place. Big, burly, muscled men are grooving. The old man appears back on the bench and nods a few times to the beat, and I wonder if he was a free man way back when the song was new. Men covered in tattoos raise their arms. There are shouts and screams and almost a sense of panic. They act like fans, and afterward, the band signs autographs, poses for pictures, shakes hands across the police tape boundary, hangs with the roadies. There are slaps on the back. There is talk about music. "I played guitar for years before I got sent here, and I loved what you did with that Stones tune, man!" For a brief time, as the music is still ringing in everyone's ears, this isn't a prison. It's just a field. Those thirty-foot walls contain only the space, not the men.

Wearing an orange vest as all visitors must, the inmates notice me. "Hey, man, you working for the band?... You the manager?... Are you the producer?... What you writing in that notebook?... Oh, you're that writer guy we heard was coming, nice to meet you, man!" I don't sign any autographs, but a few of them open up to me, the difference between music and the word I guess. They are excited by the musicians, "Hell yeah, man! That rocked!" But with me, they relax a bit, are almost vulnerable. "Man, I fucked up. How am I ever going to look my mom in the eye when she visits here? And my woman..." He is a short, almost tiny, black man in for armed robbery and murder, and his voice cracks a bit and trails off into nothing. If we were drinking beers in a bar, he would shed tears. I would put my arm around him—"Don't worry, man. Someday this will all be behind you"—and then I'd motion to the bartender for a couple shots of tequila.

He's possibly here for life, though, just like most of the roadie crew. What can I say to any of them? That day when it's all behind them may never come. Yeah, maybe they fucked up, maybe they deserve to be here for the crimes they committed, but seeing a forty-year-old man doing life for murder beg for autographs from the twenty-something Asian rockers in the Slants touches the heart. And it wasn't just him. The old man turned up, the one who had disappeared. He wanted an autograph, as did Charles. It makes me want to believe that no matter the crime, no matter the monster that once showed itself, there's a human in there too, a bit of the child that, hopefully, we all retain over the course of our lives, and seeing such locked behind walls wrenches the gut a bit. All we have here is time, and not much of it, and doing time is not life; it is not living. It is rather a kind of death.

In some moments, I do have regrets for the things I've fucked up, for the people I've hurt or disappointed, or both, the opportunities I've had in my grasp but that somehow slipped through the proverbial fingers, the lost loves and the ensuing agonies, but being in here for just a few hours, I'm happy for all of that because it happened out there. A life can shatter in a second, shatter in the reaction, say, of finding a lover with someone else, or in an email one receives and the sentence it brings, so Katie was right about the meaning in Star's song, only this moment matters, capturing it, remembering it, changing it. The Slants pack up their gear. I close my notebook. We leave. We drive north toward all that follows, all those cumulative moments out there beyond the walls where there are no guns aimed at those dressed in only blue, but also no orange vests to offer any protection.

CHAPTER 16

I LOOK UP AT THE SIGN: Rorschach Tattoos. I walk in. Straight ahead, there's a woman with blond hair behind a counter of white wood. She smiles. The counter wraps around to my left, and following it I see a chair and a stool and a desk and bottles of ink and drawings, a lamp with a Darth Vader head as its base. There's a bald guy sitting at a desk fiddling with some bottles. He turns his head.

"Hey, what can we do for you?"

"Want to get a tattoo."

"All right, man. Come on back and have a seat." The woman opens a gate in the counter, and I walk back, sit down. "So what do you want?"

I pull up my shirt, "I want to have this touched up, and I want to add a little horseshoe just above and to the right, meaning your left." I point to the spot on my chest. The tattoo I want touched up is a skull with roses growing out of it that I thought looked pretty cool way back in my early twenties. It still does, but it's faded, and I figure if I'm going to add the horseshoe so close to it, then I should freshen up the colors of the skull. I chose this place because it's close to my apartment and because it's at Alki Beach, which meant I could take a walk along the water. I did that half hoping the little kid who gave me the finger would show up. It would have been good for a laugh, but he wasn't around, so I made my way up and down without any memorable incidents before sitting on a bench for a while to think about Greg and Katie.

They made up. Greg called her, and they got back together. While I was in prison feeling the bruises, she was in bed with him, which I guess is the way it goes in prison. She apologized to me via text that night, said she had no regrets about our evening together, but she loved him and had to try to make it work. Truth be told, it did sting, doubly so because it should never have happened. Greg is a friend. She is too. What does that make me? I don't think she told him, but it's awkward for me now when Greg and I head to the Beveridge Place for a drink while she's working. We all talk, but they flirt and even hold hands across the bar when she isn't busy. I just listen to the music in those times and wonder if I should apologize to both of them or if I should just keep on with my way of saying nothing.

"Yeah, we can do that. How big you want the horseshoe? I'm Eric, by the way." We shake hands. He's the owner and chief artist here, which I know from their website. I suppose he's the one who named this place, and I must say I like his choice. It doesn't try to be too cool or edgy as many tattoo shops do, and it acknowledges the fact that sometimes people see what they want in a tattoo or rather only what they're able to see.

"I think about this big." I hold up my fingers trying to approximate the size, "Maybe a square inch, all black, no color." It makes me think about Katie's elephant. When I saw it above her right breast, I had the same sensation I get when looking at the cover of the book. I kept expecting it to fall, but it never did. It was just there, upside down, defying gravity. It seemed a little lonely.

"All right. The skull needs a little shading, some green for the stems and leaves, red for the roses, and we can make these roses a little bigger so the color holds longer. We'll say seventy for that, and, uh, another forty for the horseshoe if that works for you."

"Sounds good to me."

With my shirt still up, Eric and the receptionist are looking at my chest, and with the way he speaks, I think she's an apprentice. "See the shading around the skull here, Gin. That's really cool. Hey man, who did this one?"

"I can't even remember her name. I got it in Detroit years ago."

Gin is about my height, a little big, voluptuous I suppose, not quite beautiful, but not unattractive, which is what makes her attractive. She has tattoos all up and down her arms as well and some poking out from her cleavage, and I must admit there's something about a tattooed woman that intrigues me. I don't mean a woman with a tattoo of a butterfly on her ankle or the ever-popular tramp stamp or—and I might be kidding myself—a woman with a simple upside down elephant on her chest. I mean a woman like this one here, tattooed up and down, a believer in ink, given over to decorating her body with something other than makeup. "I like this one. Is there any meaning in it?" she asks.

"Nah. I just liked it when I saw a drawing. The horseshoe is related to the title of my book."

"Nice." She doesn't ask about the book or anything. Instead she traces the outline a little, and then some of the shading at the back of the skull, and I look at her tattoos. There are some tribal markings on the left bicep under a Chinese dragon. There's a Joshua tree with some stars over it on the other arm, a quote of something that I can't quite read, four lines, a poem or a song probably. There's a *Dark Side of the Moon* prism. I wonder if the quote is a Pink Floyd lyric. There are more, but I don't want to stare or ask right now. No woman I've ever been with has had more than one tattoo, but I've always thought it would be cool in a moment of passion to look down and see a whole variety of creatures and drawings looking up at me. She continues speaking. "You should add a rose going up to the horseshoe, maybe like holding on to it."

"Yeah, man," Eric says, "that'd be cool, and I'll tell you what. If you let Gin here do the work, we'll drop it to seventy and give you the horseshoe on the house. She's learning so she needs the experience." Gin and I make eye contact.

"That I do. What do you say?"

"Seventy? Sounds good to me. You have any time on Friday?"

I pull my shirt down, and they go over to look through the appointment book. I follow them. "How about five?" she asks.

"Great!" I reach out to shake her hand. "Rob."

"Gin. Actually, Genny with a G, but it got shortened to Gin when I was in high school." This seems like a little more information than she would tell just any customer. Or maybe I'm just hopeful. "What's your email and phone number so we can send you a reminder."

I write down the information and shake hands with her again, and Eric too. "Thanks for coming in." He has a strong grip but a delicate touch judging from the photos of his work on display. "See you then."

"Okay." As I turn to leave, I glance back. She's watching me. She smiles again. I wonder. She nods her head a little.

"See you Friday."

CHAPTER 17

I LEAVE WORK AT TWO, jump in the car and head home. The best thing about my job is that my boss is fairly lax, so long as I get my work done, which means I can sometimes take off in the early afternoon, and I do whenever I can. The consequence, of course, was that at my last performance review I was graded as average, told I didn't show much initiative. Screw initiative. I have no desire to move up in the company and climb the corporate ladder to positions in management and beyond. The corporate dream is not mine, but until music or writing can pay the bills, it's a paycheck and benefits as I haven't yet drummed up the courage to be like Manny and simply quit to go my own way.

There's a long screech of tires, and I lurch forward before coming to a halt a few blocks away from my apartment where a raccoon is leisurely crossing the road. It looks at my car, considers it for a second, moves on. It's the kind of thing that should give one a measure of perspective, the near death experience, or nearly being the cause of death. Some folks might think they're just happy to be alive and witness the backside of the raccoon escaping unscathed into the bushes, happy not to have to clean it off the street, happy to be breathing, to not be run down themselves by a Jetta on a side street in West Seattle at two fifteen on a Tuesday afternoon, content to have a job and drift through life not being dead. Others, though, would sense emergency, energy, maybe momentum, the shift of unstoppable time, and so the need would arise to be at home in the living room delving into the words, writing away the afternoon sun before pulling out the guitar to pound out the night, to be, for a few hours, as far away from the cubicle as possible.

At home, I sit down with a Blue Moon and boot my laptop. It's hot outside, so the door is open and a little breeze comes in every so often, one of which brings a leaf that settles right in front of the screen door. It's green, looks like it fell a little early, maybe a suicide, and while staring at the leaf, a black cat with three white feet crawls under the fence out front and walks toward the door. It peers in through the screen, tests the roughly two-inch gap underneath, first with a head, then the front right paw, the non-white one, but not being able to get through just looks in at me for a bit before going off with a meow. I'm sorry to see it go. If he comes back, I'll let him in. I pick up the acoustic and start to strum random collections of notes, a few chords, a few riffs. It's a meandering thing from G to A to E to F and wherever the mood takes me, and to whichever key, and I end up somehow on Iron Maiden's "Phantom of the Opera," which was the very first song of theirs that struck me, the first one that made me think them as more than just a good metal band, that made me think, even in seventh grade, though I didn't yet know it, of things adding up to five when they should only be four. There's the opening riff, haunting and heavy and beautiful in its way as it slides down to a B each time around. I play it, slide to that B, pause a little longer each time so that I can linger in the anticipation of the next riff to come, and as one B fades on the edge of the first verse, I sip my beer and enjoy the silence. Then there's a sound at the door.

Meow.

I look over. The cat is back.

Meow?

His voice trails up into expectation like a question.

"Hey, there, little buddy!" I set the guitar down and get up, walk to the door half expecting him to run away as I approach, but he doesn't.

Meow?

Maybe he likes Iron Maiden and wants to hear more. I open the door, and he comes in. He rubs his head against my leg, circles around, does it again, purrs. I bend down and scratch his neck. No collar, somewhat dirty, a little thin. He plops down on his back, rolls over, looks up at me in that knowing way cats do when they're trying to be cute.

"Welcome home, little guy."

CHAPTER 18

The keys of the laptop do not click
tonight. The cat does not
purr. The bass leans against the wall
next to the unpowered
Trace Elliot, the blue guitar
snug in its case. Even the refrigerator
respects the quiet of a moon
obscured by clouds as it cools
water
beer
soju
with no
hum.

Some nights are for creating,
some for just being,
some for watching
TV or
movies or
porn.
Some for cleaning
the apartment, for looking through
CDs without playing them, fingering
the air guitar with
the imagined chords,

E minor, D, E minor, D,
and hearing Eddie in my brain
singing about swallowing poison
until growing immune,
for rearranging books without rereading
them, flipping the words quickly and setting
them unreread upon the shelf.

and some...
some nights are for remembering
things lost,
like the Detroit friend who did not believe
I could get angry, "I told people
to call me if you do because I want to see it,"
he'd say.
He's dead now, car accident, drunk.
RIP. Chuck.
Or like the only band in which I switched
my bass for a guitar and where I
was told some of my noodlings
resembled those of Jerry Garcia.
"This one's called All I Want,"
our singer would speak
into the microphone, and the song
would start, and I would noodle,
and the band would unceremoniously break
up only a few months later.
Or all the women who heard
me say it,
"I love you,"
even those who did not respond in kind
with those same eight letters,
two spaces,
and a period.

Of course there was much
that did not happen. A woman
on her back on my bed

and arms up circling her hair
years ago in Detroit after bars
and beers for the evening,
but there was no sex, nothing to hold
onto the next morning. I wanted
to rip her clothes off and ravish
her but found a lack of courage
like all those doubts on stage,
thought maybe I'd left it at the bar
like a lost wallet, an unclosed
tab that I could pick up the next day.
We talked instead of my post-high school
trip to Europe. I showed her pictures.
She left. One more of the many things
that floated past just out of reach,
that slipped through fingers
though fingers
were clamped tight as possible.

I squeezed and clenched
those fingers last year
after lost love,
after all the coffee
in the world at the first
post-coital breakfast.
With five cups finished
she said with shaking
hands, "I need to take things slowly,"
and then motioned for a refill.
"Uh, okay."
I ordered some Baileys
for my coffee, and we talked about the Cult,
and I smiled at what I hoped
I'd found in her.
It was our last moment where everything
felt new, the first of the beginning of the end
as I have only one speed,

a speed that quickly pushed her
out of my life.

But we shared things
whispered things
touched things

changed things

And so these remembering nights are
a pleasure, the hushed, solitary
beer at 1:37 in the morning,
rotating the blue and gold cap
in my hand, noticing the birthday card
from her still on the shelf,
a dusty unreread relic
next to the unreread books,
her picture face down
on the desk
where it will stay until I get
the energy to put it
in the closet,
one more name lingering in the dark
amongst former lovers
and floating in the poems
of my past. I walk over
to stand in front of the world
map on the wall and trace
the bottle cap over places I've lived,
pause over
Seoul
and smile that the map, printed
in Des Moines, Iowa,
has it misspelled as
Soul,
something I must correct
with a pen in blue ink.

서울

I find Columbus,
Detroit, Seattle.
Love was here,
but it's past tense,
a present that slipped
into memory,
a memory that
fragmented into verse
so that the song
continues
in a different key
even as it is dead.

I lift my drink,
to the map,
"Cheers."

I could be anywhere
in the world tonight,
with anyone
speaking any language,
but I am here
speaking
the only language
I know.

And smiling at the pain
that things did float,
things did
slip, keys changed,
songs ended,
but things
happened…
things
happened.

CHAPTER 19

THERE'S A KNOCK on the door, a twist to the knob, a head peeking in. It's Greg. He takes a couple steps and stops, remembers this is still a shoeless house. Meow. He looks down at the cat. "Hey, this must be Soju." There's the trill of a purr, a head rubbed against his shin. Maybe it can be said of most kinds of booze, but a couple shots of soju will certainly take the edge off, and that's what the cat has done for me these past few days, so last night when I had a bottle on the coffee table, I read the label aloud, "Chamisul Soju," and said to the cat, "That's what we'll name you, Soju." I did another shot, and the little guy meowed, which I took as a sign of acceptance. He's been sleeping in the bed with me since he moved in, kneading the spare pillow, purring as I drift off. There's a comfort in those tiny motorboat sounds that makes sleep come with ease, perhaps too easy as I haven't got much done this week other than nap with him on the couch before dinner, after dinner, before bedtime, and then sleep in bed. He's given me a respite so I've decided to change my idea for a tattoo from a horseshoe to soju as it's written in Korean:

소주

It's a reminder to live in the present tense, to feel good about what I have, what I will create, what I will find, and I can draw it up to look arty and yet simple enough for someone without any knowledge of Korean to make sense of the design and for Genny to apply it to my skin in the proper way.

"So, you ready to go?" Greg asks.

"Yeah. Where's Katie?"

"I'm going to pick her up after I drop you off." He's giving me a ride to Rorschach Tattoos because my car is in the shop for some bodywork. It was parked in the street out front and was hit late Tuesday night or early Wednesday morning. I didn't hear when it happened. I was either asleep or up writing with the headphones on and the volume up. I discovered it when I left for work. The back end was smashed in. It could be unsmashed, thankfully, but I'd be without a car for at least a few days.

"I appreciate it." After I get the tattoo, Greg, Katie, and I will head into Seattle to see a band called Sightseer at the High Dive where a lot of up-and-comers play. I've seen and written about Sightseer before when they played the Skylark a few months back, but they're good enough to see and write about again, and again, Star Anna good, which is a little funny because Star's bass player and guitar player used to play with the lead singer of Sightseer, P.A. Mathison. All concerned are better for it, though. Star's music is awesome, and P.A. found some new musicians and formed a new band that played its first gig after only ten days together. Bands are like marriages. You have to find the right fit. Star and P.A. have, and now Sightseer is one of the best-kept secrets in Seattle. Elena is the only person I've met who has mentioned liking the band. I smile. Elena in her Cheap Trick tee shirt and her painting of the empty bench in Central Park. I'd forgotten about her. She never sent me a link to her paintings. Or was I supposed to contact her? I can't remember. Maybe I'll have to seek her out at another Jesus Rehab show.

I remember thinking back in the Third Stone days that we were the best-kept secret in Columbus. We played the Southberg at least once a month for a couple years, but our crowds never seemed to get much bigger than eighty people, a hundred or so a few times. There was a core of regular fans who were always there for the shows and the parties afterward, but it was steady. If a few graduated and stopped coming, a few more replaced them, but only a few, the rush and surge of fans never happened. It could have been the dungeon-like vibe of the bar. People went there because they knew something, not because they happened by, and the Southberg was at the southern edge of campus past all the dance clubs, frat houses, and pickup joints, a far walk for the musically unadventurous. Columbus just wasn't much of a scene. It was a city that somehow fancied itself the next Seattle with a few bands that signed with the majors, but those bands went nowhere. They broke up or turned into cover bands as the years rolled on and the hairlines receded. Or perhaps the crowds stayed away because of our music. The heavy psychedelic of Third Stone didn't fit in. Walking around the Ohio State campus, one was more likely to hear the Grateful Dead or Nirvana blasting from cars and apartments and dorms. We rocked like one of those bands, droned on like the other, and though there were those who understood, those who got lost in some of our never-ending jams, they weren't many. We figured the reason was simple. The right people hadn't seen us, but then, every struggling band thinks such. There isn't much to do in that situation, though, except keep on playing those E chords and G chords and those extended twenty-minute outros. We stayed true to what we believed in the moment. We didn't try to please anyone but ourselves. Failure was an option, but compromise was not. Sightseer is in a similar boat. They should have as many fans as Pearl Jam, but sadly, they're still playing the High Dive and struggling to fill the venue.

On the way to the tattoo shop, Greg pops in a Smashing Pumpkins CD, *Siamese Dream*, their last truly great effort. "Cherub Rock" kicks in. Creative genius doesn't often last long. These guys had two spectacular albums, which is better than zero, but then they became very hit or miss, almost ordinary. Where does it go? I wonder if they wonder, if they sit around saying to one another, "Man, we're just not creating on the same level as we were back in the day." All one can ever do, though, is try to get it down, to keep at it as the years roll on, to keep working for the next masterpiece. It's easier when you've had the kind of success they once had. They have money. The need for the day job has been removed. Maybe that's it. Maybe the drive is gone. Maybe it's about putting food on the table rather than creating a work of art, writing something to move sales numbers rather than hearts and souls. I still have hope for Smashing Pumpkins as there were some good tracks on 2007's *Zeitgeist*. I listened to that CD more than a few times during my morning and evening commutes, but now I'd be at a loss to describe anything on it. It just didn't stick. I want them to write another gem, though I do, but I'm just not expecting it. Even Radiohead let me down with their last one. *The King of Limbs* didn't do anything for me. It sounded as if they were trying too hard not to repeat themselves, and in that case they succeeded, but in the process the music fell to the floor without a pulse. "Cherub Rock" fades out and I stare out the window for a few moments. We drive past the Skylark and under the West Seattle Bridge. The downtown skyline is off to our right. It's overcast, quiet. We come to a stop light in front of a Wells Fargo bank near Admiral Junction in the northern part of West Seattle. There's a homeless man sleeping in front of the ATM with a cardboard sign that reads, "Will work for beer." At least he's honest.

"Dude, hello?"

"What?"

"Man, I swear, sometimes I think you're deaf." I hadn't even realized it, but there was no sound. The ringing always increases in those moments, drowns out all other sounds, but not this time. The thought scares me.

"Deaf? Nah, I was just a little lost in thought."

"You seem to do that a lot."

"Lots to think about."

"So anyway, what's up with the new ink? What are you getting?"

"Don't feel like saying just yet. You'll have to wait until it heals to see it."

"That'll be a few days. What the fuck? You can tell me."

"Sorry, can't."

"I'll get it out of you before the night's over."

I will show him, of course, but not tonight. I just want to keep it to myself for a couple days, hold on to the secret while lounging on the couch with Soju and strumming songs on the acoustic, maybe Smashing Pumpkins' "Rhinoceros" as that was always a favorite for the soft sweetness of its verses. We get to the tattoo shop. I get out. "We'll be up the street. Text us when you're done."

Genny smiles and walks around the counter to greet me, "Hi. Eric had to take off, so it'll just be you and me. Hope you don't mind."

"Not at all." How could I? She'll be leaning in front of me with her hands on my chest guiding the needle with no one else around. The place is cold from the air conditioning, so she's wearing a black hoodie and jeans. We walk back around the counter. "We had a few cancellations, so I'm all ready if you want to get started." She motions to the chair. I take off my shirt and set my notebook and pen on the desk next to the Darth Vader lamp. I notice it now has a peace sign drawn on its forehead. "You want any music?"

"The radio's fine." She has on the local hard rock station, KISW. The afternoon show is something called the Men's Room, which is four guys who basically just talk about their lives and drinking and music and drinking. It's a man's perspective on things with an often juvenile sense of humor, but they are funny and sometimes insightful. They come across as very personable guys, likeable, average in the sense that they don't seem like radio personalities or like they're putting on a show. They seem genuine, and they drink a lot, so a guy like me can identify with much of what they have to say. Just after five every evening, they do something called the "Shot of the Day" in which they do an actual shot on air after making a toast to someone who has done something newsworthy and stupid. They're just getting to it today with shots courtesy of Aha Toro Tequila, the reposado, one of my favorites. Today's story is read by Men's Room DJ, Steve "The Thrill" Hill. He's black, no hair, tattoos. Like me, he plays bass and likes Black Sabbath and Iron Maiden. He's the edgier one of the bunch, and he doesn't pull punches. He'll lay into things straight away. It'd be cool to sit down with him and talk about music and bass and tattoos. He clears his throat and reads the story.

"Okay, today we honor twenty-seven-year-old Vernon Fisher of Olathe, Kansas. Two weeks ago, he walked into a music store and proceeded to put a brand new Gibson Les Paul into his pants, yes, into his pants. He slid the neck of the guitar down the right leg and did the stiff-leg hobble when store employees were distracted with other customers. Now, here's the thing. He could have gotten away with it, but last week he took the same guitar back to the same store and tried to sell it back to them as used. The *same* store. Here's a quote from the arresting officer: 'We believe the suspect may have forgotten where he stole the guitar because of drug-related reasons.'

Geez, ya think?" There's some laughter on air as they make jokes at
Vernon's expense.

Genny laughs. "These guys crack me up sometimes."

"Yeah, me too." I sit in the chair, lean back, prepare for pain. She
looks at my chest in a way that I might look at page one of a story,
the first blank page wherein lies all possibility for colors and words
applied just so.

"This might hurt a little."

"I know."

"We'll start with the skull and then the roses and then the
horseshoe."

"Oh, yeah. No horseshoe. When we get to that point, let's pause
and I'll show you what I want."

"Okay."

She gets to it. I wince. She smiles, seems to dig a little deeper.
Nirvana's "In Bloom" comes on the radio, and she sings along
quietly for a little bit.

"So how'd you get into doing tattoos?"

"I've always been good at drawing, and after getting a couple
pieces done here..." She pauses, wipes the blood from my skin,
continues jabbing me with the needle. "I got to talking to Eric
about it, and he offered to teach me, so I figured what the hell.
When I'm ready, I hope to open my own shop, but you know, even
if I stay here doing the receptionist thing and tattooing when I
can, it beats the hell out of being in a cubicle, which is where I
was." She dabs the blood again, blows on the work in progress,
dabs, blows, considers. Dabs and blows again. It reminds me of
someone drawing with a pencil and blowing away the shreds of
eraser. Maybe pencil is her preferred medium so it's just a habit.
Dab and blow.

"Most things do beat the cubicle." She dips the needle in some ink,
continues shading roses. "I know I want to get out."

"You should. I did. I made more money before, but I was miserable. I felt like a fake."

"Maybe I will one of these days." She gets to working with the
green of the stems. "You from around here?"

"Born and bred. I love Seattle. It's so unassuming, so easy just to
be yourself. What about you?"

"I've lived in a few places, spent a few years overseas, but I agree with you. Seattle is home."

"Where overseas?"

"Korea?"

"Were you in the army?"

"Me? Hardly. I'm not the soldier type. I taught English." She pauses, looks at me. We hold eye contact for a moment. "River of Deceit" by Mad Season is playing on the radio, summoning Layne Staley's voice from the grave to sing about pain being self-chosen. She turns her head toward the radio. I smile to see that she's tapping a foot and ever so slightly mouthing the words. The song means something to her. The tattoo pauses, but that's okay. We all should stop what we're doing at times and just listen to music. When the song ends, they break to commercial.

Genny looks at me. "Yeah," she says, "you don't seem military. Not that you couldn't be tough if need be, but you seem more... gentle." She gets back to jabbing me with a needle.

"Thanks. You like Mad Season?"

She keeps working, doesn't look up, "Yeah, I saw them once at the Moore with my dad before he died. They were awesome. Layne Staley's voice always went straight to my heart, my dad's too."

"Sorry about your dad."

"It's okay. He sang that song to me from his hospital bed trying to cheer me up. He was the most honest and selfless person I ever knew." She closes her eyes briefly. The song is still in her head, and her dad too, harmonizing with Layne Staley. She sighs, "So, got any big plans for the weekend?" she asks.

"Going to see a band later."

"Who?"

I wince.

"Sorry."

"Sightseer. They're a local band. I'm writing about them."

"You write? That's cool. For who?"

"Seattle Subsonic."

"Never heard of it."

"I'm not surprised."

"Where's the band playing?"

"The High Dive up in Fremont."

"Nice. I hang out up there all the time at a place called the Red Door. Good friend of mine is one of the bartenders. What time do they go on? Maybe I'll stop in if I head that way later."

"They're first, so right about ten."

"Okay."

"Ouch."

"Sorry." She finishes up, dabs it with a cloth, blows on it again, repeats to my delight. "So what's this other thing you want?"

I open my notebook and point to a place where I'd written the Korean letters as artfully way as I'm capable.

소주

"What's that?"

"It's Korean. It's pronounced *so*" — I point to the first symbol and then the second — "*ju*... It's a kind of alcohol, but it's also my cat's name."

"You named your cat after a kind of booze?"

"Yeah."

"Funny." She looks at my writing. "Okay, we can do this. Can I tear this page from the notebook?" She doesn't wait for my answer and just rips it out and holds it up to my chest while motioning her hand in the shape of the letters, then she changes the needle in the tattoo gun, dabs it in some black ink, smiles. "Here we go." She digs the needle in my skin while I try to watch upside down. "So what kind of music does this band play?"

"In generic terms, they're alt-indie rock with a touch of country, but I guess a better way to describe it would be that they sound like the love child of the Black Crowes and the Cowboy Junkies."

"Interesting. I love the Black Crowes."

"Me too. I saw them years ago in Detroit, the *Southern Harmony* tour. Very cool."

"I'm jealous. 'Remedy' is great, of course, but I think my favorite on that album is 'My Morning Song.' "

"Sightseer plays that sometimes actually. You'd dig 'em." Soundgarden's "Spoonman" comes on.

"Okay, done. You can check it out in the mirror." That was quick, but it's really only nine tiny lines, no color, no shading. I get up and walk to the mirror. I blink a few times, look back at her, look back in the mirror. My jaw drops. I've become that person, the guy with the misspelled Asian-language tattoo. In her free-handing of the letters, and I guess in being distracted by conversation, she got it wrong. It is supposed to be

소주

but instead she has etched something else into my skin.

수조

It reads "Sujo," and I just don't know what to do about it. I close my eyes. *This can't be happening.* But when I look again, it is. It's right there staring back at me from the mirror.

수조

Fuck. It is happening. In one way of thinking, it doesn't matter since I doubt that a Korean will ever see my chest again, so I guess I can pretend it's correct or make up a meaning for it. Or maybe I can rename the cat. "Here, Sujo. Good kitty." He probably wouldn't notice. He'd just purr and rub up against the dragon. He's taken to doing that when I write. I'll sit down and start typing, and then he's there at my feet. He'll meow, jump, rub, and purr. It has me thinking about moving the dragon for fear he'll knock it over. I touch my chest next to the new marks and move my index finger in the way the letters should be. No, I can't pretend it's correct. I'd know for the rest of my life that it wasn't, that Sujo's name changed only because of a permanent typo, and, anyway, it's too close to Cujo, and I imagine that would draw questions. "Sujo? Wasn't it Cujo? And wasn't it a rabid St. Bernard?" So then what do I do? Do I get pissed now? Do I shout, "What the fuck is this shit?" and threaten not to pay? Or do I ignore it and just get it covered up eventually, and if so, what the hell would I cover it with? One thing I know is that it can't be fixed. The lines are too different, too small. I look back at her, and she's cleaning up her stuff but perhaps sensing my stare speaks without turning her head toward me, "How's it look?"

"Great," I lie. I'll have to cover it up eventually, so there's no point in ruining the possibility of this evening.

"Come here. We'll put a bandage over it so you can get to the High Dive."

"Okay." I sit back down in the chair, and she rubs some lotion on the new ink. Her touch is soft now, more of a caress, almost sensual. She leans in close inspecting her handiwork, and I feel her breath on my skin, goose bumps. "Looks good," she says. Then she places a bandage over it. I put my shirt back on, stand up. Ozzy's "Suicide

Solution" comes on the radio, and memories of sixth grade come flooding back. I used to put *The Blizzard of Oz* on the record player and prance around my bedroom playing air guitar hoping and dreaming of the day I'd step on stage. I had no idea at that young age what the lyrics meant. I mean I knew what suicide meant, but I didn't understand it, not really, and certainly not how people got to that point, which wasn't even a point of the song. For me in those days, it was just melody and heavy guitar and thumping bass. What did I know of suicide or the things people do to sustain themselves throughout life? All I knew then was that as each song would end, the imagined crowd would roar, and there were no doubts because I wasn't actually doing anything. I was supremely confident. My air guitar was flawless.

"So then…"

"Seventy dollars, right?"

"Yeah."

"Here's eighty."

"Thanks. I have a few more appointments, but maybe I'll try to make it to that show later. Sightseer, right?"

"Yeah, come on out." We shake hands and pause with our palms still pressed together, and there's Randy Rhodes cranking out those massive chords that still move me all these years after his death. I always liked that there was no solo in this song, even the outro bit is just high notes and bends shaken and stirred by a whammy bar, and then it fades and there's the Men's Room again speaking in voices that I can't quite pick out. After a second, we let go of each other's hands, and our eyes meet. I know I'm getting this wrong. She did screw up, but I allowed it to happen.

수조

I don't know what to do so I guess I'm doing nothing and already kicking myself for it. "If you can make it to the show, text me because I might be in the back of the club talking to the band." I know she has my number since I left it here before.

"Will do. See ya."

I like that response. *See ya*. It isn't anything, but it feels like a confirmation.

Outside I walk up the beach for a couple minutes before calling Greg. He answers but doesn't even say hello. "Sorry, dude, we can't make it back. Shit's fucked up. Let's meet later at the High Dive."

"Okay. You all right?"

"Yeah, I'm fine. Katie's just nuts. I know I did this kind of thing that day I was supposed to meet you at the Space Needle, but I just don't think I can be with her anymore."

"What happened?"

"I'll tell you about it later. How'd the tat come out?"

What do I say to that? I know that I can't fake it, that I can't go around saying it's cool, it's great, just what I wanted, and then suddenly get it covered up. Or can I? The ink is permanent but not the idea. If it's meant to mean something to me in the now of my life, then who's to say I can't change my mind in two weeks. Life moves quickly. Ideas change. People change. Relationships change. Why not tattoos? I'll give it a little time then get it covered up. "It came out well. Maybe I'll show you later."

"You'd better. Meet there around nine?"

"Sounds good." And with that I catch a cab home. The driver is not one of those cabbies inclined to start a conversation. He's just out to drive and make his money, and I'm glad for it. In the back seat, I hold my hand lightly to the typo on my chest and wonder what happened between Katie and Greg. It's the second time they've split up just before meeting me. Maybe I'm the problem. I should probably say something to her, to him, to both of them together.

I get home, and Soju greets me at the door. Meow. He rubs against my legs, then jumps on the desk and rubs against the dragon. I wonder if he remembers his previous life, other legs and furniture and statues to rub against, other fingers that scratched his cheeks. I plop on the couch thinking I might need a nap before going out tonight, but then there's Soju on my stomach, then my chest. He's found the spot where the bandage resides over the tattoo and begins to do his kneading thing right there, right over the skull and roses and misdrawn letters, and he knows where to dig. I wince, but he just stays there, kneading, purring, staring at me.

"Meow," I say.

No reply, no pause, he just keeps at it. Maybe there's a smell, something akin to blood that he feels somehow he can help to heal with a little applied pressure. My stomach rumbles one, two, three times, and I think about enchiladas and tacos and burritos. I need some food, but there's nothing here as I usually eat out. I used to cook more. I used to like it actually, back when I had someone to cook for, but then living alone and without a girlfriend, it doesn't make much sense to whip up a batch of twelve chicken enchiladas, which was at one time a specialty of mine. I made that on my first birthday in Korea way back in 1998, my twenty-ninth. The Koreans I knew then had never had enchiladas, had never had any Mexican food, and I thought that a crime so I cooked for them. "Enchilada good," one woman said. One of the guys there, a college student whom I was tutoring illegally, put on a CD of a Korean rock band called Lydian.

"Whoa, they're pretty cool," I said. There was an instrumental that started soft and then shot up into an excellent solo that tonally reminded me of Zappa's *Joe's Garage*, and that faded into some open, clean chords that brought to mind Ozzy's "You Can't Kill Rock and Roll," and though I didn't speak any Korean yet, I dug the music and the melodies. The voice was just an arrangement of notes in a pattern repeated with variation, and I liked the whole CD so much that I sought out the band a couple months later at a show in Seoul and wound up befriending the singer/lead guitar player. He knew only a little English, and with my slowly increasing Korean vocabulary we spoke in broken sentences about music and then went back to my apartment for tacos with a couple of young Korean beauties whose names I cannot now recall. I wonder if they can mine. The Ozzy-like song I liked so much was called "Eurosay," and I learned that night that it was about a kind of utopia with a great big sea and sky that would swallow all things bad, leaving only peace and calm and solitude. It always makes me think of the East Sea (what Koreans call the Sea of Japan) and sitting there one New Year's morning for the sunrise and looking out at the water toward Japan and America beyond. I sing a line for Soju on my chest.

"난 거기 가고 싶어" (*Nan gogi gago ship aw*. I want to go there)

"Sounds pretty good, huh, Soju? Eurosay?" He's quiet, has stopped kneading my chest and is now just curled up on my stomach, which rumbles yet again. I get a hankering suddenly to do a bit of cooking, and after easing Soju down, I go quickly into the kitchen with a meow following me.

"What do you think? Is it an enchilada night, a taco night, or a burrito night?" No answer. I open the refrigerator and smile to see its minimal contents. There will be no cooking before going to the store. I have no chicken or beans or tortillas, only a few spices, half an onion, some lettuce, five beers, two bottles of soju and some I Can't Believe It's Not Butter. I stand there with the refrigerator door open and consider the idea of grocery shopping on a Friday night before meeting a Katie-less Greg out at the High Dive but then remember I can't go to the store now. My car is in the shop. "Looks like I'll be taking the bus, Soju." I fill my blue guitar coffee mug with water and drink it down then look at the cup. My last gift from the old love, the only gift, and other than a few pictures, the only reminder I have of the fact that she was ever in my life. In some ways, it's a little more special than even the pictures because she once held it, she once bought it with me in mind. I sometimes imagine her in a store standing in the checkout line with a smile to think that I'd like the mug. She probably knew that I'd cherish it even years after she was out of my life for the joy of a few happy moments shared. I set the cup down on the counter a little harder than I intend, which gives me a shudder for fear of breaking it, but I check, and it's fine, no cracks, no chips, just a blue guitar on a white background, the memories intact, so I look up the transit schedule online and put some food in Soju's bowl. "You be good now." He just stares at me from the couch with a look that shows both his disinterest because he's a cat, but also his desire for attention and a good scratch on top of the head because he's a cat. I give him such. He purrs. I leave.

CHAPTER 20

I GET TO THE HIGH DIVE a little after eight and enter to see Officer Adams standing just inside the door. I should probably just think of him as Wilson and be casual about it, but considering how we met, it comes to me in the more formal sense. If we turn out to be good friends, though, I can see myself calling him Officer. "Hey, Officer, grab me a beer while you're in the kitchen." I wonder if he'd mind. He's wearing jeans and a black AC/DC tee shirt with the *Highway to Hell* album cover on it. The shirt is a little too short so that if he bends over we'll get a good view of his back, and maybe his crack too. He looks up, motions me to come over. It isn't unexpected to see him here. We talked briefly at McDonald's that night about meeting for a show, and tonight is the first time. We'll see how this goes. "Good to see you," he says. "Can I buy you a drink?"

He could have had me on a DUI when our paths first crossed. Now, he's here at the High Dive and offering to buy the first round, one of life's weird turns. Meeting him shifted my trajectory into some other universe where I don't end up in jail, where I haven't yet been held accountable for anything, where I've been given warnings, possible hints of the future, but I've done nothing to change my actions. I'm either too dumb to get it or I just don't give a damn about anything except music and writing. Maybe both. "No, man, I got it," I say. I'll buy the drinks. I owe him at least that much.

"Sounds good to me. I read your review of this band but decided to take your advice and not listen to any of the music beforehand."

"Cool. The recordings are good, but live is the thing. They're a little more rocking. They won't disappoint."

"They better not." He laughs a little, and we go to the bar and order a couple Manny's. He struggles to sit on a barstool, and I think he's either been here a while or is just showing signs of that awkwardness I witnessed when I first met him.

We clink glasses. "Can I ask you a question?"

"Sure."

"That night you woke me up downtown, why didn't you arrest me or at least test me for DUI?" He sips his drink for a moment while considering the question.

"Nine times out of ten I would have, but I guess there were two reasons. First, you didn't *seem* drunk, and well, I was honestly a little embarrassed at falling over. I'm not in the shape I once was." He lifts his shirt and pats the whiteness of his belly a couple times.

"And the second reason?"

"Sometimes I like to do the right thing, and by that I don't mean according to the law but just as a person if I have a good feeling about someone." He pauses. I wait for him to go on. "If you'd slurred your speech or fallen down or something, I wouldn't have hesitated, but you didn't, and every once in a while, I do let someone go who I should probably question more, maybe even arrest."

"Cheers to that." I raise my glass. He nods.

"The thing is that when I was seventeen, I was pulled over once after I'd had too many. I wasn't stumbling drunk, but I, uh, I would have failed any sobriety tests and most certainly a breathalyzer, and I'm pretty sure the officer knew. He looked in the car window. I could see he smelled it. We'd drunk Old Milwaukee that night and then gone to White Castle. I grew up in Illinois. Anyway, the car must have reeked of cheap beer and even cheaper hamburgers, but he didn't ask me to get out. He just asked for my license and registration. I gave them to him, and while looking at them he asked if I knew why he pulled me over. I said, 'No, sir,' so he told me he clocked me doing fifteen in a thirty-five zone, thought there might be a problem, and then he looked up at me and asked, 'Is there anything wrong, Mr. Adams?' " He gives a little laugh, a slight shake of his head. "Man, I tried to conceal the fact that my heart was just racing so in the steadiest voice I could muster I said, 'Wrong? No,

I'm just heading home after some White Castle.' You ever had any White Castle?" he asks me.

"Regrettably, yes. It's never pretty the next day."

"Indeed. So there we were. He was standing next to my car, and I expected him to ask me to get out and do the little sobriety dance. I mean who goes to White Castle just after midnight except someone who's been drinking? But he just shined his flashlight in my face, in the front seat, then back, and seeing nothing must have decided to cut me a break. I don't know. He handed me back my license and registration and said, 'I think you should head home now, Mr. Adams.' Can't say exactly why he did it, and in the moment I didn't question it, of course, so I thanked him and drove off. I'm pretty sure he followed me, but I got home without incident, and then years later when I became a cop, I told myself I'd do the same sometimes, because I knew that if he'd arrested me things would have been very different for the next year of my life. Who knows how things would have wound up? Everyone needs a break now and again, so if it seems like the right thing to do in a moment, I will."

"Did you follow me home that night?"

"Yeah, I did."

"Oh." I try to remember it, the drive home, Radiohead playing, the looks in the rearview. I didn't see anything, though. There was open road ahead and behind. How could I have missed him?

"I just wanted to make sure you got home okay. It's kind of like protecting an investment. If you'd swerved too much I would have had to pull you over, but you only did a couple of times, and then you made it home."

"Wow. Thanks."

"It just… it feels good to give someone the benefit of the doubt sometimes. It helps me maintain perspective. Or what do I mean? Uh, maybe balance is a better word. Life isn't a black and white thing. It can go a million different ways."

"That it can." We drink, and I start to feel a little guilty. He let me go, and I didn't learn anything from it. I knew even in that moment that I should have. I remember having the thought on the way home that there should be more cabs in my future, but I swerved as I thought it. Hell, I shouldn't have been driving when I saw him at McDonald's. He knows. He has to know I was drunk on both occasions, just not shitfaced. There's a difference, but in either case, one should not drive. It makes me feel like I owe him something. "Can I buy you a shot?"

"Why the hell not?"

It makes me wonder if he's driving tonight, but I don't ask. I'll check later before he goes. We get two shots of Aha Toro Añejo, down them, order two more beers. We look at the stage where Sightseer is setting up. The guitar player, Jason Lightfoot, is there towering above P.A. He's easily fifteen inches taller than she is. They're speaking on stage while tuning guitars. They both laugh, both seem quite at ease going through the pre-gig ritual. I wonder if they get nervous. The keyboard player and drummer step up to the stage. I haven't met them yet but plan to tonight. The bass player is nowhere to be seen. Jason finishes tuning his Les Paul and switches to a Telecaster. I emailed him earlier this week to remind him who I was and that I wanted to write about the show. His reply came quickly: "Awesome, man! Got you on the list with a plus one. See you Friday."

"I'm going to go talk to the band for a bit when they're done sound checking. You want to come backstage or just wait here?" Officer considers this for a moment.

"Can you get me backstage?"

"We're at the High Dive. Anyone can get backstage." This place is on the small side, maybe two hundred and fifty max capacity, just a long narrow room that widens a little at the back where the stage is. The bathrooms are to the left at the far end, as is the band room, the backstage area, but "backstage" is a generous term here. It's just a little room, right across from the bathrooms, where bands store their gear before and after sets and where they hang out when trying to get away from the crowd. The room is graffitied and postered. There are flyers and stickers from many bands I've never heard of, but the last time I was in there, I saw "Like Lightning" written in black marker on one wall, a picture of a band called Furniture Girls taped to the back of the door but partially covered by a flyer for some other band. There was a Jesus Rehab sticker under which someone had written, "Time for Jesus to enter a facility." I remember thinking in that moment that it's music that saves, not Jesus. I've been to church a few times in my life, but it was never more than a bunch of people standing up and sitting down and singing badly and listening to an old man go on about something. It was dull and lifeless and the people kept standing up and down and up and down, and nothing ever happened. There was no miracle, no joy, no conversion, just a bunch of people who, I imagined, wanted to leave early to get home for the football games as I did. Yeah, there was music, but it was drowned in dogma. It couldn't be free. It couldn't breathe, and in the High Dive backstage room, I thought of a Furniture Girls song called "Symply Sid" and a lyric from its second verse, "A ticking bomb set to implode leaving dreams and chaos in his wake." It was about Syd Barrett of Pink Floyd, but also about his music. Art is all chaos and dreams. It shakes things up, creates disruption, but also order, beauty, horror, tragedy, joy. It is a ticking time bomb. There's no way to say when it will go off, but go off it will, and what will happen then no one can say, but those are the best moments, those explosions. Those are the moments that make life worth living.

A guy carrying a guitar case goes scurrying past us. He disappears backstage for a few moments, and then emerges on stage carrying a bass, a black and white Fender Jazz, but he isn't the same bass player they had last time. That guy had a beard, was balding a little, wore cowboy boots. He didn't move much on stage, seemed soft-spoken, a little uncomfortable in the spotlight, which is something I can certainly identify with at times. He looked up at the ceiling a lot, but he was a decent player, and it was his style that really added a definite country element to the band. Where a player with a more rock feel would ride on the root note AC/DC-like sometimes, he would bounce with the kick drum between roots and fifths and tap his feet as if he imagined he was dancing. The thing was, though, that as good as they were that first night, I imagined they'd be a lot better if they rocked more. The music was there, the melodies, the players. The energy was already high, and the power, but I wanted more. Maybe it was the bass player. He could play well, but his style wasn't the best thing for the band. I wonder what the new guy will do. He rivals P.A.'s height. Hell, the bass he straps on seems bigger than he is, but he plugs in and plays a few riffs, and the sounds are good. He lets loose a groove that starts on the Red Hot Chili Peppers' "Suck My Kiss" and then morphs into a few other things, pauses to tune. P.A. says, "Hey, we're ready to sound check if you are." The sound guy speaks into his talkback mic so only the band can hear. P.A. nods her head. "Okay then." She turns to the band, "Red Eye Haze?" whereupon Jason starts a descending guitar line that resolves to an F# chord, and everyone else joins in. It's one of their songs, one of their many about whisky, or rather whisky-inspired. "I woke up in a red eye haze, been drifting through for a thousand days…" It's a rock tune with a strong country vibe. There's a rolling, galloping snare and the one-two of the bass accenting, keeping time with the kick drum, and then the chorus. "I don't care if you go, and I don't care if you stay, 'cause I'm already gone, in a red eye haze." And then they stop. It's just a sound check for them, a teaser for the rest of us, but the melody is there, implanted, catchy and booming in our brains, "I don't care if you go…"

"Damn, that was pretty fucking awesome," Officer says. He motions to the bartender, orders two more drinks. "I think you may be right about these guys."

"Just wait until you hear the second half of that song."

"Rob!"

I turn around to see stayC Meyer, singer for Furniture Girls, that ticking bomb of a rock group. They are at times funky, at times heavy, always danceable. They use loops to augment their sound, and their bass player, Jim Watkins, is one of those who just makes me go, "Wow!" He plays the instrument with an ease and grace I've never had and is arguably one of the best in the city. This is evidenced by the funky heaviness of a song called "Drool," which has a bass line that would do Flea proud, one of those bass lines that always floors me and instills in me the desire to become a better bass player myself. stayC gives me a hug. She's a badass on stage, a sweetheart off. "How you doing?"

"Good. You?"

"Can't complain. Thanks for the great review by the way."

"No problem. Thanks for the great music. Can I buy you a beer?"

"Sure."

"What kind?"

"Never met one I didn't like. Well, except for Corona."

I order a couple Manny's. We drink for a second, look at the stage. The sound guy is up there fiddling with the drum mics. The band must be in back getting ready for the show. "You going to get up and sing with them tonight?" Last time I saw Sightseer, stayC sang backup on a couple songs.

"Hell, yeah."

"So when are we going to see you guys down at the Crocodile or the Showbox?"

"It'd be great to play those places, but fuck if I know. All we're trying to do now is find ways to make music anywhere we can."

"You guys make a living at it?" Officer asks. "I'm Wilson by the way."

"Sorry. I should have introduced you guys."

"stayC." They shake hands. "It'd be great if we could make a living at it, but it is what it is. Everyone in the band is too old to have red carpet fantasies. We just want to play. If that means the Showbox, great. If it means the Rendezvous or the High Dive, that's great too."

"Maybe we should go to a table," I suggest. We pick up our drinks and do that. "I agree completely. It isn't about millions or accolades. It's about doing it, just the simple act of stepping on stage and singing a few lines, playing a few chords." She nods her head. "Can I ask you something? You ever get any stage fright? I mean, if you've read my writing, you know I used to play, but there were times when getting up there was hard, and I was just so full of doubt, not about the music but about me, my own abilities. You ever get that kind of feeling or think about giving up music to pursue a more normal life?"

"I always have a little self-doubt. That's good, though. It makes me push myself more so that quitting isn't even an option. I can't even imagine a life without performing. I'll always do something musical in some capacity. I can't not. It's in my blood, or maybe it's better to say it is my blood."

"What about stage fright?" I ask.

"Stage fright? I do still get nervous sometimes, even after all these years. It's kind of weird. You think I'd be used to it by now. The only way to deal with it, though, is to channel that nervous energy and let it ignite you."

Thane Mitchell comes to the table. He's Furniture Girls' drummer. He has blond dreadlocks that go halfway down his back and has been known to play shows wearing nothing but ladies underpants, not for anything sexual, mind you, just to be a little goofy, a little odd, slightly shocking. He isn't a hard-hitting drummer. He's more of a finesse player. He's solid, though, and the rhythms are good. The rhythmic heaviness comes not from pounding but from the combination of his drums and the loops they use and Jim's bass. He plays for the music, for the band. He squeezes his own nipples, makes a little squeaky sound, does a little jig, hugs stayC. "Mr. Murphy." We shake hands. "I'm going to head backstage. See you guys in a bit." He walks off.

"I think I'll join him." stayC follows, and watching her I remember seeing them at the Tractor about month ago. They'd recently added a second vocalist, Kate Bradley, and that only made the chorus of "Symply Sid" take off over an uncharacteristically simple bass line. It was the harmonies. It made me wish I could sing better. "Rise up, Pull yourself up, 'Cause the hands that help you out are fading fast." I'll have to put that song on later.

"So you like her band?" Officer asks.

"Yeah, they're one of Seattle's best-kept secrets. Sightseer is too. They should be the two most popular bands in the city."

"What do they sound like?"

"Furniture Girls?"

"Yeah."

"Well, when I first saw them, they had two guitar players, and combined with the samples they used, they had a great Faith No More kind of vibe. It's a little more subdued now, still rocks, but they added another singer when one of the guitar players left, so the vocals cover a lot more ground, which I suppose is obvious. I guess they have more dynamic range now. There's a great ballad called 'I See Red' that always makes me think about having a drink in an empty bar just after someone has left your life. It isn't a happy drink, but not sad either. It's grateful, free, glad to have been seen, truly seen, if only for a little while. It's a beautiful piece of music. You should look them up online. Actually, that tall Sightseer guitar player also plays in the band."

"Interesting. I suppose it says something of his playing if you think his two bands should be the most popular in the city."

"It does indeed." I glance toward the bar and see Faustine from the Young Evils and Stephanie from Like Lightning sitting next to each other at the bar, but since they don't know each other, they're just minding their own business, sipping their drinks, tapping their phones.

"I'm going to go say hey to those two," I say to Officer.

"Think I'll head out to the car to smoke a bowl."

"You?"

"Yep. Wanna come?"

Things with this guy are just weird. There was the Alabaster song that saddened me so, the booze, the Dream Girls sign, the taps on my window. *I can't feel anything anymore.* If it hadn't been for that song, I would have stayed. I would have hung with the band afterward. I might have driven home drunk, or drunker than I finally wound up being. And then tonight, he said he likes to let people off sometimes to give them a chance to right themselves, to pay a little forward to karma. I guess that song saved me because he found my car and then fell over, and that meant I didn't go to jail. And now we're here almost friends, maybe already friends, drinking and talking about getting high. I should never have met him, but I did. It was the song. Music will do that.

"Yeah, maybe I'll join you in a bit."

"Okay. Remember my car?"

"Yep."

"Cool. I'm a block over that way, 35th and Evanston, a half-block from the rocket." He points toward the back of the bar, "If I'm not back by the time Sightseer goes on, text me."

"Will do."

He leaves, and I walk over to the bar and tap Stephanie and Faustine on the shoulders at the same time. They turn.

"Hi."

"Hey."

"What's up?"

"Do you guys know each other?" They look at each other, introduce themselves, shake hands.

"Hi, Stephanie."

"Faustine."

"Oh, from the Young Evils. I read Rob's bit about you guys, been meaning to come check you out."

"Thanks."

"Stephanie plays in a cool band called Like Lightning."

"Okay. Yeah, Rob liked your song called 'Disappear.' I read that one." I'm not surprised that they've both read at least some of my stuff. After I write about a band, some or all of its musicians will read other things I've written. It's curiosity about the writing and the other musical happenings around town, maybe even a little about the writer.

"That I do. You guys should do a show together."

"Maybe sometime."

"Yeah."

At the prospect of a show featuring their two bands, the Young Evils' lyric comes to mind. "This rock and roll city, this rock and roll city is done." It is. There's no music for me in the moment, which is like saying there's no sound. What is a musician without music? Maybe I'm not one anymore. Maybe I never was. I'm just writing about it all these days, observing, critiquing. I need to participate. I need to step on a stage and hear the roar of a crowd again. Things appear very different when looking out at a sea of bodies, heads, and hands bouncing in time to the beat, shouting and singing along. The world is a fine place in such moments, the finest. I remember that Third Stone gig all those years ago. Once the music kicked in, once I hit the right notes, it all fell into place. There was order in the world, in the universe, and all because a few metal strings and vocal chords vibrated. It wasn't even ruined by a few bad notes because everything that followed was perfect. There was order, melody, harmony. There was music. Sound comes back. I hadn't even realized it was gone. Is that how it's going to be? I'll wake up deaf some morning and not even realize it until I flush the toilet or crack open a beer. Stephanie and Faustine are talking.

"My best moment on stage?" Faustine asks. "Oh, man, so many come to mind. I was down in San Francisco once with a dear friend having the raddest vacation ever. We went and had a few drinks at Vesuvio, Jack Kerouac's infamous hang-out place, and picked the bartender's brain on where to go see some dirty old grimy blues. He led us up about a block or two to a place called the Saloon. Now, during this period in my life I was really into carrying around this old recorder, and whenever I would go to a show or a place where I thought the sound was something I wanted to remember, I would set the recorder up and hit record and leave it there through the night, basically journaling through sound instead of writing. Well, there was this blues jam happening with a bunch of old dudes, and one of their wives saw me set my recorder on top of a shelf and hit the button. Let me just say that did not sit well with the locals, and after being given the eye from pretty much every regular in that bar—mind you, there was a good forty-plus-year gap—I turned it off and found myself having to explain that I wasn't there to 'bootleg' their jam yadda yadda. My friend looked at me in that moment of inferno and calmly told me to go and offer the main musician the tape, so I took the tape out of the machine, walked up to the main dude, and handed it to him. He continued to harass and degrade me, and after about three solid minutes of him being an asshole, I piped in and said, 'Listen, man, here's your tape. I don't want it. I'm a drummer on vacation just documenting it for myself, but before you go on yelling at me, why don't you find yourself a drummer who can actually play a shuffle because I have yet to see it in this city.' And it was that moment that things went from bad to questionable. I wasn't sure what was gonna happen. He seemed to think I was joking at first, but I just kept staring him in the eye, and so after a moment, he asked me if I wanted to sit in. And it was after the first song I played that he introduced me as 'Faustine, his friend from Seattle visiting to sit in.' So I guess that may have been some of the best and worst all in one."

"What about the other guy who was playing drums? He must have been a little put out."

"Honestly, I don't know. I suppose he drifted off. People with no confidence will do that. If the same happened to me, I'd talk to the drummer. Maybe we could show each other a few things. I don't have an ego about my playing. There's always something more to learn, but this guy just disappeared." She turns to Stephanie. "So what about you? Best stage moment?"

"I've had a lot of great moments with my bands over the years, but I guess my favorites have been when performing classical music. I played the entire Ravel "Sonatine" for a recital in college. Anyone familiar with this work will know what a special piece of music it is."

"I must admit," I say, "that I'm not familiar with it. Is it a difficult piece?" She laughs a little.

"It took me probably nine months or so to learn it, and in those days, I practiced four hours a day, so the time, effort, and commitment to learning the piece was epic."

"Congrats on that," Faustine says. "So tell us about the recital."

"Well, I played it on a concert Steinway in an amazing auditorium, but there weren't too many people. Piano student recitals, when you are in music school at least, are a dime a dozen. The audience is only your other piano major friends, your teacher, and maybe one or two other faculty, and maybe your family. My parents came, bless their hearts. Christ, how many recitals did they attend in their lifetime, one hundred? Two hundred? I still, to this day, even though there were so few folks in the audience, remember being totally terrified. My hands and legs shook. When I sat down at the piano, my leg was shaking so badly that I had a hard time pedaling. I remember playing pretty well, despite the shaking, and that was because I had prepared well, I knew the piece inside and out. It didn't mean I wasn't nervous. I was, but I was still confident."

I probably would have been a quivering mass of jelly. I get nervous enough when playing with a full band, but to be the only one on stage would be a scary thing. I'd fuck up for sure. I suppose it's something I should force myself to do someday. Maybe she's right. With enough preparation, I might just be able to get through it unscathed.

"And I think the reason this recital stands out for me is that, looking back, it represented a culmination of years and years of effort. I started piano at five, took lessons all through high school, then went on to music school. By the time of this recital, I was twenty and had been a serious piano student for fifteen years, and learning the Ravel had taken an enormous amount of effort. I do think that the amount of time getting your art or your work finished can contribute to its relative importance when you look back over your creative life. I say this because, sometimes, creative folk can get confused and think the show was great or not great depending on feedback from others. I've learned in hindsight that listeners' opinions, good and bad, fade, and what's left is pride in hard work and dedication to craft."

"I completely agree," Faustine says. "The show is what you make of it, not what others think, and a show doesn't have to be perfect for it to be good. It's just how it feels, what you take away at the end of the night."

"I played a gig a long time ago where I screwed up a couple of times, but what I've brought with me over the years is that the show was still great. I have some issues with nervousness on stage, but we nailed the end of that show, and that's what everyone remembered." I wonder if anyone can still recall that night. The woman who went home with me, Deon working the door, the band, anyone in the audience, the bartender. I might well be the only one, and it's because of my mistakes. The fears always come, but not the fuckups. I've played many now forgotten shows that were every bit as good as the best parts of that one, but they've faded, and at some future point, it will be as if the band never existed, people dead, memories lost, CDs discarded by spouses and grandkids. I'll probably be the last one holding on. There in the hospice waiting for death, I'll somehow manage to slip in the old CD and say to the nurses, "This was my old band. There was this show one night in Columbus…" And they'll turn down the volume and guide me back to bed. "Just try to get some rest, Mr. Murphy." I'll lie down and stare out the window, knowing that more than just my life will soon be expiring. "This was my old band…"

"As long as you use the mistakes as motivation to get better and keep at it, then no harm done. It's rock and roll."

"Easier to gloss over a mistake in a rock band, though. The classical audiences are much less forgiving."

"That's understandable," I say. "When music's written out like that it's aiming at a level of perfection. Music these days is more about the emotional impact. Not that I'm against a certain level of perfection. What was the name of the Ravel piece again? I'll have to check it out."

" 'Sonatine,' but you should also check out 'La Valse.' "

"Will do. I've always been partial to the Beethoven stuff. You ever play that?"

"I've played 'Pathetique' for years although these days I could probably only play the second and third movements. I don't much practice the first one anymore since it makes my left hand hurt." She laughs a little, flexes her left hand a few times.

"You playing in any bands these days?" Faustine asks me.

"Nope. I'd love to, of course, but I haven't found the right thing yet so I'm just writing."

"You could always just do your own thing," Stephanie suggests, "maybe some solo acoustic stuff."

"I'd love to if I could sing, but I can't."

"Maybe you just haven't found your range."

"You might be right, but then, the larger issue is the idea of stepping on stage solo. I've never done that."

"Then you definitely should. Or maybe you could add a percussionist to fill out the sound a little."

"You free?"

"Well, possibly. If you arrange something, and I'm not busy, I might just be game."

"I'll keep it in mind." My phone buzzes, a call from Officer. I don't answer, but I do decide to go out to meet him. "I have to meet a friend outside. I'll catch up with you guys after the show."

"Sure thing."

"Okay."

CHAPTER 21

WHEN I EXIT THE BAR, Genny is standing there looking like she's deciding whether she should enter or not. She sees me. "Hi."

"Hey."

"I was just thinking to go in."

"The show won't start for about another half hour, so I was going to go over and meet a friend. He's waiting in his car over near the rocket. Want to come?" The rocket is attached to a building at the corner of 35th and Evanston and was acquired in 1991 by the Fremont Business Association when they learned of the availability of a 1950s' cold war rocket fuselage. They bought it and three years later successfully installed it in its current location. It's fifty-three feet tall and pointing skyward and inscribed with the motto, "De Libertas Quirkas," which means "Freedom to be Peculiar." It competes with the Fremont Troll under the Aurora Bridge and the statue of Lenin, which is only a block over on 36th, for the most unique landmark in this neighborhood, a place that bills itself as the "Center of the Universe." It seems more like its own universe though. Troll? Rocket? Statue of Lenin? There's also the parade of naked bikers—bicycles not motorcycles—that comes through every year for the summer solstice celebration. Some of them paint themselves, some just leave the clothes at home, but it's all for a laugh, all in the spirit of being unusual and carefree, and all very much a family-friendly affair.

"Uh, sure."

"Do you... smoke?" I mimic smoking a joint.

She nods. "Lead the way." We head up the block.

"Thanks for coming."

"Sure. How's the chest feeling?"

"Fine. Even if it hurt, I've had a couple beers already, so it's no worry. We'll see how I feel in the morning." We walk a block and turn at the rocket. Officer's car is a half-block up. "It's that one," I say pointing to it. We cross the street and approach from the passenger side, tap on the window. He unlocks the doors and we get in, me in front, Genny in back.

"It's about time, dude." He passes me a joint. I take a hit.

"This is Genny." I hand her the joint. They shake hands.

"Pleasure."

"Likewise." She gives the joint back to Officer.

"His name is Wilson. She just did my new tattoo."

"Oh, cool. Let's see it."

"Not yet. I'm waiting for it to heal before I show anyone."

"As your tattoo artist, I say you should show him." Officer hands the joint back to her. "Thanks."

"Yeah, she's right." I look at her. She smiles then exhales out the back window.

"Uh, okay." I lift up my shirt, peel the bandage half back. Officer leans in.

"What the hell is that? Is it Chinese?"

"Korean. Soju," I lie, and the other, the actual, goes through my head. *Sujo. Damn.* "It's the name of my cat and a type of Korean alcohol."

"Interesting. Why that?"

"It's unusual, something I've never heard for a pet's name before. Plus, I like to drink soju sometimes." My phone buzzes, a text from Katie. "What time will you be home? Mind if I come over later?" I reply that I'm not sure and that maybe we can meet tomorrow. "You have any tattoos?"

"Just one. Got my mother's name on my arm." He taps his right bicep. "Her name was Anita, but she always went by Nita." He pulls up his sleeve. Nita. It's in blue ink and a freehand script. It's spelled correctly. "It might seem an obvious thing for a tattoo, but I did it after she died a few years ago."

"Sorry for your loss and nothing wrong with the obvious thing," Genny says. She pulls a joint from a cigarette case in her back pocket, lights it. "Next one's mine to share." We pass it around.

"Thanks. It's okay, though. It's inevitable that one's parents will die. I mean, she was in a lot of pain at the end, lung cancer. It ain't no way to live being drugged up on pain killers and just waiting to die."

"I hear ya there."

"Yeah, but it's still living, being alive." I hand the joint to Officer. "I guess I just have a hard time with the idea of death. I can't wrap my head around the finality. I can't imagine being bedridden and waiting to die, maybe feeling those last few breaths coming on, struggling to make the lungs move, the heart beat, knowing this is the last moment, afraid to close your eyes because they might never open again."

"No way around it, though, man. When it's my time, I'll just laugh as I lie there on the bed. I'll pinch the ass of every nurse that comes by and have friends and relatives sneak me in some booze."

"I think the lingering expectation would be worse than death," Genny says. "I don't want to be confined to a bed just waiting for my last breath. I'd off myself. I'd rather go out instantly in a car crash or something."

"In a way, I would too, but then, so long as you're alive, there's the hope of a cure, or at least of a few good moments, the possibility that something will happen to make the time worthwhile."

"Like what?"

"I don't know. Like making someone laughing, or laughing yourself. Maybe a song will come over the radio and bring back a good memory, maybe of someone you once loved." I remember thinking about that, the future memory of lost love in the hospice, showing the nurses that picture atop the Space Needle and saying, "She was the one!" I will be happy when that time comes, and I'll fight like hell to keep my eyes open for another hour, a day, a week, maybe a month. A month of just looking at that picture and remembering sounds pretty good. "If I was in such a situation, I'd probably just write. I'd get down every last little story I have in my head. I wouldn't be able to do that if I died in a sudden accident."

"Can you ever really do that?" I look back at her. She's right. There will always be some stories that don't get told. I wonder what that would be like, having more to share but not being able to. Maybe it would be better to die then. "And anyway, you should do that as you go along through life so that there are no regrets at the end, no rush to get it all down."

"Yeah."

"That's impossible, though. I mean most people try. I write. I play music when I can, but I have to work and such. There's no time to do everything I want."

"It isn't about doing everything," Officer says. "It's just about doing as much as you can. At the end you should think that maybe you didn't do a few things, but that doesn't matter since you did all these other things. You can call it good and close your eyes and let go."

"Easier said than done."

"I agree with you to a point, but he's got me thinking about it," Genny says to Officer. "I'll never close my eyes willingly in that situation, never call it good because he's right. Something can happen in a moment, some kind of magic or miracle, and when you die, that's it. Nothing more can happen. In my moment, I'll be thinking, 'What am I going to miss tomorrow?' I'd be dead the next day, of course, but you know what I mean. There will always be something." She sighs, and I wonder if she's the first person I've ever convinced of anything. A minute ago, she was ready to go out in a fireball, but now she wants her goodbyes. I like her for that. That kind of fear makes us want to live. My phone buzzes with another text from Katie. "Okay. I'll call you tomorrow."

"Man, I'm stoned," Officer says. "This is some good shit. I think it's even better than mine."

"We should get back into the bar. Sightseer will be starting soon."

We get out of the car, and walking back, I get a little bold and put my arm around Genny. She doesn't squirm away or resist at all. "Thanks again for coming."

"Sure."

Officer is a few steps ahead of us walking in a not-so-straight line toward the bar and the music. I have my arm around Genny's shoulder. We're all high. We will all die. But I'm beginning to think that at least for this night, I will not sleep alone.

When we get back to the High Dive, the show is beginning, "Hello, we're Sightseer. Thanks for coming." There are shouts from the crowd: "Sightseer!" Some claps. "Give us a sec to tune up." We situate ourselves at the bar, order a few beers, and I start taking notes about the crowd, the band, the bar, the show. I'm writing about tonight, playing critic, but also participating, everything going through my eyes and ears, through my filters and pen as I try to get down just a smidgen of things as they are, and as I am within them. I hate reviews that try to describe things from a detached perspective. How is that possible? What I care about most is how the music makes me feel. The technical details are important to a degree, and I do report on them, but in the end they don't matter. E chord, A chord, G chord. They're all the same, just a collection of notes played at the same time, and yet they are everything, and how can one possibly describe everything? We can only describe our perception of such. There is so much we miss, so much we over-look, so much that escapes us, and the only thing I know for sure is that I'm here. Even my memory of the past is clouded, changed. Some details I've kept to myself, some changed in the writing. What matters is not so much what happened but how we carry it forward, how it changes the present.

There's the click of a hi-hat on stage. "One, two, three, four," and then a big G. They're opening with the Black Crowes' "My Morning Song" and nailing it. P.A. can truly do the gospel-esque rock thing that Chris Robinson has mastered. The band is in their element, and it rouses the crowd, lifts the mood. The song enables, and there are lots of cheers when it's done. "It's the weekend tomorrow, so drink up!" P.A. says. More cheers.

They play a few of their songs next, and I note they are bluesier, more rocking, more Crowsey so to speak, than they had been at the Skylark, where the term of alternative-countryish rock would have been more appropriate. Tonight, the country element is subdued, and even with it they were one of my favorites in Seattle, but I like this more. They've gotten better, beefed up their origi-nals. "Red Eye Haze" pushes with more weight, more drive, more urgency. I scribble an almost illegible note, "Lots of B.C. feel but still all Sightseer!"

Five songs into the set, Officer says, "These guys are great, but I need a smoke. I'm gonna get one now so I don't miss the end of the set."

"I could use a smoke too," Genny says. "You mind?"

"Nope. I'll be here."

They leave, and I turn my eyes to the stage. P.A. leans into the microphone. "Uh, where's stayC Meyer. You need to come up here for this one." There are some claps from their regular fans, a small but loyal crowd. I look around. Maybe fifty people. There should be more, five times that number, ten times, a thousand. Where are they? Why am I the only critic in town enamored with this band? Why am I the only one who can hear the beauty and power? I'm doing what I can in writing about them, but, so far as I know, Officer is the only one who's paid attention. Elena too. Elena in her in her Cheap Trick tee shirt. I never contacted her, and it seems too late now. Lost opportunity. Maybe the timing was wrong. Maybe it just wasn't meant to be. Someone shouts, "Woo hoo!" as stayC walks up on stage. She grabs Lightfoot's microphone and stands next to P.A. There are a couple more cheers. "This one's called 'Read It & Weep.' "P.A. starts in on the acoustic, F#, D, B, E. It's a simple thing, a thousand rock songs probably have the same chord progression, but she plays it just so, soft with a hint of the harshness and heartache to come, and we know it's coming, but we're pulled in anyway. We're ready for it, anxious even. Who doesn't want a little heartache in the form of a song? P.A. sings.

Well, it's dead outside
and it pains me
you won't pass this way again.

...

Knife in the back
a fork in the road
took a girl out west
and I watched you go

...

A million days
and a thousand miles
won't help this fade to black.
I can see her in the bedroom
dragging nails down your back…

And then there's the chorus, big, an explosion of distortion in F♯, and stayC, who had been grooving next to Lightfoot up until this moment, lifts her microphone and joins in. The combined vocals boom. They resound. They fill up space.

Oh, lonesome me
crying out to you.
Your letter lies on the table
What can I do
but read it and weep?

There's another heavy F♯ then, one reminiscent of Judas Priest's "Metal Gods" with the accent of the low E note, and then a descending fast blues riff and right back into the openness of the verse. It isn't rocket science, but it takes us places farther away than any rocket ever could. By the time the last chorus comes, we're all singing, "Oh, lonesome me…" Fifty people, band, bartenders, all melt into one. "…But read it and weep." The song ends. We all stand. We all clap, cheer, shout. There are goose bumps. I feel sorry for Genny and Officer for missing this moment for the sake of a smoke. stayC hugs P.A. and Lightfoot before leaving the stage. "stayC Meyer, ladies and gentlemen!" More applause.

A woman sits next to me in Officer's unoccupied seat, pushes his beer away from the edge of the bar. I'm about to say something when I realize she looks familiar. Elena?

"Elena. Hi."

"You never looked me up."

"I'm sorry. I just spaced out on that. I'd still love to see your paintings."

"No worries. It just surprised me is all. I was wondering if you'd be here tonight."

"Here I am. You here with anyone?"

"Yeah, I'm here with a guy, a first date kind of thing, figured it'd be a safe choice in case the conversation wasn't good since we could just listen to the music."

"That's cool. So how's the conversation?"

"Not great. Not awful. We'll see how it turns out. He's in the bathroom now, so I just wanted to say hi and remind you to look me up."

"Will do. Sorry about that."

"Okay then. Talk to you soon." She goes back to a table toward the front, looks over when she sits down, but is soon joined by a guy. I'd watch them, but Genny and Officer come back, and the music starts again, Zeppelin's "When the Levee Breaks," itself a cover tune, and as with the Black Crowes' cover, they nail it. I've never seen another band play "Levee," and to hear Sightseer do it, I don't want to. It's just too damn good with those booming intro drums and a violin played by the other guitar player. He takes a long solo at the end. More applause. "Jason Welling everyone!" They are ramping up the night. The power is there through the next few songs. Almost everyone in attendance moves forward. Proximity helps. It's easier to grab hold of the notes when standing right in front of the stage. Bodies move and arms are raised, but then the band shifts for the ending. They tone it down with a mellow acoustic number, "Biggest Storms," one of those thoughtful tunes that when done as a closer leaves the audience feeling not pumped so much as lifted, brought in, not a climax but rather the comfort of a post-orgasmic moment, the settling after release. It's just P.A. on the acoustic and Mr. Welling on the violin. There's a hush, and people honor the song. They stop speaking. They listen, let themselves be taken by the sounds, the melody, the words.

> *The silence of this room is deafening*
> *I can hear the creaking of my bones*
> *I can hear the dust dancin' in sunbeams*
> *Lord, I wish you didn't go*
> *And ain't it funny how*
> *the biggest storms don't make a sound.*

We sway in time. We drink. Men hold their women, and some women hold their women. Genny and I make brief eye contact, but neither of us speaks. It's too soon for dancing, and I think we both have the same idea. *Just listen. Let the music do its thing.* If it's meant to be, there will be plenty of time later for dancing.

And who knows what tomorrow brings
A gypsy's curse on angel's wings
And no one can predict these things
And this is what I found
The biggest storms don't make a sound.

And then the set is over. "Thanks a lot for coming out tonight. We'll see you next time." The band starts to tear down equipment, but the audience just watches for about five minutes. They want more, and yet they're satisfied. They're just letting the last few notes run their course before they get on to the business of more drinking. "Wow!" Genny says. "That was pretty fucking awesome. Smoke?" They go out for another smoke, so I finish my beer and look at my phone. There's a text from Katie. "What time tomorrow?" It makes me wonder what she's up to this evening, but I guess it's probably drinking alone. Greg must be too. He never showed up, never called or texted. I have no idea what happened between them, but maybe they'll be back together tomorrow. I reply to Katie. "Early afternoon, say around 2," and after a few minutes of no reply from her, I put the phone in my pocket. I look around but think Elena has left. So has the bass player. He went quickly just as he'd entered late. It's odd for sure. Maybe he's new, or maybe he's just filling in. I'll ask them later, maybe tomorrow. I know I should go back and talk to the band, but I'm just not in the mood. The last mellow song has brought me down.

The guitar player for the next band is tuning by ear rather than using a tuner. He stops, plays a few measures of "Remedy" to show he knows some Black Crowes. He's still slightly out of tune, though, and the sounds are brittle. They crash upon my head, but he seems satisfied, sets his guitar back on its stand and walks off the stage.

"Let's get out of here," Officer says coming up behind me. "I don't want to stay and hear anything that guy plays."

"I couldn't agree more." We pay up and exit the bar. There's a group of people smoking outside. A few taxis go by, pedestrians walking both ways up and down the sidewalk. The statue of Lenin is right across the street. "I have some beers and soju at my place. You guys want to come back for a drink?"

"Sure," Officer says. "I'll drive."

Genny looks at me, pulls out a cigarette. "I don't know. Can I smoke there?"

"Outside."

In Officer's car on the way to my place, Genny is again in back with the window rolled down and a cigarette dangling out of it. I'm looking through a stack of CDs that was in the glove box. There are no cases for them, no covers of any kind, just a pile of discs waiting to be scratched with every movement of the car, every movement of my handling them. Does no one take care of their music? I'm a little drunk, though, so I'm not my ordinary careful self. I flip though them with little thought, and Officer seems not to mind. Black Sabbath's *Heaven and Hell* is first. Great CD. I'm one of those that loves Ozzy and Dio Sabbaths equally, two sides of the same coin, both awesome, but I'm not in the mood for it after that last Sightseer song which I still have running through my brain, "... ain't it funny how, the biggest storms don't make a sound." I rotate CDs to the bottom of the pile as I go. After a few home-burned and unlabeled CDs, there's Smashing Pumpkins' *Siamese Dream*. Wow. It's seems ages ago that I was riding in the car with Greg on the way to see Genny when he put this one on. I keep flipping and come across *Colossal Head* by Los Lobos. What a wonderful album, so balanced in the mix. I saw them open for Dave Matthews way back in my Columbus days, and they ended with an extended version of "Mas y Mas" that blew everything from Dave Mathews clear away, but then, I've never been a fan of Dave's music. He's talented and the musicians in the band are talented, but his music is hollow. It's sterile, over-clean, scrubbed of any grime. I'm about to put on Los Lobos when I notice the CD under it is Moby's *Hotel*, which is perfect for my mood after "Biggest Storms." I put it in and click forward to track six, "Temptation," a cover of a New Order song that is more than a little better than the original. The New Order version, at least as I've seen in live footage on YouTube, is a high-energy thromp that moves only the pelvis, but Moby owns it in his arrangement. He slows it down, spreads it out, has a woman sing it. And she has an awesome voice, a breathy, sexy voice that whispers in the ear and runs down the spine and gives me chills every time I hear it. The song starts, and as we hit the West Seattle Bridge, that beautiful voice starts singing of walking alone and finding her soul as she goes home.

"I love this tune," Genny says.

"Me too. One of my favorite covers ever."

"Play it again."

Officer doesn't say anything.

I hit repeat, and Genny squeezes my shoulder as the female vocalist, Laura Dawn, sings now of never having met someone quite like you, the unnamed you that is in so many songs. And it repeats. And it makes me wonder what's going to happen because it seems too soon to be squeezing shoulders. The song ends, but Genny keeps squeezing. Maybe she just wants to get my attention. I turn around.

"Turn it up and play it again," she says.

"Okay."

When we get to my place, Officer parks in front, and we listen until the song ends, then he kills the engine. "I never much liked that song until now," he says.

"Many times you just have to hear a song in the right moment or it might just slide right past."

"I agree." Officer and I don't turn back while she speaks. We just keep looking straight ahead. Hypnotized by the end of the song, the silence of the neighborhood. I imagine Genny still smoking, still looking out the window. "I first heard this album when an old roommate had it. She liked to play it when smoking pot, and she always had pot."

"Yeah, music is often about context. If I'd first heard it on the radio while at work or while in rush hour, I wouldn't have gotten it. It would have been just another forgotten song in a forgotten moment, but it was a late-night drive home with a borrowed CD, and I can still remember the moment. It was ordinary. I'd driven home thousands of times, of course, but the song seeped in under my skin and made it a special moment that I still remember. I mean, how many times do you remember the drive home?"

"I might remember this one." She turns her gaze left out the window. "What I mean is that I haven't heard that song in a few years, so it's a little like new, and it made the drive, uh…"

"Memorable?"

"It made the drive a part of the evening rather than just a transition from one place to another."

"One moment that will stick for me is that sound check song," Officer says. "What was it called again?"

" 'Red Eye Haze.' "

"Yeah, that was cool, unexpected and very… powerful, I guess, powerful and catchy. I still have the chorus in my head, so I have to say you were right. I was a little nervous because sometimes you read a review, and the writer says the band is awesome, so you go and check out said band, but then they suck."

"I don't disagree. I've been asked to review plenty of bands, and many times they do indeed blow."

"But you seem to like every band you write about."

"I don't want to waste my time writing about shit. I'd rather tell people where to go than where not to go. If I don't like a band, then I have no connection and so nothing to write about. It would be a waste of my time. We only have so many nights on this earth. Why rehash something I didn't like? I don't think the reader wants to read about my dislikes unless they already don't like the band."

"Understandable," Officer says. "I don't know how critics do it. Even if you don't write about it, you still have to go hear it, and as many good bands as there are, I imagine there are far more bad ones."

"Any kind of art is like that," Genny says.

"Most of the bands I go to see are in the middle somewhere, not awful, but not great. Ordinary is the word, I guess. They can play their instruments well enough, but the music just sits there. It doesn't take the listener anywhere. Sometimes it's tone, too. I've seen bands where the music might be fine, but the guitar player insists on setting the tone of his amp to something brittle and excruciating, like that guy in the second band tonight, or the bass player just cranks up the bass tone all the way and crushes the mids and highs so that it's just a rumbly mess."

"Yeah, there was something very off about the tone from that guy in the next band."

"And he was also a little out of tune. I feel a little sorry for the sound guy having to deal with that. Recording studios have it bad as well, probably worse than the critic, especially the small studios that cater to local musicians. Every band that's just getting started wants to go in and do their demo, but some of them must be near-impossible for the recording engineer to endure. The critic can leave a show, but in the studio the engineer has to stay and record, mix, and sometimes even master the music. No escape."

"You guys want to go inside? I need to go to the bathroom."

"I think I'm just gonna head home, maybe get some McDonald's on the way. You hungry at all?"

"Tempting, but I'm good."

Genny opens the door, gets out. "I have to go to the bathroom." She leans back in the window. "Nice to meet you."

"Likewise." He looks to me. "Let's do another show soon."

"Indeed." He turns the key and brings the car to life. The music starts again, but he clicks forward to "I Like It," track ten. "The other one's good, but I still prefer this one. That woman's voice is sexy as hell."

"It is. I'll see you." I get out, and he drives off. I open the gate, and Genny follows me into the apartment. I turn on the light and take off my shoes. She follows suit without even asking and then looks around.

"Where's the bathroom?"

"That door back there by the kitchen." She runs off. Soju comes out of the bedroom and walks over. I bend down and scratch his head and back while he turns circles. There's the sound of the toilet flushing, and Genny emerges from the bathroom. She walks over and sits on the couch. I stand up, "Want a beer?"

"Sure. Aww. This must be Soju." There's a meow. He hops up on the couch next to her. She scratches his neck. I bring the beers over and sit down. Then we're just quiet for a minute drinking and petting Soju. "I probably shouldn't be here, but I was a little drunk to drive, and honestly, I have a good feeling about you. Can you give me a ride to my car tomorrow?"

"I would, but my car's in the shop. The bus comes right by here, though, so we can catch it in the morning. I can go with you if you want."

Meow.

"Okay. He's so adorable." She scratches his head. "How's the tattoo feel?"

I put my hand to my chest. "Fine. You ever had any soju?"

"Nope. Never even heard of it until today."

"Do a shot?"

"Sure." She shrugs her shoulders. "Why not? I wrote it into your chest. Might as well try it." I wince a little on the inside to think that she didn't actually write it on my chest, that she etched something else entirely, but again, what can I do in the moment? I get a bottle and two shot glasses, pour, give one to her.

"Cheers." We clink. I down mine, shake my head a tad like I always do after a shot. She does the same.

"Ooh. Fuck that's harsh." She lets out a little cough. Soju jumps off the couch and up to the desk, rubs his cheeks against the dragon, sits next to it. I move a little closer to Genny. She doesn't say anything as I reach over with my left arm and trail my fingers up over her right ear and down to her shoulder. As I lean in to kiss her, she leans forward too, puts her left hand up on my shoulder. We kiss to the sound of a car door closing outside, and a few seconds later, the latch of the gate clicking. It opens and shuts with another click, and then there are three knocks. Genny, Soju, and I all look at the door, but only my heart sinks for there is but one person it can be. It's the kind of moment when one knows something bad will happen, something horrible, something regrettable, something that one cannot stop.

"Who's that?"

"Uh, I don't know, probably just a friend. I'll see." I'm hoping it's Officer come back with cheeseburgers or Greg or just any male presence I can easily explain and who offers no threat to the current situation. I walk to the door, pause for a heartbeat afraid to look out the peephole. I open it. Katie. *Well*, I think to myself, *this will be interesting*. She'd said she wanted to come over, but even though

I pushed that off until tomorrow I should have texted that I was staying at a friend's, that I would be anywhere else, just in case, but I wasn't that smart. I know she finds it difficult to be alone. It's why Greg says she's needy, a latcher-on. If she expresses the desire to come over in the wee hours, then she will, and if her self-invite has been rejected, she hopes it'll be a welcome late-night surprise, that there'll be smiles and kind words, "Ah, I was hoping you'd come." I don't say anything to her, though. I just stand in the doorway between her and Genny.

"Who is it?" Genny asks again.

Katie is holding two bottles of soju and had been smiling but her face goes cold at the sound of Genny's voice. She pushes in past me and stands next to the desk. She sets the bottles down with a thud that makes me think they might break, and the sound frightens Soju, so he run runs off to the bedroom with a screech in that way cats have of exploding at the speed of light when it's time to be somewhere else. Katie stumbles, has to use the desk to steady herself, so I know she's already drunk. Drunk, lonely, upset, depressed. I guess that would be an apt description of myself these past few months, even now. Why else would I have slept with her during that brief split she had with Greg? I'm supposed to be his friend, and hers, but a friend wouldn't do that, or at least not a friend in his right mind. Maybe I'm the one who is fucked up. Genny stands up, looks at me.

"Who the fuck are you?" Katie asks.

It's uncharacteristic of Katie to swear like that. She's in a bad moment, though, and the comforting she'd hoped to find here is elsewhere, if it even exists. She clenches a fist, and I think it will all come out. I'm hoping for tears and sobs, that she'll collapse on the couch and that I can explain to Genny the whole situation. I could say something to diffuse the tension. I could step in between them, put an arm around Katie and guide her to the desk chair, offer to pour some shots, introduce them, try to make them friends, or at least not enemies. But I do nothing. I just stand by the door. It's still open and a slight breeze comes in. It feels cool, and I close my eyes for a second to enjoy the comfort of it knowing it'll be the last comfort I feel this evening. I'd squeeze my hand as hard as I could, clench it into a fist, but I'm still holding the shot glass. Genny is too, and I suddenly want to look back outside across the street because

I'm wondering if there's a similar tension at this moment in that apartment where the shadows fight in the window, wondering if that young couple who I'd seen merrily run from their car late that night when Greg and Katie first hooked up is loving now, or fighting, or even still together. Love falls apart everywhere, always, or just doesn't connect. The lasting thing is the exception. Katie lunges at Genny who lunges back, and they fall toward the desk shaking everything on it. The dragon teeters, falls, breaks its left leg and the end of the bass with a crack. I let out a slight gasp as the girls wrestle for a moment. One of them has come here hoping to find a little love, or at least a little loving, the other having just lost it, maybe seeking some too. And then there's me, clueless me. They fall to the floor and roll apart and end up facing each other, huffing, faces red, eyes angry and confused at how things turned out this way. Not knowing what else to do, I set down the shot glass and twist open one of Katie's bottles. I take a swig trying to find the words to right this all, to mend hearts, to ease hearts, to save a moment, a friendship, a possible burgeoning love, but when I set the bottle down, I have no idea what to say. They are both looking at me for the answers, but I have nothing to offer. I am empty, and the only words coming to mind are those of others, phrases that contain melodies I have within but cannot sing, and one... one a sentence I have not heard from a voice I cannot remember.

I don't want to disappear.

I can't feel anything anymore.

I woke up in a red eye haze.

This just isn't working.

PART 3

Chapter 22

I'M A PHOTOGRAPHER TODAY for Pain in the Grass at White River Amphitheater, which is in Auburn, a little south of Seattle. It's the main outdoor venue for the summer festivals in this area and isn't bad as such venues go. There's the covered area in front of the stage where there are reserved seats and then the lawn stretching back and up. Bands look pretty small from up there, but then one can have the comfort of spreading a blanket and chilling to the tunes while munching on a hotdog. I saw Radiohead from up there. It was their tour for *In Rainbows*, and it was spectacular, but the thing I remember most about the show was Thom Yorke fucking up the beginning of "Faust Arp." That song starts with an acoustic guitar and his singing and nothing else, and he started plucking out the notes but missed a few, stopped, laughed, apologized, "Uh, sorry 'bout that." The audience laughed in response. Some people clapped. "Let's try again, shall we?" He got it the second time around, and just like that Third Stone show years ago, I realized that maybe people don't care if you screw up. Hell, many times they don't even know. People will forgive so long as what comes next gets it right.

I look at my left wrist, at the green wristband there. "Photo" is written on it in black ink. It's my photographer credential, but of course an eight-year-old could have made it. The enterprising mind might buy a number of wristbands, say red, green, blue, pink, yellow, orange, and such, and bring them to the show. One look at the photographers would indicate the color of the day, and there it would be, instant pass, access to the photo pit. I'm not much of a visual person, never been any good with a camera, but I need pictures to go with the written word, so I asked for a photo pass, and they gave me one. I laughed, though, when they approved me, because I don't even own a camera. I have only a phone that often takes blurry photos, which is either the phone's fault or my own. Funny that the old guy atop the Space Needle steadied his hands enough to take a perfectly clear picture, or I guess lucky is a better word. I put my hand over my pocket and feel the phone there and the picture it contains. I do still look at it from time to time. Why not? It was a great moment. I wonder if I will end up showing my grandkids, if I ever get around to having any, my prospects for a partner being pretty dim at the moment.

With no camera, I had to borrow one from Officer, but what he loaned me isn't much better, just a standard digital camera, a little point and click, tiny, minuscule by professional standards. It's better than nothing, though, so after a quick, early beer, I make my way toward the main stage where Queensryche will perform a short acoustic set to get the show going. I walk to the entrance of the photo pit, which is a little aisle between the stage and the crowd barrier. The security guards hang there and the photographers work around them while bands play. Small timers such as me only get to stay there for the first three songs of each band's set. Then, we have to scatter and take pictures of other things, or as I will do, drink beer and scribble a few notes. I show my wristband and am admitted, and the inadequacy sets in. I feel small. The other photographers have monster-sized cameras with long, wide lenses. Some of them have two such cameras, some three, and they all have bags that house even more lenses and film and who knows what all. I can nearly envelop Officer's camera with one hand. Sigh. Queensryche comes out, and they settle on some stools with Geoff Tate in the middle. We all start snapping photos. There is much twisting of lenses and zooming and angling for light and angles. I point and click. One of the guys on stage has a twelve string guitar. He's tuning it. Geoff Tate speaks.

"Uh, you about ready there, Eddie?"

"Yeah, in a sec." Eddie continues tuning.

"We kind of have a show to do, Eddie."

"Hey, I got more strings than everyone else." Laughter from the crowd. Eddie finishes tuning, and they play three songs ending with "Silent Lucidity," which is the expected closer for an acoustic set. I look back around at the crowd of maybe only a thousand for the early performance. The lawn is still pretty empty, but the people here now want one more song. I hear shouts for "Suite Sister Mary" and "Eyes of a Stranger" and "I Don't Believe in Love." But I'm okay with them stopping since the mellowness of "Silent Lucidity" put Sightseer in my head: "Ain't it funny how... the biggest storms don't make a sound." Queensryche leaves the stage, and as I leave the photo pit I'm approached by a female staffer.

"Uh, sir, who are you with?" It strikes me as an odd question since I'm with no one, but then I understand.

"Seattle Subsonic." I say it with authority as if Seattle Subsonic is on par with the likes of *Rolling Stone*. I hold up my wrist to show that my band is the right shade of green and has "photo" written on it.

"Oh, okay. Well, I saw your little camera there and wondered. I hope you don't mind."

"No problem," I say walking off, but as I make my way toward the beer garden, I hope it will be the last time ever a woman questions my size. I get another nine-dollar beer and try to take some notes, but I'm distracted. That woman's voice is in my head.

"I saw your little..."

And it goes on like that. Before and after the Loaded set—Loaded being Duff McKagan's band, good live rock but a little nondescript, no phrases to grab hold of—I am questioned, once by a man, "Are you supposed to be here?" and once again by a woman, "What's that you're using? It's *so* small." It isn't the way I want her to phrase it. No man ever wants to hear a woman say, "It's *so* small." I just show my credentials though, and they let me stay and shoot with the big boys.

After Loaded, I go to the special BBQ area where the bands and the KISW DJs can mingle with fans who paid a little extra and photographers like me. There's a table set up for serving hot dogs and burgers and chicken. There are people milling about drinking and eating. I'd been hoping that Queensryche would be here but they must be backstage out of the sun, and since this isn't the High

Dive, I don't have access there. This is as close as I'll get. I get in the long-ass beer line, the slow-moving kind of line where people get right back in after they get a beer, and I notice in front of me Miles from the Men's Room. Genny and my typo briefly come to mind, but I don't want to think about that now.

"Miles. Hi."

"Well, hey! You are?" We shake hands.

"Rob Murphy. I'm the one who wrote about your beer."

"Oh, yeah, man. Thanks! We appreciate it."

"You guys are doing a cool thing. Happy to help in my own small way. I heard you guys say on air that no one had written about it so it was a pleasure to do the research."

"Ha, ha. I bet it was. We're just happy to be a part of it. We drink beer and the listeners drink beer and the Fisher House gets a ton of cash."

There's a pause in our conversation then. I hate imposing upon someone because they have a little bit of celebrity, and I suppose he gets drawn into many random conversations with his listeners who imagine themselves his friend. "Anyway, nice to finally meet you."

"Nice to meet you too, man. I'll try to check your blog out from time to time." He's probably just being nice to say that, but I like hearing it. Any artist will get a tinge of excitement from the possible fan or even the casual supporter, especially if that supporter has an audience of his own. He looks at his friend, "Sam , this is Rob. Rob, Sam." Sam and I shake hands and exchange greetings. "Again, thanks for listening, and hopefully I'll be able to get another beer before this decade is over. Christ almighty!" They turn forward as we move but a few inches closer to getting a drink. There's a voice behind me.

"Hey, I couldn't help overhearing you and Miles." I turn around. It's Ted Smith, also of the Men's Room. He's the slightly goofy one on the show, actually goes by the moniker of "Thee" Ted Smith in a joking way to give himself an exaggerated self-importance, calls his blog the World's Greatest TV Blog, or at least he did at one point. I only read it a few times, and grammar and punctuation were not big concerns of his. Speaking and laughing are more his things. He likes to work out, often talks about it on air, but being in the Men's Room, he also likes drinking beer. Looking at him, I get the feeling that he prefers the beer. No problem there. I do too. He's the only one on the show, a show on a hard rock station, that proudly proclaims to be a fan of Justin Timberlake. One has to respect him for that. He is comfortable in his shoes and can poke fun at himself. We shake hands. "Thanks for writing about the beer. You writing about today as well?"

"Yes, I am."

"Nice. Be sure to mention my style." I look at his style and make note of it as he motions his hands and smiles in a check-this-out kind of way. He's wearing a Seattle Sounders jersey, colored in what the Sounders term as "Sounder Blue and Rave Green" (both colors on the lighter side of their spectrums), tan shorts, and sunglasses. He has no hair and a beer in hand, makes me wonder if he's one of the ones who is perpetually in line, probably. I don't know if his outfit qualifies as style, but he seems comfortable, and I've always thought that more important than the look of an outfit. There's an easy manner about him in the way he's smiling. He seems on the verge of laughter. That's how he sounds on the radio, too, like he's always thinking about something funny even when he's trying to be serious. "You know, you should get a pic for your article." From most people, that would seem a very ego driven comment, but not from him. He knows what he looks like. I hadn't planned to take his picture, but what the hell? I whip out the point and click and snap one.

"Sounders fan, eh?"

"Of course, man. You?"

"I don't know. I wouldn't even know where to go watch a game. I mean in a bar as opposed to going to the stadium."

"I sometimes go to a place in Fremont called the George and Dragon. You should check it out sometime."

"Yeah, maybe I will." I scribble the name in my notebook and make a mental note to google it or maybe just look it up on Facebook. That reminds me of Elena. I must be the biggest idiot ever because she asked me to contact her, to search for her, even when she was out on a date, she said it, "Look me up," but after what happened the night of the Sightseer show, I haven't contacted any women. Well, I've tried a couple, but to no avail.

"You should. I can send you an email next time they're playing. Games are fun, lots of beer drinking."

"Sounds good, and please do." I'm not sure what I'm getting myself into. I've never been a soccer fan. It's just a game that I don't know much about as I grew up playing football and baseball and basketball. Ted seems a genuine guy, though, someone who'd be cool to hang with for a few beers. Maybe I'll meet him for a soccer game sometime, if he emails, which I doubt he will. Not that he isn't being honest in the moment, but he's had a few. I've had a few. We all say many such things when drinking. I certainly won't hold it against him if he doesn't contact me.

"Holy hell, this line is slow."

"Fuck yeah," I agree.

Another band is taking the stage, playing their brand of heavy rock. I decide to skip them as they're nondescript. The guitars are loud and the drums booming, and those are good things, things I love, but the music isn't... well, it just isn't moving. It's odd because it has so much energy, but it just goes nowhere. Instead of 2 + 2, it's 2 – 2, zero. I'd rather stay here in the never-ending beer line where I think I may in fact die. Miles is talking to his friend. Ted here has his finger in his ear.

"You know, I'd save a lot of time and money at these things if I didn't drink," I say.

Ted ponders it for a moment and then speaks. "Hell, I'd own a home if I didn't drink." We both laugh. It's probably true of me too, but priorities, priorities. His phone rings and he grabs it and starts laughing into it, but the line gets a sudden sense of movement and in a few minutes I have a beer.

"Nice to meet you," I say to Ted before heading off. He nods his head, chugs the last of his beer and gets another, then makes his way back to the end of the line. I lean against a pole and look around for a moment. There are a number of other KISW DJs here, and what they call the Rock Girls, models who wear the skimpiest of KISW clothing and appear at these kinds of events. Most of them have tattoos. I approach two of them, a short blonde and a tall blonde with a red streak in her hair. They're both wearing black tank tops cut off just below the breasts and shorts that are just that. "Uh, hi. Mind if I get a picture? I'm writing about the show today." I've never done this before, asking for such an obvious photograph. Music writer seeks photo with scantily clad models. It makes me wonder if I'm falling into cliché.

"Sure thing, hon."

"Yeah."

I ask a guy walking by to take the picture with one of them on either side of me. He does, and then he walks away to my left as the girls head right. I look at the photo on the camera. *Fucking Christ.* I must be drunk. I look too happy in the picture, and a little dumb. I can see the caption now, "Guy takes picture with models, thinks he has a chance, models laugh about him later." I know I didn't have a chance. I know that, but it did feel nice with one of them under each arm. It was false, though. This whole show is false with the nine-dollar beers and the slow-ass beer lines, even for the VIP ticket holders, and the way it just goes on and on with one average band after another. People come here to be seen, to buy tee shirts and say, "I was there." They are hoping to meet the musicians, the DJs, the Rock Girls, hoping to get laid. And I'm one of them. I look so god-damned happy in the picture that my drunk feeling just goes away. Where did that smile come from? I need to go. There's nothing for me here except maybe more innuendo about a small penis if I go back out there with my borrowed camera.

Miles walks up to me, and without saying a word, and for no reason I can think of, he grabs my notebook and writes the following: "Her thigh was wet with pussy juice as Don lifted her skirt and fondled her. She exhaled with delight as his finger worked between her moist lips. She quivered before grabbing his cock in his tight Wrangler jeans. Sadly, his penis was very small."

He hands it back to me, and I read it. We laugh. I can only guess he saw me talking to the Rock Girls, saw them walk away, my dis-appointment in the photograph. I don't know. Maybe he's prone to writing about penises in the notebooks of strangers. Maybe he heard me talking to Ted about writing and wanted contribute to the article. We sip our drinks, and he thanks me again for writing about the Men's Room Original Red. "No problem," I say. He goes backstage, and I'm left to wonder at the coincidence of what he wrote. What is it with size today?

It's so small.

I leave then after making a note to delete the picture later. Some happy moments are worth remembering. Some not. When I'm older, I want the Space Needle to have meant something, not the Rock

Girls. I still hear it in my head: "Sure thing, hon." I think about that night at the Little Red Hen, sitting in the car hoping, gesticulating, needing to hear a certain voice, "Rob?" but now all I can hear is Geoff Tate in a low, sexy whisper, "Rob?"

I hate forgetting, but it seems I have. I try to remember, but there's only the silence from the day at the post office.

"..."

So I let Geoff's voice take over. I pop Queensryche in the CD player, *Operation Mindcrime*, and on the way home sing along about revolution, about a woman named Mary, about not believing in love. And it's beautiful, of course, beautiful in the way music is while driving alone with the windows down as the sun sets, leaving the crowds behind for the comfort of a few solitary chords and melodies. I skip around, hit repeat, turn it up. I love the bass tone on this album. It isn't warm. It isn't brittle. It growls, it rumbles, it bites, it drives, especially in the brief moment between the first chorus and the second verse of "I Don't Believe in Love." It rolls on a D there, pops out of the mix, builds, and just slices through everything, and there's nothing better, nothing so filling, nothing more I need. It soothes forgetfulness as I hit repeat again and again.

CHAPTER 23

ON THE WAY HOME, I pick up four twenty-two-ounce bottles of Men's Room Original Red and think about size, about bass tone, about what Miles wrote in my notebook, about charitable beer drinking, which is what the Men's Room beer is all about. I open one of the bottles, take a good long hit, swish it around my mouth before swallowing. It makes me curious to reread what I wrote about them, so I look it up online and read it aloud for Soju while he rubs against my feet.

> The Men's Room likes to drink. I'll repeat. They. Like. To. Drink. Men after my own heart for sure. One of the people who edited early versions of my book said of the main character, "Man, he's drinking *all* the time." That's the Men's Room, but there are four of them, which means four times the booze. So what do four guys who have a radio show and a fondness for beer do? Well, when they're friends with the guys at Elysian Brewing, they get drunk with said friends and do what any beer lover would do. They make the suggestion, "You know, we'd love to have our own beer." The guys at Elysian just happened to like the idea, or maybe the beer in them liked the idea, so it was born out of a drunken moment, and I imagine, an arm around a shoulder, some leaning in. "You know, man, we really got to do this. I can *feel* it." But

it wasn't just another of those late-night drunken ideas that dissipates in the sobriety of the following morning. It didn't turn into a lifetime full of maybes and regrets, "Man, that would have been awesome if only we'd fucking done it." The beer was made, and then, being a physical thing, the idea assumed a life of its own.

It was the audience. I know it's hard to imagine, but the people who like the Men's Room seem to have a fondness for beer, so it sold quickly. Originally, Elysian made a pale ale, but when the idea started to take off, when the beer sold and the money started coming in, it was switched to the current amber brew, slightly hoppy, a bit of a malt finish. It wasn't just about beer, though. It was about opportunity. The guys in the Men's Room saw a chance to give to those less fortunate than themselves, so it was decided that a portion of the profits from the beer would go to help support the families of military vets through the VA Puget Sound Fisher House and the Ft. Lewis Fisher House, two facilities that help wounded vets and their families. Drinking beer was suddenly a charitable activity, enough so that they were able to visit the Fisher House in May and give them a check for $94,000. That's a lot of beers drunk. Cheers indeed to that! And to the fact that for 2011 the projected total of donations is expected to reach $200,000. Hats off to both the Men's Room and Elysian brewing for doing a great thing.

When I finish, I listen to a steady soundtrack of KISW staples. Judas Priest. Black Sabbath. Deep Purple. Pearl Jam. Lots of Pearl Jam. Their music has aged well. And then I call Genny. No answer. I try Katie too. No answer. Then there is Pink Floyd and Alabaster and a group from Finland called Kingston Wall, a heavy psyche-delic and progressive group that I would have given much to have seen live. I put Queensryche on, the Jesus Rehab, Furniture Girls, Sightseer. It strikes me that I don't know much of anything about current popular music, even hard rock. What I like is mostly old or local.

I finally turn off the music and sit on the sofa with a Men's Room Red in hand, Soju under the other, and I'm glad I came home. I much prefer the small show. I like to sit at the end of the bar and watch an unknown band swing for the fence. It's better to discover music that way, more personal than radio, more intimate than a festival with all its distractions. Not that there aren't great bands playing festivals and stadiums, but in the small clubs, it's all about the music, *only* the music. The crowd and the personalities and the sponsors fall away. All that matters, the only thing that matters, is the sound that emanates from the stage.

Soju meows and rolls his head over, looks at me upside down. I scratch his cheek, his chin, his head.

All that matters is the sound that emanates from the stage.

My phone buzzes. It's Officer. "Hey, man, what's up?"

"I'm downtown at Buckley's, but was thinking about heading over to Dream Girls. Why don't you come out?" Leaving the concert, I was ready for a quiet beer, a quiet night alone, maybe a little porn, but this might be better. Even if it's hands-off and no booze, the women are at least live.

"Yeah, sure, man, sounds good. I'll meet you out front in fifteen minutes or so. Oh, but first I'll load the pictures from your camera to my laptop, so give me twenty minutes at least."

"Sure thing. See you then."

I get downtown in about forty minutes and park in roughly the same spot I had the night Officer first tapped on my window. The Dream Girls sign is there again, beckoning, trying to sell the dream. I hope it isn't crowded, but it's a Saturday, so that hope is thin at best. Officer walks up behind me. "I was beginning to think you weren't going to show."

"It took a little time to transfer the pics and look at a few. Here you go. Thanks, again." I hand him the camera. He puts it in his pocket.

"No problem. Glad to help.

"Were you out at Buckley's alone?"

"Had a date, but it didn't work out so well. She took off when I went to the bathroom, so I've just been drinking."

"Why do you think she'd do that?"

"No fucking clue, man. I suppose she was cutting her losses. Seems rude, but whatever. In a way it's better not to drag it out with awkward goodbyes and such. How was White River?"

"Okay. I left early. It just got tiring after a while. Maybe I've just gotten old. Since I'm supposed to write about it, I might just have to make shit up about the last few bands. It wouldn't be a first actually. I've had some nights where my notes were completely illegible, so all I had to go on was a general sense of what I'd felt about the music."

"Any shows in particular?"

"Helmet was one. I got pretty drunk, but it was because all the opening bands were complete crap. I made up some shit and then said Helmet was good. I think they were, but I don't remember. There was someone who commented, though, who didn't like what I wrote, and though I can barely remember the article, I remember very clearly what he posted in the comments. 'This article, your writing and your attitude all suck. Sissies like you should just stay home.' "

"That's awesome. I'll have to look up that one."

"He was partially right. I phoned that one in, so perhaps it showed through in the writing." We both look up the street toward our destination. "Shall we?"

"Sure." We start walking. "So tell me, man, what the fuck happened that night after I dropped you guys off? I mean I know what happened, but you haven't told me details."

This is the first time I've seen Officer since he didn't come into my apartment that night. I wish he had. Things wouldn't have gone that way with Genny, and then it wouldn't have mattered when Katie showed up. We all would have had drinks and listened to music. There might have been some flirting, maybe even some awkward sexual tension, but there wouldn't have been the profanities, the pushes and shoves, the grappling and heavy breathing, the accusing eyes. When I hesitated to say the right things, when I hesitated to say anything, Genny stood up. "I'm outta here." She put her shoes on and left without even looking at me, and I let her go without a word. She did mumble something as she walked out the door, but I couldn't catch it, and to think about it now, she obviously wanted me to say something, do something, offer some sort of explanation. Often just doing the simplest of things, showing the slightest bit of concern, will save such a moment, and that was my last opportunity to rescue it all. I could have grabbed her arm, asked her not to go, explained the whole situation to her, but I didn't, and she left, and I think what she muttered was "asshole." I'm not sure, though. It may just have been my own thoughts about myself.

Katie sat on the floor for a little while. I had another shot of the soju she brought over and looked around for the cat—nothing like a soft, cuddly pet to cure the awkwardness—but he made no appearance. I took another swig from the bottle. It went down easier each time.

"So who was she?"

"Someone I was hoping to get to know better."

"Sorry."

"It's okay. How are you?" I took another drink and offered the unopened bottle to her. She took it, opened it, drank an impressive amount.

"I'm fine. It's just hard in moments. Sorry if I ruined your night."

"No worries."

"I should never have slept with Greg. It's always a bad thing to sleep with customers."

"Well, that's not your fault."

"I never should have slept with you, either."

I was hoping to avoid that. I should have offered an apology before she had a chance to say anything, but all I did was hope it wouldn't come up. It wouldn't have been hard to string the right few words together and speak them, but then, it is. It can be. Sometimes a sentence is a scary thing, so I hesitated. I didn't say a syllable, but in the moment, since she already said it, I had no choice but to say something, "I'm the one who owes you an apology on that account, you and Greg."

"I think he's okay with it where you're concerned. I told him."

"Oh." I thought she might be wrong but didn't question her about it.

"Listen, could you put some music on? I want to talk a little, but I want the sound, too." I put Alice in Chains on, *Sap*, without asking her what she'd like to hear. "I honestly like music a little more since I've been reading your writing. I can see what you're trying to do, and I love the way you experience music, but I question it too, what you're trying to do, that is."

"Why?"

"It seems a little like you're using the music of others for your own ends."

"Not true. I love the music I write about."

"That's what I mean. You don't write about music you don't like, so it seems either a little dishonest or a little cowardly. You have to give some bad reviews now and then, otherwise no one will trust you."

"Look, I know what you're saying, but…"

"You know what it is? It's that in the overall sense, I know what I'm going to read before I read it. You'll like the band and the music and probably talk to a hot woman who doesn't go home with you. You'll repeat a few lyrics from the songs, drink a couple beers, and then you'll go on and on about that woman you used to love or still love or whatever. What was her name anyway? You never say it."

"I don't tell anyone. It'd be like giving her some kind of power, some kind of place here in my present rather than in my past."

"I disagree. With no name, she's mysterious to you as well as everyone you know. It gives her more power." We both took a drink. Soju came back out of the bedroom and rubbed up against Katie's leg then jumped up and sat next to her. "She's the Voldemort of your writing. You should give her a name and then kill her. People with names are easier to let go." I don't say anything. "Look, I'm sorry to be so blunt, but she isn't coming back."

"I know."

"So kill her."

It was almost funny to hear her speak that way, as if we were playing a game, planning the murder of someone who was preventing us from being together. I decided to see where it would go, "How?"

"A knife through the heart. It's the only way." She was right. Some sort of killing is always involved. I opened two more bottles of soju and sat next to her and Soju, who then scampered off to the litter box. We didn't speak as he did his thing, as he made an unusual fuss of spreading the litter around. This was followed by a stink, which made me think the lid for the box must have come off a little. "Right

Turn" came on. It's credited to Alice Mudgarden in the liner notes of the CD with Mark Arm and Chris Cornell appearing on the track and apparently contributing to the songwriting effort. It's a beautifully dark tune. The whole album is. It half makes me think Alice in Chains should have played only acoustic, but only half, of course, because of songs like "Them Bones" and its ripping guitar tone. It's heavy and smooth all at once in the ascending chords under the verses, and it chugs and chunks with a little extra oomph being that they tuned down a half step and then into drop D. It isn't a happy song by any stretch of the imagination, but it makes the prospect of someday being nothing more than a big pile of bones almost bearable, something to be faced head on. I thought it might be a song for the hospice days, and that made me smile. What would the nurses do if I rode the E string tuned down to C# and sang that one? So I decided that when *Sap* finished, I'd put *Dirt* on. Katie and I both felt alone. Maybe the song would do us good. But then the outro chorus of "Right Turn" came in with its refrain about not being right, and we just started kissing. There were no moves, no lines, no convincing, just two lonely people reaching for something intimate no matter how temporary or wrong it might be. We groped. We disrobed, but somewhere during the act, I whispered a name, the *wrong* name, the unwritten name, "Rita." Thankfully, I was humming it in there, and Katie was enjoying it well enough, loud enough, or at least she seemed to be, maybe, so she didn't hear the name. Her eyes were closed. She moaned, and I grunted as I watched her body shaking beneath me. I slowed down then. I wanted the moment to last as long as possible, so I shifted her to my left a little. She understood.

"Where do you want me?"

"Right there."

We continued slowly with our eyes open, and there was release, the sexual kind, yes, but also the name. Even though she didn't hear it, it was out there, and it flew away.

When I woke up, Katie was gone, and Soju was hiding somewhere. I felt like my brain was trying to murder me, like it was scraping the inside of my scalp with a guitar pick, trying to pluck out a droning

tune amongst the bone and membranes. I cupped my head in my
hands and curled up but to no avail. The song's throbbing rhythm
continued, so I momentarily considered hair of the dog in the form
of a beer or two, a nap, a lost day but perhaps a day without a
hangover. I got up and made my way to the kitchen, opened the
fridge, briefly considered the growler of Manny's that was sitting
there next to the milk when the door opened. I turned around to see
Katie and Greg enter. They had a bag of McDonald's. Katie smiled
as if it were the most normal thing. "We got breakfast." I would
have preferred champagne like last time.

"Great, I'll put some coffee on."

"No need to," Greg said. "We're not staying."

"Oh." Katie placed the contents of the McDonald's bag on the
desk, and they both sat down on the sofa. I looked at the food, two
breakfast burritos with hot sauce and a Sausage McMuffin. I opened
the muffin, took a bite, sat down. "When did you leave?" I asked
Katie. I didn't know what she'd told him but figured I'd just get it
out there. The muffin tasted awesome.

"After you fell asleep, I went to Greg's."

"Oh." I took another bite.

"Look, no hard feelings here," Greg said. "The first time we broke
up was because I thought Katie had a thing for you. Turns out I
was right. And I knew you dug her, so there were some things for
us to work, though. And I think we have, finally, as we've been up
all night, well, all morning I guess. What time did you come over?"

"Around five."

"Yeah, and anyway we've been talking, and the only solution
is…" He paused. I took another bite and had never tasted anything
better. I knew what was coming, what he was going to say, but with
that headache, I just wanted to be quiet and eat. "… We… we all
can't be friends, or at least not like we have been." I noticed that she
had a tear in her eye. I finished the muffin and wondered if I would
cry after they left. "I wanted to tell you in person. You deserve that.
The three of us just don't work together. Not now at least."

"I'm sorry." I didn't know what else to say.

"Me too," Katie said. She took his hand then, squeezed. "I'm so
sorry." They hugged. I grabbed a burrito and started to unwrap it.
They stood up at the noise. He reached out his hand. I took it.

"Like I said, no hard feelings, just time to take new paths."

"It's okay." Katie stepped in, hugged me. "Bye."

Then they left.

New paths. The three of us don't work together. I was reminded of some other words.

This just isn't working.

Maybe nothing ever does.

My headache was gone but that was the least of my problems. I remembered telling Greg and Katie about what people do when they're depressed. They listen to music. I had been. I wondered again where the Radiohead was. There was one song I wanted badly to hear, a song that might have made the moment bearable, but there was no CD, no melody. There was just a growler of beer. It was just after ten, early, but I didn't care. I went to the kitchen and poured myself a glass. Soju came up to me, meowed twice as if to ask, "Where'd they go? Where are they?"

"I don't know, buddy, I don't know." I scratched his head and neck, took a sip of the beer. "I don't know where anybody is."

CHAPTER 24

WE'RE STANDING IN FRONT of Dream Girls when I finish the story. "Dude, I'm sorry to hear it, but this will be perfect for you tonight." He's right. This place will be perfect for me. Hell, it might even be too good for me. I check my phone for messages, and there's a Facebook notification. I tap it. "You're checking Facebook now? Here?"

"Just give me a second." It's a friend request from Elena, and I wonder if it's one of those that artists and musicians do, the friend request for numbers, reaching for a possible new fan rather than an actual friend. Still, I accept and then think to send her a message. "Good to hear from you. What's your number? Maybe we can meet for coffee sometime and finally look at your paintings." Officer picks a copy of the *Seattle Weekly* off the ground and leafs through it while I text, while I wait for a response. It comes in a few minutes, a smiley face and a phone number. I look at Officer reading the adult classifieds in the back of the paper. I can feel the glow and buzz of the sign above me. I can hear the thump of the music in the club. I think it's "Pour Some Sugar on Me," which is, of course, expected in such a place. I would go in except for one thing. I now have a phone number and a new friend. I dial her number. If she's out and feels like meeting up, I'll ditch this place.

"Who you calling?"

"A woman."

"Genny?"

"Nah, someone else." It rings four times, and then a message kicks.

"Hiiiii. This is Elena. I'm sorry I missed you, but I don't have any more appointments tonight. Please try tomorrow, though, as I want to satisfy your every need. Full service: Sixty dollars an hour," and then very breathy, "Bye." It was a sexy voice, but it wasn't the Elena I know.

"What the?"

"Wrong number?"

"I don't think so." I check the number she sent against what I dialed, and they're the same. "Hmm, she must have mistyped her number."

"Here." He hands me the classifieds. "Call one of these women. They'll answer." I look at the ads. They're for massages, for two women at once, for in-call or out, for full service, for overweight women, for older women, for all kinds of shit. And most of the ads give a name. There's Lolita, Serenity, Jade, Sparkle, Divine, Elena.

Elena?

"What the?"

"What?"

"Look at this ad. It says, 'Feeling Stressed? Lonely? Treat yourself to the best Sensual Massage. Private—Discreet—Experienced. Call Elena.' I... this, uh, that's the number this woman just sent me." It is. Elena sent me the number for this other Elena who apparently offers professional massage "services." I show my phone to Officer. He compares the numbers, reads the ad again, busts out laughing.

"Ha! I don't know who this chick is, but she's cool."

"Yeah, but this number. What the hell?"

"Look, just message her tomorrow. Let's go in." There's a brief pause, and since I don't have any argument against it, we enter the club. I can't help wondering as we pay the cover and find a table if this is a joke or if Elena's upset that I never contacted her. I guess I'll check tomorrow. If we're still virtual friends, I'll message her.

The music playing now is Queen's "Fat-bottomed Girls," which is a cool song, but it can't mask the fact that this is a depressing place, dark with white, orange, and red flashes from the stage that seem in time with the beat, lonely men at their tables, women grinding on some of them. There's a large-chested woman up on the stage who's trying to be sexy but is succeeding only in illustrating the sadness of this endeavor. A waitress brings a couple of Cokes, and we pay ten dollars each. Officer has a Dream Girl on him in a few seconds. It's quick, almost like she knows him. She's blonde and fake in all the expected ways. They walk off to the VIP section leaving me to sip my ten-dollar Coke and listen to the end of the song. Next is Nine Inch Nails' "Closer," another strip club staple, but an awesome song even if it isn't one to raise the spirits. In fact, I prefer it to the strippers. I turn away three of them in favor of just listening. I suppose the others get the message as no more come. No matter. I have Trent to keep me company.

I down my Coke and order one more, pay another ten bucks while listening to the rest of the song. The woman on stage has removed her top and is writhing about on the floor and grinding an imaginary lover off-beat. It's the most unsexy thing I've ever seen. She grabs her ankles and pulls her legs back, arches on her stomach and rocks a few times and the song diminishes in the beautiful soft notes of the keyboard outro. She rolls over, gets up, walks offstage. There is applause, but I don't get it. There isn't even a shred of illusion in this place unless you come with blinders on, but then that is the point. It makes me feel not a little foolish for coming. I finish my drink and leave quickly before another song begins. Don't get me wrong. I like dancing women, naked women too, but I was wrong. "Closer" does raise the spirits. It shines a light on what matters, and what matters is not emanating from this stage.

Outside, I walk to my car thinking to message Officer tomorrow to make sure he got home okay and to apologize for leaving him alone in there. I'm alone, but so what? I have a cat at home, a guitar, a bass, a few beers in the fridge. I get to my car, start it up, drive with the stereo off and the only sound is that of the tires on the road. It's exquisite after all the music of the day. It's a song in its own right, something like John Cage's 4:11, but this isn't a performance piece meant to shock or surprise. It's just rubber on pavement and the absence of all else, a low hum, a meditation. When I get to the West Seattle Bridge, I see some red and blue lights in the rearview and pull over hoping they will pass, and quickly they do until first the sound dies, then the flashing colors. I sit there for a few moments happy that the emergency is elsewhere.

CHAPTER 25

WHEN I GET HOME, I get it in my head to find the missing Radiohead CD. I don't even make it to the refrigerator to grab a beer. I just go straight to the shelf and start looking through cases. I even leave disks on the floor, on the shelf, on the desk. The cases are scattered in the same manner, some lie open, others shut. After going through about fifty, hell, maybe a hundred, I give up. I gather the CDs into a stack so they won't be scratched, but I don't put them in their cases. I leave those where they are. Maybe I'll get to them later. Pink Floyd's *Dark Side of the Moon* is on top of the pile. I consider it briefly, but I'm in more of an "Echoes" mood, so I pull *Meddle* off the shelf, and while "Echoes" begins its slow churn I pull the *I Might Be Wrong Case* from the shelf and try it for what must be the fiftieth time. Still empty. "Where is it, Soju?"

Meow.

It seems like he's saying, "Hell if I know." With the music going, I start looking around. I check behind the shelf and under it, behind the TV, in the bedroom, the bathroom, the toilet. Yes, I look in the toilet. Instinctive, I suppose, when searching for something in the bathroom to simply grab the lid and look in. No CD, thankfully, as that would have been a real trip trying to figure out how it got in there and remained unnoticed all this time. I keep looking. Refrigerator. No. Trash. No. Car. No. Closet. No. Underwear drawer. No. I look everywhere except one place, the litter box, which is in the laundry room next to the broom, the mop, the Bounce. I walk over to it at the end of the kitchen and grab a beer on the way. The CD is nowhere else. If not in there, then it has simply disappeared.

The litter box has a black arched cover with an entrance on the front. According to the product description online, it's for cats "who believe in going in style," so Soju goes in privacy and comfort. He's very good about that. Never makes a mess. I pause next to the box, take that quick deep breath one does before opening an uncertain door. I take the top off and find all the stuff one would expect to find, lots of it really. "Ugh." I suppose I should clean it, but not yet. Finding Radiohead is a more important matter. I put the top back on and go out to the living room. I sit next to Soju and scratch his head for a bit. He squirms, makes his neck more available. I set my beer on the coffee table not having taken even one sip and let sleep come over me in spite of the hunger that comes from not having eaten dinner. What does food matter anyway? The CD is gone.

I wake a little after four and look around. No Soju. He must be in the bedroom, so I get up and look in at the bed for the little guy hoping for a meow that does not come. He stands up, yawns with arched back, steps in slow motion from the king size blue pillow to the other king size blue pillow where he turns once and settles himself into a perfect black and white circle of fur, eyes peeking up at me, telling me, educating me that there is nothing else to do in these waning hours, maybe ever. I hit play again on the stereo, and "Echoes" resumes. I lie next to Soju, my head on the first blue pillow. It's still warm. The pulse of the music mixes with purrs and lyrics as morning comes, as stomach forgets its hunger, and the only things that need doing are breathing and sleeping.

Meow!

And feeding the cat.

I get up, pour food in the bowl, but I don't go back to the bedroom. Instead, I sit with the music and boot the laptop, and I remember that

in my thirties, there was
all that
which prevented me
from doing,
from writing,
and I was one

of those people.
"I want to write,"
I'd say,
"but there's work,
an oil change,
and the girlfriend
wants to spend Saturday
at IKEA before cooking
cabbage rolls
and watching DVDs."

Now,
all I do
is write,
and there is no
girlfriend,
no Saturdays whiled away
shopping for made-to-put-together furniture,
no evenings given
to cabbage rolls
or enchiladas
or various stews
as I rarely cook for one,
no moments on the couch
wrapped in arms
that can't be still
as movies are ignored
and clothes come off.

It is the words
rather that light up
the night, that keep
the walls from closing
in, that make the hours
something to remember
as phrases are typed
and read and reread
and shouted to the heavens

with arms upraised
for the beauty and joy
I hope
others will experience
when they read them.

This, of course,
is followed
by the doubts
that seep in
after lowering arms
and looking
around to see,
again,

there is
no other
here.

The bars
and the bartenders
and the beers on tap
call then. "I'm here,"
they say. "The beauties
are here,"
they say.

But I'm strong
now,
finally.
And though I do want
someone here,
need
someone here,
as there are moments of ache,
trembling, loneliness,
despair,
they are only

moments, and they
will pass,
like me someday.
Music fades
and I sit.
I breathe
in, out
in, out.
I twist open
another beer,
notice the indentations on the cap
match the permanent ones
on my thumb and index finger.
I give the bottle
a good long hit.
I do have my sorrows,
but there are
no regrets as I smile
at my good fortune
in this life,
the freedom
to remember beauty,
to place a name on it,
and from its loss
create
type
live
here
in the wee hours
of the present tense
knowing unknown beauty
of one form or another
awaits on the next page.

CHAPTER 26

WHILE THE COFFEE IS BREWING, I put a tortilla in a pan, heat it up, munch it down plain while waiting for the caffeine to be ready. There are the usual sounds of gurgling liquid dripping down into the pot, the meow of Soju over on the couch, a bus driving by outside, and then there's a Christmas song in my brain, "God Rest Ye Merry Gentlemen." Where the hell did this come from? And why in September? I'm powerless against it, though, so I sing a little, "God rest ye merry gentlemen. Let nothing you dismay." I let it trail off. I'm tired. I wish I could sleep for a week, but there's work and writing and music to listen to and write about, to sing, "Remember Christ our savior was born on Christmas day." Soju comes over and rolls on the floor. He looks up at me. Meow. It's an invigorating sound, playful, daring, joyous even. His tongue is sticking out. He's purring.

"Good morning to you, too."

When the coffee's done, I pour some in a cup and then consider it for a moment. The blue guitar is fading a little. More of the Christmas song comes to mind. "To save us all from Satan's power when we were gone astray."

The whole idea of religion has never made much sense to me with its whole afterlife thing of burning in hell or halos and wings. I've just never been able to shake the idea that there is nothing at the end, that death is death, infinite darkness. It's why I turned to music early on and to writing these days. These things bring joy now. They bring consolation now. They bring meaning now, *before* the darkness. Sometimes, they even bring women. I think about the ending of *Hard-Boiled Wonderland* again and just can't help thinking it spot-on. If I knew the end was near, was at hand, a drive to the coast where the music could mix with the waves would be ideal, but perhaps a mix tape would be in order, or rather a mix CD, cassette tape being a thing of the past. Maybe that best of Pearl Jam CD that Lindsay had in her car that night in the Skylark parking lot. Or perhaps something that includes much of what I've written about, music important to me in the present tense.

I put both hands around the mug and take a sip, and then another. Hell, I'd probably take this cup out in the car on that last day and sip some Manny's or Blue Moon from it as the songs play and the breathing slows. I turn to walk back into the living room humming some more of the Christmas song, but Soju is there right behind me.

Meow!

Trying not to step on him or trip over him, I lurch forward and stumble, but it's no good. I lose my balance and fall. The cup slips from my hands, and as I hit the floor, I'm met with a shower of both very hot coffee and pieces of porcelain. The sound of the mug smashing into the floor is the worst, something akin to the shattering of a smile. I don't give a damn about any other glass or cup in this apartment, but the one I drop, the one in pieces in a pool of coffee has to be this one. I'd curse and swear and shout, but I don't have the energy. I lie quietly for a few moments. There is pain in my shoulder and right arm from the fall but more from the broken cup. It's one more thing gone, one more thing that slipped through my fingers. I look at the fragments and see the handle completely intact so I reach out to touch it. Soju comes over, sniffs, goes back to the sofa.

Meow.

After a few minutes, three, maybe five, I'm not sure, I think to pour myself some more coffee but then decide to go to Starbucks over at Alki. Staring at the water will do me good now, even without the CD made. I get up. I look down at the mess, and not in the mood to clean, I just leave it. I get dressed, pull my hair back, and grab the laptop thinking I'll clean up later. I walk to the door and open it, give a push to the outside screen door but then pause. The pieces are sharp. Soju might cut himself. I shouldn't leave it. I look back at Soju. He's staring out the door with his body crouched and poised. I turn to see what he sees. There's a cat, a gray tabby. It's absolutely still with eyes fixed back at Soju. After a couple seconds, it gives a quick glance up at me and then bolts under the fence and is gone. Soju follows before I can shut the screen door.

"Soju!" I take a fearfully slow step, and then I hear it, the screech of tires, a yowling meow cut in half. Silence. I freeze thinking, *Please let it be the other cat, please let it be the other cat.* A car door opens and shuts. I stand still while my heart drops it into fifth and punches it. I can't see anything through the fence, and I usually appreciate that for the fact that passersby can't see in. Now, I appreciate it for the opposite. I listen instead. Nothing. The silence after the storm. I take a step, pause, listen, take one more and then open the gate.

And there's suddenly a cop car. Out of nowhere there's one with lights flashing red and blue in the early a.m. of Sunday. It's as if it's been waiting here for something to happen. There's a maroon sedan of some sort in the street with a woman standing next to the front driver's side tire. She has her head bowed. The cop car is behind hers with headlights clearly illuminating something in the street. That empty feeling comes to me. I want to know, but I don't want to know. *Please let it be the other cat.* I sit down and lean against the fence and feel the tears well as the officer walks toward me. The woman by her car seems to be shaking a little. The officer speaks.

"Sir, is that your cat there in the street?"

I look left, away from the officer, toward downtown, and see the gray tabby staring out of some bushes with red and blue flashing in its eyes. It waits for a second and then turns and is gone. It is the way of the world. All good things do end, but somehow, and I have no idea how, we manage this. Life does go on and on and on. I think I'll make that CD later, just in case. The officer speaks again.

"Sir?"

I don't answer. I just have that stupid song in my head. "Tidings of comfort and joy, comfort and joy..." Fucking hell to that. I go back into my place and grab a beer, sit on the sofa. The door is still open. The cop follows.

"Sir?"

Goodbye, little buddy.

CHAPTER 27

THE DAY AFTER SOJU DIED, Elena messaged me on Facebook. I got the notification around ten in the morning but waited until somewhere around eight in the evening to read it. "Hey, there. Sorry about the phone number thing. I couldn't resist. Just a joke. Call me." She gave me a different number. I wrote it down, deleted the message, and then didn't call. I wasn't trying to be a dick and play at being mad about calling the escort or prostitute or whatever that other Elena actually labeled herself. That was pretty funny actually. I just didn't have the stomach for anything other than beer, certainly not people. I poured out my last few bottles of soju and didn't buy any more. I skipped a few shows that I'd said I'd write about, didn't answer the phone when it rang. I put my hand to my chest every time I lay down and remembered Soju pawing me just after the tattoo, kneading, helping me heal the only way he knew how. After a week of me not calling Elena, I realized I was afraid of her, or rather the possibility of her, the possibility that she could make me forget a voice I'd already forgotten, make me stop trying to remember certain looks and gestures and sounds, details, nights and smiles that only I knew, and for me, forgetting was a fearful thing. It reminded me of death, of the absence of sound. Does that which we have forgotten ever happen?

And now, I'm left to wonder if whole parts of my life, parts of me, will vanish even before I do. I remember being tickled one night. I was laughing while curled up in a ball on the floor. It went on for some time, but I can't even remember what color the carpet was, and more important, who had tickled me. Was it Rita? Someone before her? I have no idea. I just remember laughing. Maybe it's a false memory. Maybe I tickled myself. I don't know. I try to remember the carpet. It was blue, I think, or green, maybe a faded gray. I have not a clue. One more moment gone, but the funny thing is that the memory will probably stay with me until the end, again in the hospice, another story for the nurse, "I was tickled… ha ha!" I just won't be able to tell them who did it, and I'll pause trying to remember, but I'll fail. Maybe I'll start weeping. "I can't remember." The nurse will guide me back to bed. "Here, why don't you take a little nap." It saddens me now since I want to think such moments mattered, that it wasn't just me having a good time and passing through events without thinking about them, that even if the good times ended that they are still remembered as such, no matter what happened afterward, that even if it wasn't working at some point, that it was at some point prior, and that the who and what and where and when and the color of the carpet will be remembered.

I call Elena at two in the afternoon. It seems a safe time. Voicemail, click. I decide to call back and wait all of five minutes to do so. Again, voicemail. I wait almost five minutes more and hit redial. After months of not doing exactly this, it's now urgent. Voicemail again. "Fuck!" *Oh, shit, did I say that out loud?* "Uh, hi Elena. Rob here. Give me a call when you're able." I hang up without leaving my number and wait a few minutes. I'd pet Soju if he were still here. I look around. Nothing. No meows, no purrs.

"…"

I lie on the couch, breathe deep, exhale. I close my eyes and wonder whether this is what it feels like to be buried alive, to be stuck in a coffin six feet under where the only movement is the beat of a slowly suffocating heart, the pulse decreasing, the body growing cold, listening to the wood of the coffin and the dirt around it, the wiggling of worms, the stretching of the roots of trees.

"…"

But no, this is… this is different. My heart is racing, pounding, thumping like those drums at the beginning of "Hot For Teacher." I shiver with excitement. I have the urge to eat nachos, Taco Bell nachos with no sour cream and inundated with Fire Sauce. I'm not in the future unhappy part of my life, though that may come. I'm in the now and will always be. The past is mutable. It is whatever I make of it. The future is the same.

My phone rings. It startles me so I sit up. I'm one of those with the old style phone sound as a ring tone. It can be jarring, but it should be. Someone is reaching out to me. When calls come unexpected, it sometimes makes me look around the room for a phone attached to the wall with a twisted cord hanging down. Mine rings again. I pick it up and see it's Elena's number. I answer and try to act as if I weren't waiting. "Hello?" but it squeaks out. It's obvious.

"Hi. It's Elena. I got your message."

"Great!" It sounds like I'm congratulating her. "Uh, I mean, thanks for calling back."

"Were you upset about that one number I gave you? Sorry if you were, but…"

"Nah, I wasn't. It made me laugh actually."

"I'm glad, but you still waited a week to call me."

"Yeah, sorry about that. I…"

"It's okay. I noticed you'd stopped posting on your blog so I thought you might be hard at work on that book you mention sometimes when writing about bands. I paint so I know how that kind of thing can go."

She noticed. She was looking for my writing and paying attention. "Well, there's always that, but I… well, uh, my cat died so I just haven't done much this past week."

"Oh, god, I'm sorry. How awful."

"Yeah, it sucked, but what can you do?" I don't want to go on about Soju, not now, not yet. "Uh, listen, I called to see if you might be interested in checking out a show tonight. Well, that, and to apologize for never looking you up in the first place."

"Honestly, that's why I gave you that number last time so maybe we can call it even."

"Fair enough. So what do you think about the show?"

And then on the evening of Saturday, November 5, I have two obligations. First, there is a birthday party at the Skylark for Troy Nelson of the Young Evils. Since I like the band, I figure to stop by and say hello, wish him a good one. Also, I feel bad for not writing about their last show. It was back on October 1 at the Tractor, but I just haven't written about any music since Soju died. The requests from bands and bars and promoters keep coming, and I still go to shows and drink and sometimes make notes, but I haven't written anything, haven't posted anything, so I head to the Skylark to support Troy on his day, and on the way over, I think about that show. Faustine was there behind the drums drumming quite well. The things I'd heard were true. She was very good. They played songs from their first CD and some new material, and the sellout crowd cheered. The new stuff was a little edgier, a little darker, less of the clean open jangle, and I try to think of how to describe it to Troy and Mackenzie and any of the other band members who might be at the Skylark, but I can't come up with the right phrase.

I get there, and it's crowded. I suppose being a DJ for KEXP and in a somewhat popular band will do that for a birthday party. Nothing wrong with that. Their music is good, and he's a pretty cool dude who wants me to record an audio version of my book, which is still out there seeking its way. I've received a few rejection letters, but that's to be expected. The only thing one can do is keep on sending it out. I go to the bar where a Manny's is waiting for me. "Cheers," Jessie says. I raise the glass to her, have a sip, look around. There are people milling about drinking, some dancing, some eating. There's a photographer in one corner, and I see Mackenzie so I go say hi. She smiles. We hug, get our picture taken. Troy walks up. "Nice to see you."

"Sure thing. Happy birthday."

"Thanks."

"How was PJ20?" They were one of two local bands invited by Pearl Jam to play the PJ20 festival. The other was Star Anna. I'm envious, of course, but both bands deserved it. I wonder if that's where the new Seattle sound is going, a mixture of Star Anna and the newer Young Evils songs, which I still can't quite describe.

"Fucking awesome, man."

"Hell yeah," Mackenzie says. "We were all on stage for the last encore of 'Rocking in the Free World.' Troy had a tambourine, and we were both shouting along with the choruses and," she pauses for a second, "and just wow." Her eyes light up like she can clearly see the moment now, thousands of fans dancing and singing along as Pearl Jam and friends play Neil Young. "I don't know exactly how many people there were, but shit, that was… just wow." She puts her hand over her heart. I know what she means. I've seen the videos on YouTube. Again, I'm envious. I should have gone and written about it. Maybe I will for PJ40.

"Listen, sorry, I haven't yet written about your last show, I dropped the ball on that."

"No worries," Troy says. "What'd you think of it?"

"I was glad I finally got to see Faustine play, and…" It comes to me then, the phrase to describe the music. "I loved it. More evil, less young. Good stuff."

"More evil, less young. Nice!" Mackenzie smiles. "Thanks."

And then more people come up to each of them for hellos and pictures and hugs and handshakes, even a few autographs. I step aside and let them in. I finish my beer and drop a ten on the bar for Jessie, wave goodbye to her, step outside half wishing there was a car here in which I could smoke pot. That not being the case, I decide to head downtown to my second obligation of the evening, Julia Massey and the Five Finger Discount at the Crocodile.

And Elena.

When we spoke that first time on the phone, she couldn't make the show that night. She had a date, another Match.com thing. I didn't press the issue, but she did say she'd love to see a band some-time so we messaged over the next few weeks. It was hard, though. Last weekend, she had a vacation in Chicago, and before that it was plans with friends. There were shows she wasn't interested in, nights when she wasn't feeling well, times when I got sucked into writing. She wasn't like Katie. She wouldn't just show up at my place with booze, although parts of me wished she would. Finally, though, we managed to agree to meet tonight, and when I get to the club, she's waiting outside. She has on a blue coat, but I can see she has the Cheap Trick tee shirt on under it. I wonder if it's on purpose, and with nothing really to base an answer on, I decide it is.

"Well, there you are finally."

"Yep, here I am. Nice shirt."

"Thanks. A few years ago I saw them in Chicago. Great show."

"I'm jealous. I never have."

"You want to go in?"

"Yeah. You're sure you don't mind me writing about tonight?"

"Not at all. Do your thing. We'll have time to talk before and after."

We enter the venue, which is one of Seattle's best. It's a roughly five hundred capacity place with a nice stage and a good sound system. There's an actual backstage too, even a green room. Pearl Jam and Nirvana and the like all played here back in the nineties, and these days it's a coveted gig. The first band is tearing down their equipment so we go to the bar and order a couple drinks. Manny's for me, Crown and Coke for her. I take out my notebook and jot a couple things down.

"It's good to see you writing. I was wondering if you actually would when you mentioned it. Not to be too forward, but I love that you write. So few people do anything, and it isn't for lack of talent but rather drive, and that's why my thought was that if you didn't contact or call me for all that time after we first met that you just weren't ready, you had other things going on. That's how artists are."

"If I'm one."

"Of course you are. Question of quality aside, you put your voice out there. Sometimes that itself is worthy of applause."

She's right. We often get hung up on what's good and what's bad that we forget what it means

just to step on stage, the bravery it takes to be like Lily Briscoe and say, "This is what I see. This is the way I paint the world."

"So what happened with the Match.com thing? No luck?"

"Nope. I do that every once in a while. I've met some interesting people, but no one I'd call a keeper. That guy I brought to the Sightseer show was the worst of them. I don't think he's ever been out to see a local band."

"I wondered where you guys went that night."

"We cut out pretty early into their set. He said he was bored so I later ditched him at a bar and caught a cab home. He probably just wanted to get laid but was too impatient to see the whole night through."

I write one more thing in my notebook, "Maybe forgetting is a good thing."

Julia Massey takes the stage with Geoff B. Gibbs (bass) and Dominic Cortese (drums, and also of the Jesus Rehab) just as we're each getting another drink, a sixteen-ounce plastic cup of Manny's for me, a Crown and Coke for her. There are light bouncy chords on the piano and some clicking of sticks and cymbals before the rhythm comes in and the bodies in the audience that are not scribbling in notebooks move to the beat. Elena looks at me, "I'm going to go up front and dance a little." The band labels themselves as cosmic folk rock, and it's an apt description in some ways, but I'm not quite sure what it means. They do use distortion sometimes, even on the bass, but as an effect, not for the overall tone. Julia plays mostly keyboards, but some acoustic guitar, and the music is never simple rock, and yet, it isn't folk or Americana or psychedelic. They're one of those rare groups that has their own sound. Cosmic folk rock is only a partial description. There's a sweetness to the music without being overly sentimental, an honesty without sharing too much, a willingness to bare all without saying, "Look at me!" They aren't pop or heavy or alternative. They aren't exactly cosmic, but they are out of this world, or rather in a world of their own, and the music bridges the gap, invites us in. Maybe *this* is the new Seattle sound. I get another beer, and the music continues a little poppy, a little spacey. They look like they feel good up on the stage, and I write things like "cool slap groove... big chords in the middle... little bass solo!" during a song called "Back Door Open."

The bass is a driving element in the band, and Gibbs is quite good at taking a dominant role, but he doesn't overshadow the others. They mix their sounds well. Massey's voice echoes Regina Spektor at times and a little of Zooey Deschanel at others. "Aghodoe" is my favorite song, which in moments reminds me of Pink Floyd's "High Hopes" in the progression underneath her plea, "Please, please, please don't forget me." I remember Stephanie from Like Lightning telling me that people hear what they like, what they're familiar with, so I wonder what another critic would say, think, write.

"Aghodoe" speaks of branches breaking and the plea of youth. There's a bounce to it—"Please, don't forget me"—but then the acceptance of age, experience, life, wanting to be a garden, sustenance, a necessary part of what came before, appreciated, but not lamented, smiled upon, and at the end the phrase changes, "Please forget, please forget, please forget, please forget me." It's a touching song, the rare kind that is beautiful and also fun. "Please forget me." It's a phrase I've never had the strength to say, or even to write, but I do now. I scribble it in my notebook.

Please forget me.

I sip my beer and read it.

Please forget me.

And suddenly life seems easy. All it takes is the length of a song, a melody of only three words, two of them repeated before dropping on the "me" as the last chords fade into silence. And that's the way of things. Pain and heartache can linger, but they can vanish in a second, in an A chord on the keyboard that fades as the applause kicks in. "Woo woo!" Maybe music is the constant. $2 + 2 + M = 4$ until the likes of Julia and Geoff and Dominic step on stage. Then it's 5. The M transforms. It's like an element that takes up two spots on the periodic table. In one, it's a stable thing, light, a component of life, always there but inert. It doesn't affect things. It's background. In the other, it's heavy, unstable, radioactive. The slightest neutron passing through its core will spark a nuclear reaction, and from there, nothing is as it was, but only as it is played out by the jangly unclean chords of the blue guitar. Everything changes, and it can all be from a simple thing, say, a bass guitar hitting a C#, fourth fret on the A string, then up to a D# and an E, and repeated as a woman asks not to be forgotten, or as someone else over a similar progression sings of high hopes. The music adheres, as do the melody and the words, and their lingering effects are not incidental. It gives me a vision of sorts, or maybe clarity is a better word, and I realize it's easier to forget people than music, easier to forget the sound of a voice than the tone of the guitars in a song, easier to live without love than music.

Please forget me.

As we leave the club, I have a nuclear reaction on my brain, specifically the sun and its process of fusion that compresses four hydrogen nuclei together to make one helium, but that single helium nucleus is not the complete sum of its parts. It's less with a mass slightly under the four units of weight one might think four hydrogens would make. This is what Einstein figured out, $E = mc^2$. That bit of lost mass is converted into energy, and a lot of it. What makes the sun so powerful is that C is a big number by itself, about 670,000,000 miles per hour, roughly Mach 900,000, and squaring it makes it all the more so. That means even small amounts of mass, say four teeny tiny hydrogen nuclei, turn into huge amounts of energy when squished together. So I wonder what would happen if a cockroach disappeared with all of its mass multiplied by the speed of light squared and transferred to the other side of the equation, or a rabbit, or a person.

Or a G chord.

Elena and I get to her car, a blue Camry with a Suziki Ichiro bobblehead on the dash. We're both a little drunk and probably shouldn't drive, but how else are we going to get anywhere? And since I'm in the mood for some quiet after the show, there's just one place I want to go. "Come back to my place for a drink?" She looks at me in a way that makes it seem as if we've been dating for a while, as if going back to my place for a drink is the obvious thing, the expected thing. There's desire, of course, but not the lust and urgency that go hand in hand with such first times. She puts her keys in the door, unlocks it, and before getting in looks at me. "I'll follow you." And so while driving, I keep her in the rearview, and for the first time in months, probably the first time in my whole life, I want to be forgotten. I want to disappear from all that was and exist only now. And not because I'm in love, or even on the verge of it, but because I'm alive. I can ask to be forgotten. I can forget. I can see something new in the rearview, and I can look forward to all the songs I've never heard.

Back at my place, we have Sightseer on, repeating at low volume. Our clothes are in a pile on the floor, and we're on the sofa spooning. Elena is singing along, "Who knows what tomorrow brings…" I'd wanted to put on Radiohead earlier, even spent some time looking for *I Might Be Wrong* while telling her how the CD had vanished. She helped a little then by pulling a few CDs from the shelf and opening them, but when she came across Sightseer, she suggested we play that instead. It was a better choice anyway, more of a common ground for us, and now, we're listening, both on our left sides. My right arm is around her, my left beginning to tingle in numbness from leaning on it too long. Elena sings some more: "… ain't it funny how the biggest storms don't make a sound." She turns around, kisses me, runs her fingers over the tattoos on my chest. "Is that Chinese? What's it mean?"

"It's Korean. Soju. It was the name of my cat." I touch the tattoo. "He was a good one."

"I'm sorry. Did you get that after he died?"

"Before. Soju's also a kind of Korean alcohol that I like to drink sometimes. That's how I came up with the name."

"Oh. Do you have any pictures?"

"Of the cat?"

"Yeah."

"Sadly not a one."

"That's too bad. Tell me about him." So I tell her what Soju looked like and the things he did. I mention the dragon and that it broke, but I don't say exactly how that happened, seems a story for another time, maybe in a bar when we're trading stories of our exes. She listens with interest, and we get to talking about other things for a while, and then she sits up. "I think I should be going. I'd like to stay, but I shouldn't." I want her to stay of course, and perhaps she sees my disappointment because she adds one more thing, "Not yet anyway."

CHAPTER 28

When I was a lad, it was baseball
that caught my fancy. George Foster
hit 52 home runs in 1977, and I thought I
wanted to do that. And I did once,
two home runs
in a game in the first two
innings. The second one sailed far over
the left field fence, and I just watched,
forgot all about that thing of circling
the bases in a slow jog until my coach
from the bench and my father
from the stands prompted me,
"Rob, run!"

I didn't want to run. I wanted
to watch that ball shoot beyond
the confines of the playing field
for we have so few moments where we can
see the actual result of our success
while people cheer and the strength
wells up inside, the arms raise,
the mouth opens,
"Hell yeah!"

That was sixth grade, back when nothing
mattered like hitting a home run.
The girls were aliens,
and art had no meaning. I knew there
was a power in the opening drums
of "I Want You to Want Me" and in the way
all those Japanese people screamed,
but I didn't play guitar then
so it wafted over me,
a mile-high jet stream
of my non-understanding.

I felt my home runs more,
my two home runs.
The kind of day a sixth grader
lingers on for a school year,
and some people their whole
lives. "I hit two home runs once!"

The older me has grown in a different
direction though. I ignore the Mariners
while drinking in the bars, have no idea
whatever happened to Mr. Foster
or the baseball card of him
I once had. These days, it's the G chord
strummed a certain way, the beautiful
turn of phrase, the line repeated
in a poem or a song,
the look a woman
has while tracing tattoos
and listening to songs
of whiskey and heartache,
the texts she sends
at midnight on nights apart,
"Are you naked :)",
the flush of the toilet
from her in my bathroom.

Elena comes out
as I hear the water
still running. She grabs
two beers from the fridge
and walks to my desk,
"Whatcha typing?"

"A love poem."

"Better be about me."

She hands me a beer
after opening it.
I sip, pause, play it cool.

"Oh it is, baby. It is. Did
I ever tell you about the time
I hit two home runs?"

"No more stories."

She grabs my hand and leads
me to the couch, puts Julia Massey
in the CD player, cranks
it up.
"Let's just
listen
a while."

Chapter 29

"**WHERE'VE YOU BEEN?** I texted you twice."

"I'm sorry, baby. I was writing."

It's our first fight. I was supposed to be at her place an hour ago, but like I told her, I was writing. I can hear Sightseer on her stereo: "Your letter lies on the table. What can I do?" There are four empty bottles of Blue Moon on her counter. That's a good pace for her. She probably would have greeted me at the door with one if I'd been on time.

"Writing?"

"Yeah. Sometimes I get to typing and just lose track of time."

"What? You couldn't call or answer my texts?" Not being given to dramatics, she says it in a very low-key way. It would be easy to think she isn't really upset, but I know she must be. We've spent the greater portion of the past three weeks together, many of them all night at my place. Relationship has started. I should have been on time.

"I'm sorry." It's all I can say.

"It just isn't like you to be the unfeeling robot guy. It's disappointing."

"I know. I'm sorry. I was working on my book, and I, uh, well…" Maybe she's right about me and the robot. It would have been easy to stop, to call, to reply to her texts and turn off the laptop, but I didn't. The urge came to write, and I went with it. I always do, like it's part of my programming, and that means there are times such as this when there's a risk of losing her because of who I am, because I need to write, but I also know I shouldn't be an asshole, especially if I care about someone. It's the balance of those that I've always had a hard time with. When I finally did stop typing, I thought to get flowers on the way over, but then I got to driving in a rush and texting at the same time. "On my way." I nearly hit two parked cars and, of course, forgot the flowers. "I'm sorry."

"I do understand about art and writing. I do. You know that, but I think I'd rather just be alone tonight so you should probably leave."

"Can I give you this?" It's a poem for her, part of the writing I was doing.

She takes it. "What's this?" She reads it out loud.

At 42
I'm all too aware
my last breath
will come some day,
some far off day,
I hope,
and though it's been
only a few weeks
for us so far,
I hope now
you
are with me
then.

She looks up at me, but before she can say anything, I do. "Don't misunderstand. I'm not saying love or trying to pressure you into anything like that. I'm just happy. I'm having fun, and no matter what happens between us, I hope at the end that the memory is still there, that's there's still a good feeling, that I haven't done anything to make you hate me. I want these memories to last."

There's a pause. The first notes of "Biggest Storms" fill the space. "I finished that Murakami book today," she says. "You were right. The end is cool, very understated, comical in a way, too, with the beer and the mother with her little girl."

"I am sorry."

"I know." She looks down at the poem, back up at me, "Text me next time, call me. I was worried you had an accident, or I thought you might be looking for your damn Radiohead CD." She snickers a little at that. "You find that thing yet?"

"No, not yet. Before I die, though, I will. It's my new quest."

"Why don't you just buy a new CD?"

"I'm stubborn, I guess."

She buries her head in my chest, squeezes me tight. "My stubborn robot. Don't be late again. I hate it when you're late."

CHAPTER 30

IT'S OUR ONE-MONTH ANNIVERSARY, and I follow the recipe to the letter. I put one pound of crab meat into a bowl and add bread crumbs, mustard, hot sauce, Cajun seasoning, eggs, onion, and mix it all up trying not to stir too much or too little. When it seems ready, I portion out four servings and shape them into hearts. This is no easy task, mind you. I can play music, but I'm no sculptor, and the heart-shaped crab cakes leave a bit to be desired where shape is concerned. Hopefully, Elena will like them. She's coming over around nine after meeting a few friends for early evening drinks. I have a flower in a vase on the table, some wine and some beer, some soju, a card for her with another little poem, no gift gifts, though, no jewelry or such, only enough to commemorate what will be a good night at the beginning of something.

At ten before nine, there's a knock on the door. She's early. I open it. "Hey, Robot," she says stepping in. We hug.

"I got you a rose." I motion to the vase. She walks over, grabs it with her thumb and middle finger and picks it up. She sniffs, smiles.

"I got you this," she says handing me a heart-shaped box that I figure must be chocolates. I open it. "Surprise!" she says grabbing my forearm. In the box, there are no chocolates. Instead there are three Trojan condoms, ribbed for her pleasure. It's the greatest one-month anniversary gift ever.

"Only three?" I ask.

"I think we'll be all right." She leans up and kisses me. "I brought some Crown, too. I'll make the drinks." We go into the kitchen, and

I put the crab cakes in the pan one by one with a spatula and turn on the burner. "Are those supposed to be heart-shaped?" she asks handing me a drink and poking me in the ribs. Being a little ticklish, I shriek and drop the spatula, thankfully not the drink. "You okay there?" she says laughing.

"Don't know. I might die."

"Wait until tomorrow at least." She picks up the spatula, hands it to me. "I'm going to the bedroom to change. I want to get out of this sweatshirt." She kisses me on the cheek, and I get to cooking while she gets to changing. I finish my drink, make another. The crab cakes are almost done when she calls from the bedroom, "Can you come here for a sec?"

"Sure." I check the food and set the burner to low and then pick up my drink and go to the bedroom. "Whoa!" The heart-shaped condom box is open and next to the bed where she's lying in nothing but a see-through red lace teddy that will not be on her body much longer.

"Happy One Month."

We're lying in bed, one of those moments of soft pillow talk that might lead to declarations of post-coital emotion. I feel on the verge of such when it hits me. "What's that smell?" We look at each other. "The crab cakes!" I sprint to the kitchen naked and open the window before turning off the burner. The crab cakes are brown on top. I turn one over and realize I could probably use it to shingle a roof. Elena walks up behind me, puts her arms around my waist. "Uh," I say, "there's a slight problem with dinner."

"I see."

"Sorry."

"You always burn something when you cook for me." It's true. I cooked for her once before and

burned two tortillas when attempting to heat them up in a pan. Thankfully, they weren't the last two so I switched to the microwave, and the bean burritos were a success.

We clean the kitchen a bit, air the place out. "It's already nine thirty. Most restaurants will close soon so I guess it's ramen noodles or McDonald's. Sorry, baby."

"No reason to be sorry." She pulls me to her, and we kiss long, passionate. She steps away, walks toward the bedroom and says without looking back at me, "Would you rather have eaten crab cakes or do what we just did?" The light goes off in the bedroom. McDonald's can wait.

We pull into McDonald's almost forty minutes later and run in quickly holding hands and feeling like a young high-school couple. Just inside we hug before walking up to the counter and ordering a large Quarter Pounder meal for me and a cheeseburger for her. "Let's just share the fries and the drink," she says patting her purse. She brought the Crown. We take our food and pour some Crown in the cup when no one is looking. Cheap Trick's "Way of the World" is playing on the restaurant's sound system. She picks up a fry, says "I like this song," dips the fry in ketchup, motions to me: "Here." I open my mouth and take the offered fry. She takes a good long drink of the Crown and Coke and leans over the table putting her lips to mine. She gives me a mouthful of the drink, and we kiss as if we're alone in my apartment. When we pull apart she says, "Let's get some apple pie." I get two apple pies and am reminded of that night I saw Officer here. I make a mental note to call him. We eat our dessert looking at each other and sipping the Crown, both of us eager to get back to my place but savoring the moment of anticipation.

"You ever think about cutting your hair?" she asks reaching out to touch it.

"Sometimes."

"Would you if I wanted you to?"

I sip the drink. I know she won't ask me to in this moment, but it's a question that speaks of her desire to know how much I care for her.

"If I love a woman, I'll cut my hair if that's what she really wants."

She smiles, sips the Crown, kisses me again, then stands up to leave as Bob Marley's "Three Little Birds" starts. "Let's bring the rest of the fries and a refill of the Coke."

CHAPTER 31

PHOTOGRAPHER STACY ALBRIGHT ARRIVES at the George and Dragon, an English pub I learned about from Ted in The Men's Room. It's in Fremont just down the street from the High Dive, and it's a dark place with the bar in the center, tables around the sides, pool table and dart board in the front corner. The décor is English soccer paraphernalia mostly focused on Arsenal since the owner is an Arsenal fan, a Gooner, I guess. There are three TVs tuned to the same soccer match, English Premier League as the clientele here is heavily English, but even the Americans who frequent this pub follow European soccer, and that's led to it being declared by some sources as one of the best soccer pubs in the city, possibly even the country. It's often filled Saturday and Sunday mornings as early as eight for EPL games, and various evenings for Seattle Sounders games. Even now, there's a large group of people in red and white Arsenal jerseys watching the game on the two TVs in the front of the bar. Our table is back near the bathrooms.

Stacy walks up. "Sorry, I'm late." She sets her camera bag down. It's big like the ones I saw at Pain in the Grass, but she needs it. She's a pro at capturing the musical moments in images just as I try to capture them in words. I first met her the morning after Thanksgiving at Easy Street Records in West Seattle for the release of Chris Cornell's *Songbook*. I was there to buy the album. She was there to see her handiwork as it's one of her pictures that was chosen for the cover, this wonderful moment at one of his solo shows where the crowd is a sea of arms reaching for him as he reaches back. We struck up a conversation when I complimented the photo and mentioned that I need photographers sometimes for my writing. It was one of those serendipitous meetings and after some talk of music and writing and photography, she suggested that I see the Missionary Position since it was one of her favorite Seattle bands. She even offered to take pictures for me if I were to write about it, so I said, "Sure," and here we are in the George a week later sharing beers with a few musicians before heading over to the Tractor for the show. I asked Elena to come too, but she wasn't in the mood to go out. She wanted a quiet evening with a book. I offered to stay home, but she wouldn't have it. "You're writing about it. You have to go. You gave your word."

"Yeah, I know, but if you want me to stay, I will."

"Go. I'll be here. If the band is good, I'll go next time."

It's a wide cast of characters we're meeting tonight. Julia Massey, Geoff Gibbs, and Jared Cortese are to my left. Jared and Julia have made it known they're engaged and will get married next year. We all congratulate them and toast and drink. To my right is Jason Welling, the keyboard-guitar-violin player from Sightseer. P.A. Mathison is next to him. Across from me are Kate from Alabaster and stayC of Furniture Girls. Stacy Albright sits next to her. I introduce her to the rest of the group and then buy a round for everyone except Kate. She's sober, gave up drinking a couple years ago.

"Thanks for the drinks, sir," Welling says. "Next round's on Beef." That's his nickname. Welling. Wellington. Before Stacy arrived, we were talking about musical starts, how we got into music, who took lessons, who taught themselves. He continues now, "So like I was saying, I started piano lessons when I was six because my parents had a piano, and I'd sit there and plunk on the keys and eventually I started to figure out chords and songs. I'd listen to their records like the soundtrack for *Close Encounters* or *Pat Boone's Christmas*. I loved 'Santa Claus Is Coming in a Whirlybird.' " He laughs a kind of hee-hee-hee laugh. "At six, why wouldn't I? And then I was teaching myself violin when I was ten, guitar at thirteen. I figured it was better that way. Unless you want to play jazz, you'll teach yourself.

It's a waste of money to pay someone to teach you to play the likes of 'Smells Like Teen Spirit' or 'Enter Sandman.' "

"I saw Metallica when I was sixteen," P.A. says. "They scared me. It was the same with Led Zeppelin when I was four and my brothers would put on 'Immigrant Song.' I'd run to my bedroom and lock the door."

"Did your brothers play instruments?" I ask.

"My family was musical, but not in the classically trained way, more of a backyard jam kind of way."

"That's cool," Julia says.

"Yeah," stayC agrees.

"It actually was. Here's to musical families." We all take a drink. "So I wanted to take violin lessons when I was young because my grandpa played—I still have his violin actually. Beef plays it on stage sometimes—so I tried to play in school, but they stuck me with a viola. I was cool with that because I could hide out in relative obscurity like you"—she looks at me—"said you do sometimes do when playing bass, hide in the groove behind the vocals and the guitars."

"I'm just not a fan of the spotlight."

"Neither am I, but look where I wound up. Anyway, I couldn't read music, I just couldn't. I'd play by ear and turn the pages on the sheet music when everyone else did. I played well enough that they recommended me for the city youth orchestra, but I knew I'd be found out, so I just kind of quit that."

"They never knew you couldn't read music?" Stacy asks.

"Nope."

"Seems like there's a story in there somewhere," I say.

"You should write it up."

"Maybe I will." It seems like interesting fodder for something, concealing the inability and succeeding. Maybe a poem would do it justice, maybe a book. I can identify with her in the sense that I don't read music either. I do it all by ear, and the thing is I've played with some very good musicians. Maybe that means I tricked them in a way even as they knew I couldn't read music. I wonder if I was the thing holding them back. Maybe there was something lacking in my depth of understanding and in my playing, but then, they chose me for their bass player, complimented my style, my riffs, my taste for knowing when to ride on the root note and when to walk a little.

And yet, I did wonder, did sometimes feel inadequate as the doubts rolled in, the fears of notes and chords hit a little off time, fingered a little wrong, maybe completely forgotten. *Which chord comes next?* It's hard to imagine I'll ever step on stage again, or if I do, it's hard to imagine not fucking it up.

"So anyway," P.A. says, "when I quit that, I thought guitar looked interesting, and then my parents gave me one for my birthday after I let it be known. From there, I just sort of figured it out enough to get by. I still feel that way I guess, like I'm just getting by. I haven't remotely reached my potential yet. I never had those days as a teenager spending hours in my room playing along to Zeppelin or whatever, and I didn't in my twenties and thirties either, because I had family and work stuff going on. Maybe someday."

"I'd say you're doing quite well with the whole potential thing." It's Julia, the young musician complimenting the older one. "I love you guys. I sing your songs all the time."

"She does," Jared says.

"He's right. I do. You were awesome at the High Dive last time."

"Thanks."

"You were at that show?" I ask. I hadn't known who she was then.

"Yeah, and now we're hooked. Interesting, Jason, about the lessons bit. I started on piano too and must have been the only kid who enjoyed piano lessons when growing up. When I started guitar, it was because I couldn't haul a piano to college, but I did what you did. I taught myself."

"Cheers to that," Beef says. We all drink, and he goes up to the bar to get another round.

"What are some of your best and worst musical moments off stage?" I ask. "I mean, something either you were doing or witnessed."

"I vividly remember seeing Julia perform for the first time and having this tingly warm feeling come over my body every time she sang a note." He's holding her hand as he speaks. "It was... I just couldn't believe it. It was just a little rock show, but it was the best concert I'd ever been too."

"The small ones often are for the intimacy, the proximity," I say. "There's just so much more to grab hold of. You can feel the music transforming like mass into energy in a way that you can't at large shows, like everything adds up to more than the sum of its parts, like 2 + 2 = 5. You guys ever think that art can change reality with the way it affects people?"

"Well," Jared says, "I'd say that art can tune you into a different reality. With how different we all are, there are essentially as many realities as there are perspectives."

"There's also the fact," Julia says, "that 2 + 2 = 4 seems completely objective, but what if the symbol for 5 actually meant 4 in an alternate universe. How about the fact that math continues to 'prove' that there ARE many other realities and dimensions? All you have to do is play with polyrhythms a little bit to see that this mathematical proposition is worth considering."

"It's a feel thing," P.A. says. "If you feel in the moment that it's 5, then it's 5. That's what music does. Why else do it?"

"I can completely get behind the idea of music changing our perception of events, time, memory," Geoff says. "Like a brilliant narrative that captures the essence of a mood through robust hyperbole or colorful evocative language, it becomes more about the feeling of an event instead of the event itself."

"I've had that exact same idea," I say.

"It's the same mechanism," he continues, "as nostalgia for memories bending them to romantic glorification. 2 + 2 still equals a resounding 4, but from the gravity caused by the evocative and emotional power of music and moment, we see the 5 through the curvature in our own personal perspectives. Reality remains The Real, and we are left with our own amazing experience of it. I suppose this could explain why people still argue ascetics and there are thousands of religions."

"It's a good and a bad thing to say the reality can change," stayC says.

"Why so?"

"Well, it's good in the sense that it can open new perspectives. Sure, things seem different, and they are in a way, but it's a dangerous thing if 2 + 2 = 5, because then things that are wrong can be right. There's justification for anything."

"It's about the energy." We all turn toward Beef. David Neilsen, Sightseer's drummer, is standing behind him with Lightfoot to his left. They're late and have apparently been listening for a bit. "It doesn't matter what you might think changes or what it adds up to just so long as it moves you. Reality doesn't alter, but music might set you on a different path. It's just a path that's always been there."

"Greetings, sirs," Beef says. We scoot our chairs a little closer to make room for them to pull two up and sit. I introduce them to Stacy. "You guys should have her shoot a Sightseer show."

"Maybe we will. You have a card?" She hands one to Lightfoot. "Thanks," he says, "but back to the conversation, my two cents would be that in some ways rock and roll was created to change the world, or at least had that idea put upon it, and it does if perception changes."

"Indeed," Kate says, "perception is all we have. You only see things the way you do, and if that changes so does the world, or rather your world, maybe just in a small way, but still it does."

There is some agreement then. Perception changes, maybe the world, but not The Real, just a different way of looking at The Real. I feel as ever like I'm missing something in this, like maybe I'm making it more complicated than it needs to be. Jane's Addiction's "Summertime Rolls" floats out of the jukebox as the soccer match ends—Arsenal won—and the sound system kicks back to music. It's such a beautiful song but easy to dismiss as simple. The thing is it's about dynamics, about simplicity and complexity, layering with a steady, constant foundation underneath. And I must say this bass line is so absolutely gorgeous. It's one of those that makes me wish I'd thought of it, one of those that I will play for the nurses in that future hospice if a bass is somehow handy, "This was Jane's Addiction." They won't know, of course. Who knows what music from these past few decades and the present moments will still be known then. I look around this table and think there are some worthy contenders here. None of them are famous yet, but they all should be. We should all be singing their songs fifty years from now. I should be able to tell those future nurses, "I knew Sightseer and Julia Massey and Furniture Girls and the Jesus Rehab," and have them recognize the names as they gently tuck me back into bed. "That's nice, Mr. Murphy."

"So to go the opposite way, what about the bad musical experiences?" I ask.

"I once completely forgot the lyrics to a song," stayC says, "three verses gone in a poof." She's laughing to tell it. "I just garbled some stuff and my face turned redder and redder. Damn, that was embarrassing."

"I have one," Julia says. "We did this show at the Nectar once, and I'd eaten a ton of cabbage that day in various forms. One was in my bowl of pho, another in a cabbage salad, and before the show I had a couple drinks. Well, this turned out to be a show-stopping combination because in the middle of our set, I was either going to poop my pants or rush to the bathroom. My band mates, of course, had no idea that I was enduring this, and so Geoff and Dominic were shocked to hear my in-between-song chatter include, 'and this is where the band keeps playing, and I take a bathroom break.' " This brings laughter. It's the kind of thing the guys in the Men's Room would joke about.

"That's awesome!" Kate says laughing. "The story would be complete, though, if the bathroom had no toilet paper."

"Thankfully, it did. Christ, if they hadn't I would have been screwed."

"I remember that," stayC says, "but you guys handled it with ease. Everyone in the audience was just looking at each other and going, 'Did she just say that?' And yet the vibe was good. Everyone was smiling with that. 'Well, I've never seen that happen before' expression."

There's some more laughter. I've had my fears and doubts on stage, but I must say I'm glad never to have had that happen. "Who are your favorite current Seattle bands?" I ask. "Local bands, I mean, not yet famous."

"Definitely, the Jesus Rehab. Since I'm a bass player, you may think this is odd, or you might think it's just because I know Dom and Jared personally, and that surely is why I originally learned of the band, but the core of my love for TJR is that there is no other two-piece that sounds like this. Most guitar/drum duos are roots rocky, a kind of blues with screaming White Stripes and Black Keys tones, and don't get me wrong, I love that sound, but TJR is like a nineties power grunge band with a little jazz thrown in. It's a sound all its own. They're manimals."

"Hell yeah!" Julia says.

"I have to agree with the assessment of most two piece guitar/drum groups. TJR is the best I've written about by far."

Julia sings a little then while looking at Jared. "And all the spaceships in her head, all those spaceships in her head, spinning round and round and round," and here the whole table joins in.

These guys know each others' songs. "… and round and round and round." We sing it a few times and end laughing.

"Yeah, thanks," Jared says, "but I like that Sightseer song." And then he starts in singing, "I don't care if you go / And I don't care if you stay." The whole table starts singing again, " 'cause I'm already gone / in this red eye haze." And then Geoff, Beef, and David start tapping rhythms on the table while stayC and P.A., of course, go into the second verse: "So tell me if I get too close / Standing at a dead end road / You don't know how hard I've tried / to fight the urge to cross that line." Jared and Julia start tapping on the table too. The rhythm picks up, begins to gallop a little. Beef and Lightfoot join in on the vocals, "When you can't hold in and you can't hold back / break it down to the simple facts / It's too late to turn back time / Steal your heart and give up mine." The rhythm makers all hit the two big accents, DUM DUM, and the drinks shake. There's a pause, then back into the table tapping chorus, "I don't care if you go / And I don't care if you stay / 'cause I'm already gone / in this red eye haze."

We pause then, smile, clap to ourselves. Others in the bar are looking at us and wondering what the hell we're doing, what we're drinking, or how much, but it doesn't matter. This is what music does. It grabs into a moment, and then nothing else matters but the need to sing those lines and bang on the table, and for that brief time, those of us sitting here are a tribe, a makeshift, spontaneous band.

"That was fun," I say.

"That definitely qualifies as one of the best musical moments I've had off stage in a long time, maybe ever," P.A. says. "Thanks, Jared."

"In honor of that song, I think we need some whisky." Jared stands up, walks to the bar, orders the whisky. When he comes back, he makes a toast, "To music."

"To *our* music," stayC adds, and we know she means our little table jam here, but also the music of the individual bands represented. Furniture Girls. The Jesus Rehab. Julia Massey and the Five-Finger Discount. Sightseer. And also the music of all those local bands doing what these guys do, getting those grooves down not for fame or money, but rather for the love of it, the need of it, the inability to not do it, the refusal to let it die as the years accumulate.

"Well, we have to get going," Julia says. "Pleasure hanging with you guys."

"Indeed it has been," P.A. replies. People stand up, and there are hugs and handshakes and goodbyes, some phone numbers exchanged, promises to do a show or two together, or to meet for more drinks and talk about music, and then Julia, Geoff, and Jared are off. I wonder if one of their bands is the next thing, Seattle's new sound. I hope so.

"So Rob," P.A. says, "one of the reasons we came out today is that we wondered since you play bass if you'd be interested in subbing for a gig. Our guy quit, and the guy who did the last show can't do it."

"Uh, sure. Of course. Are you kidding? I love you guys. When's the show?" stayC is smiling like she knew they would ask this. She raises her glass to me, drinks.

"Two weeks from today over in Bremerton at a place called Hi-Fidelity Lounge," Lightfoot says. "It's a small bar, almost feels like playing in someone's living room or basement since they have a sofa, love seat, and coffee table along one wall. The ceilings are low, and there's a lamp on the coffee table and décor seems seventies-ish with velvet paintings on the walls, tile floors, but always fun to play there."

"Sounds good to me."

"Nice," Beef says. "To our celebrity guest bass player." We all drink to that.

"Thanks, but I think celebrity is pushing it a bit."

"Think you can learn fifteen songs in that time?"

"Guess we'll find out."

"Cool. We practice Tuesdays and Thursdays so we can get four rehearsals in before the show."

And it's settled. I have a gig. Everyone in the band gives me their phone numbers, and Lightfoot writes down the names of the songs I should learn. "What about 'Biggest Storms'?" I ask, and they tell me if we do that one, it'll be acoustic, just P.A. and a guitar. I like that. Strip it down to its bare minimum, its bare beauty. That way I can just watch. I can listen. Sightseer finishes their drinks and leaves then after more hugs and handshakes. "See you guys Tuesday," and then it's just me with Stacy and stayC and Kate.

"Sorry, for this," I say to Stacy. "I should have told you we'd be meeting people."

"It's fine. I like to listen to musicians talk about music and their experiences playing. It sheds some light on them as people and helps me capture better photos of them when they play."

"You should shoot the Sightseer show I'm playing."

"I would, but I'm already booked that night. Maybe some other time."

"Sure thing."

"Congratulations," Kate says, "on getting the Chris Cornell cover."

"Yeah, that was cool."

"Thanks. That was such an awesome moment. I love his music, and I'd been taking pictures all evening with my good camera, but then I put that away right there at the end and as an afterthought pulled out my little point and click and just snapped a few. Funny how it goes sometimes. And picture or not, it was awesome to witness, the cheering, all those hands reaching toward Chris, him reaching back, and click, I got it. There's just something about the live musical moment that is so special. It's like nothing else in the amount of energy produced. The sound, the electricity."

"I agree," I say. She's put Einstein into my brain. I remember thinking about it after Julia's show, the transformative power of music, especially live music. It can solidify things, or shatter them, and thinking about this energy, I'm again doubtful of my whole 2 + 2 = 5 idea. The past is mutable, but I don't think anything, even music, can add up to more than the sum of its parts. Things change, but they always add up.

"Cheers to that." stayC clinks Stacy's glass, then my own. We drink as Kate raises her coffee mug. It's empty, but she goes through the motion to be a part of the moment.

"I guess I've found inspiration in the Seattle music scene. It saved my life. It *changed* my life. I'm so incredibly moved by live performances, being up close, snapping the micro moments that cannot be seen from the back row. It's an honor to capture the power of the musicians and their emotional release on stage. It's right where I'm supposed to be."

"Nice," Kate says. Sadly it's a hard thing for people to find where they're supposed to be. Many never do. Many never even think about it. They just live. Stacy and stayC and Kate have it right. One takes pictures. One sings. One plays guitar. These days I take notes. I wonder if this is where I'm supposed to be, if the musical ship has sailed, if my thing now, my place, is writing, describing the phrases, measures, and melodies rather than playing them. I guess in two weeks I'll find out.

"What I really like to do," Stacy continues, "is photograph a band a few times. You learn their movements that way. I see a lot up there, and later, when I read about a show, I learn the backstory that I didn't know at the time, things I might not have seen or heard at the show."

"I get that the other way around. When I write about a show, I often miss things because I'm looking down at my notebook and scribbling, drawing pictures or maybe ordering a beer at the bar. I'll see the photos later and wonder, 'When did that happen? And if I missed that, what else did I miss?' The photographer becomes my eyes for the night, eyes on the band in a way I never could. In a way, it's almost like being in a band. The writer has to trust the photographer, the photographer the writer. There are a thousand photographers just like there are a thousand guitar players. You have to work with the right one and trust that they'll nail it." Tonight will be our first time working together, but I have a good feeling. The Missionary Position. Her pictures. My words. It's going to turn out well. Stacy gets up to go to the bathroom.

"So, you nervous?" stayC asks.

"For what?"

"The Sightseer show, of course."

"In a nutshell, yes."

"You shouldn't be."

"I know, but I always am. I remember this one show I did with my band years ago where I fucked up. I wasn't too drunk or anything, I just thought about it too much in the moment. I feared fucking up so that's exactly what I did."

"And you will," Kate says, "if you start thinking up there."

"Yeah, I've battled my own stage fright issues, especially the first few times I tried to sing, but you have to channel that. I think what it comes down to is that people are supportive. They want you to do well. Nobody wants to go to a show to see the band fuck up, and so even if you do fuck up, they'll be forgiving, they'll laugh it off, but only if you do too. If you crawl into a hole and die and destroy the whole performance, then they'll turn on you. Remember just breathe, let it go." That's a Pearl Jam song, 'Just Breathe,' and I know that stayC and Eddie are right. People want to close their eyes and get lost in the music and the words. They just want to breathe, and to live, and they want the music and the words to make it easier to continue doing so.

When Stacy comes back, stayC stands up, "Sorry to say, but I have to go now too. I'm catching a show at the High Dive tonight, band called Christa Says Yay. You guys should check them out sometime, a little bluesy, a little soulful. Good stuff."

"Maybe, I'll head over with you," Kate says. There are still more hugs as we all get up to leave. Stacy looks at me.

"We should get to the Tractor."

Chapter 32

WE ENTER THE TRACTOR just as The Missionary Position is getting ready to go on, and I notice there is no bass player on stage. That reminds me of the first time I saw the Young Evils and my thought that I'd inquire about playing bass if I liked them. What would they have said? Thankfully, I had the good judgment not to ask. I must admit that sometimes it's better not to play, that sometimes it's better to be in the audience listening or taking notes with a pen and a beer at the corner of the bar, that it's better to wait for the right thing to come along, and as if to prove the point, I have an upcoming gig with Sightseer. If it goes well, I wonder if they'll ask me to join the band.

I get a Manny's, settle in at the bar, and tell Stacy I'll be here for the whole show, and that I'll find her when it's over. She goes off to do her photography thing, and I watch her for a few moments taking some pictures of the stage, of the crowd. When The Missionary Position starts, they're wearing white tux coats and have a good Morphine vibe with a sax and the keyboard bass parts. I once had a girlfriend who was a huge Morphine fan tell me Mark Sandman's voice was a "fuck me" voice for how hot it made her. I imagine some women might feel the same about Jeff Angell for the way his voice oozes a gritty kind of confidence, and as the show goes on, there are moments when it sounds a little like Pink Floyd's "Shine on You Crazy Diamond" or bits of the Doors here and AC/DC there. They play some new kind of blues-infused rock, modern with electronic elements, heavy grooves, and textures from the hips that cause audience, photographers, even writers, to shake a bit.

I take notes in my customary way, separating myself from the moment, becoming the observer, but that's a good place to be because the music comes at me full force since I shut all else out. And the music does come, and in one moment near the end of their set, it brings me down, way down. There is a song called "All My Mistakes," the first on their 2009 CD, *Diamonds in a Dead Sky*. It is a mellow tune, soulful, a little gospel-like. Angell sings.

> *For years I've been looking for answers at the bottom of a glass*
> *How 'bout another round of the good times, baby,*
> *'cause you know they never last.*
> *And there used to be something you liked about me…*
> *And I think about what could have been*
> *And who I couldn't be.*

I wonder if the "you" in the lyric is a reference to anyone in particular, if the song was meant for an actual past love or just the idea we all have of it, a replacement for a name, that lost thing we couldn't keep because we weren't the right people to do so. The book isn't published yet, but I've already added a dedication to the manuscript: "For Rita." She's a woman I let down because of who I couldn't be, meaning I couldn't be the right person. I could only be myself. And that was the pain. My self was rejected, and the words come again as the song continues and the audience sways more, "And I think about what could have been. And who I couldn't be," and it makes me sad. Music, like no other art, can grab hold of a moment and echo out bits of the listener's life; the refrain, the phrase, can lift or drag down, but it has to be played by the right group of musicians, and these guys are the right ones.

So I'm tempted to leave when the song ends, much as I did the night of the Alabaster show. There was a different phrase then. *I can't feel anything anymore.* But these days I can, and though a song such as this might take me back to a moment, I can let it go when the song is over and look forward to whatever chords come next. For the Missionary Position, that's an uptempo bass line played by Benjamin Anderson on the keyboard, the *bum tch bum tch* of the kick drum and hi-hat, some swells and fades on guitar. Every head in the audience is bobbing in time with the kick, some up and down, some side to side. The guitar fades, and the vocals come in over bass and drums, "There's no time like the present." The pace is quick. It shakes things. When the chorus comes in, it leaps up with Angell's distorted guitar doubling the bass line, the snare on each beat, another repeated phrase: "Let's start a fire!" Indeed, I want to. "If you feel the hands around your throat, let's start a fire!" not for sadness or anger or anything else in my life, but for the joy of the moment, for the sake of lighting up the night. "If you're wondering what's going to happen next, let's start a fire!" The crowd is bouncing, circling, swinging, and I sing along with almost two hundred others, "Let's start a fire!" Let's burn away all that was, shine a light on all that will be.

As I'm paying my tab, there's a text from Officer "You at the Tractor?" I'd asked him to come, but he's on duty tonight.

"Yeah."

"How was the band?"

"Great. You'll have to catch them next time."

"Indeed. Be careful driving home."

"I will. Watch out for people sleeping in back seats."

"Always do. Let's catch up next week."

"You got it."

I say bye to Stacy after confirming that she'll have the images to me within a few days, and then I leave, and on the drive home, I keep the stereo off. My ears are ringing pretty badly. It's a sound, though, and I'm grateful for that. I hum along and try to determine the pitch. C perhaps, but no, that's the first chord of "All My Mistakes." F isn't quite right. A. Yes, it's A. I'm sure of it, so I try to think of a song that starts with that. Sightseer's "Athabasca" comes to mind. It's a song about going home to small town life in Canada. P.A. is Canadian. The song starts acoustic with the plucked notes of an A chord, a run from B to C# to D, back to the A a few times around before the verse and the rest of the instruments come in. It's a beautiful poetic tune about what you get by going back, about what you can't get. I love

Sightseer's rocking tunes. "Read It & Weep" caught my attention for those Judas Priest-like F# chords and a descending blues riff, and well, "Red Eye Haze" is one of the best sing-along jams ever, ever, but in their mellow songs, their acoustic songs, their ballads, they have two home runs—"Did I ever tell you about the time I hit two home runs?"—in "Biggest Storms" and "Athabasca." Radio stations should be falling over themselves to play this stuff. Record companies should be scrambling to woo the band for the privilege of recording them. Fans should be screaming for that soft closer to float home on. I drive along 99 South and sing softly.

> *I've learned a few things about heartache...*
> *I can admit you were right,*
> *you were right...*
> *You can't hold time*
> *Making up lost years in one single night*
> *You can't go back*
> *Keep yesterday in the palm of your hand.*
> *It slips away...*
> *We're a long way from home*
> *Athabasca*

Memories are like small towns where we grew up, where we color things as we see fit, where we know everyone. They are sweet dreams in a jar. Sometimes it's hard to escape, but all roads do eventually lead away to other towns, other people, other songs, and sometimes there's a pang in the words.

> *We're a long way from home*

And sometimes a joy to realize it.

> *We're a long way from home*

A joy at the start of something. I run the melody over in my brain and imagine playing the bass parts in fourteen days. B, C#, D, E, followed by the name of the town. The mellow sparse songs are harder to play because every note must be perfect. Every note must ring, must hold its place. Fuckups can't be covered by a quick run of notes to the next chord change. I would usually be nervous about that, but I'm not now. It's just a run of notes in the abbreviated alphabet of music. I'll play them and look out from the stage, and when it's over, there will be applause. I know this already. It's a good fit. It's the right time. The music found me just as I found it.

I look in the rearview now and again, and there's a car lingering, tailing, switching lanes and roads as I do. It follows me down 99 to the West Seattle Bridge, exits with me past the Skylark and on toward my apartment. There are lights on top, not flashing, but they're there. It can only be Officer for the way he's hanging back, following, making sure I get home okay. Seems I have a guardian angel of sorts, one that wears a badge and smokes pot, one that likes late-night cheeseburgers and strippers, one that deserves a shot and a handshake, and maybe even a hug, next time I see him.

When I get home, Elena's asleep in the bedroom, but on the table there's a painting of a cat that looks very much like Soju. There's a note next to it. "Still drying. Don't touch." I see now why she didn't want to go to the show. I get a beer from the fridge and sit and look at the painting for a while. It makes me glad I never took any pictures of Soju because she might not have done this for me. But then, I know too that as the years go by, this is what Soju will look like in my mind. I'll forget the differences that I can see now. This cat is a little overweight, the tail too short. Soju had a little splotch of white on his left side that I never told her about. I suppose I'll forget that someday, maybe that far-off day when I'm in a hospice clinging to this painting. "See. This was my cat." I'll point, and the nurse will say, "Aw, he's so cute," while rolling her eyes because I told her the same thing the day before. And I'll keep pointing and say, "Look. He was black. The only white was there on the paws." I'll point again forgetting all about that splotch. The nurse will nod, "That's right, Mr. Murphy. Now, let's put this back over on the table." And she'll do that, and I'll forget. So now, when I can remember, I look. I mark the differences. I drink a toast to Soju, and then I notice that in the bottom left corner, Elena's written his name wrong. It's right if going by what's on my chest, but I'm the only one who knows that. I stare at the Korean letters.

수조

I wonder if I'll forget that too, if I'll tell that future nurse, "That's my cat, Sujo." She'll tilt her head and say, "Sujo? What kind of name is that?" And I won't be able to tell her. I'll just point and repeat myself, "That's my cat, Sujo."

I finish my beer and go to bed being careful not to wake Elena, and as I drift off to sleep, I wish Sujo were here purring, taking up one of the pillows so that we'd have to position ourselves around him. I listen to Elena breathing and try to commit that sound to memory. It's better than the sounds she makes during sex. Inhale. Exhale. Inhale. Exhale. Breathe. Live. Relish. Remember while I can. I decide to take a picture of her tomorrow so that maybe I can tell the nurse, "See? She was the one."

I wake up with an idea, get quietly out of bed, and walk to the printer in the living room. It's under my desk, and I notice a French fry when I kneel next to it. I smile to think it must be from our one-month anniversary, but I have no idea how it got here. I pick it up and set it on the chair. The printer is one of those multi-function things, a printer/scanner/copier, and I open the top slowly as if something might leap out. Nothing does, but something is there, some long lost thing, my live CD, *I Might Be Wrong*. When I woke up, it popped into my head. I remembered wanting to write something about Radiohead a while ago, almost a year, and I'd thought then to scan the image of the CD to accompany the writing. I just plain forgot. I laugh at myself for how I've looked everywhere else in this apartment and my car and at work, and here it was all the time. CD in hand, I walk to the kitchen and grab a Blue Moon from the fridge. I take a sip and smile to think that though the past does not alter, the poem does.

...I give the bottle
a good, long hit.
I do have my sorrows,
but there are

no regrets as I smile
at my good fortune
in this life,
the freedom
to remember beauty,
to place names on it,
and from its loss
create
type
live
here
in the present tense
knowing beauty,
known beauty,
is curled up
asleep in the bedroom,
breathing,
dreaming,
comfortable
in the knowledge
that she is
the next page.

I place the empty bottle on the counter and the put the CD in the stereo and skip to track eight, the one I've been wanting to hear all this while, the one that's just Thom York and an acoustic guitar, "True Love Waits." The guitar comes in, and it swallows me along with the voice that sings of true love waiting in haunted attics, and a plea, not asking to be forgotten, but rather asking one not to leave.

I set the song on repeat at a low volume and go back to the bedroom. I crawl in next to Elena. She's on her right side facing the wall with me behind her. I put my arm over her positioning my hand deliberately over her breast, her chest, her heart. She breathes deep, pulls my arm snug, whispers without looking back, without, I imagine, even opening her eyes, "You found it."

CHAPTER 33

TONIGHT, WE'RE IN RICHLAND, WASHINGTON, the Tri-Cities, a Friday night on the road. A week ago, I was filling in on bass for Sightseer at the Hi-Fidelity Lounge in Bremerton for the second time as I'd been the substitute bass player for a string of shows over the past few months. They kept asking, "Can you do one more in Bremerton? How about the Skylark? And, oh yeah, we have a weekend in the Tri-Cities." I said yes to them all, and then in the Hi-Fidelity, we finished "Read It & Weep," and I looked out at the forty odd people in the audience and felt not the need to sip my beer, nor close my eyes to make the fears and doubts go away. My face didn't redden, and I didn't need to pretend to adjust the volume of my amplifier. It was easy. I let it go. I just breathed, and when the applause died down, P.A. turned back, gave me a quick look, and then she spoke to the audience.

"You know, Rob here," she pointed to me and half-turned back, "has been good enough to help us out for a few shows, and being that this whole band thing is like a relationship, a marriage, so to speak… with five people…"

"Group sex!" came a shout from the audience. There was some laughter, and I began to sense what was going to happen, and then I smiled like one who knows something, or rather one who sees something wanted coming.

P.A. cocked her head a little. "Exactly… but with instruments rather than body parts." Some more laughter.

"Anyway," Lightfoot stepped up speaking into his microphone, "we wanted to extend a hand to Rob and ask him to be number five, to be the guy." There were some claps and shouts in the audience. Lightfoot turned back to me. "What do you say?"

I'd never been proposed to before, and now it was in public, on stage, three songs into a set in which I'd gone into thinking I was filling in, a sub, an honorary member for the evening. I'd practiced with them and hauled equipment and sound checked hoping for a few more musical moments on stage, a few last ones, before my hearing goes for good, if it does. Thankfully, it hasn't gone when we've been playing, but it still happens at home, sometimes while driving, sometimes during sex, but I don't think Elena knows. And then there while everyone in the band and audience was looking at me, it got quiet. I looked out at stayC. She raised a glass. There was Stacy taking pictures. Furniture Girls' Jim and Thane were there clapping. I wondered whether any of them knew of this before I did. Kate was there with her fist raised. She was saying something, cheering. Elena was on one of the sofas sipping a Crown and Coke. She had her right hand on her chest, was smiling at me. She would congratulate me privately later.

I looked at the band. David behind the kit, Beef behind his keyboard. P.A. and Lightfoot at their microphones looking back and smiling at me. I looked down at the set list. The next song would be "Bitter Blue," a new one. While rehearsing the previous week, Lightfoot mentioned that he liked chords on the bass so I started playing some, A, A, D. I added a little ascending bit after the D and then went back to A and repeated the progression changing the ascending bit each time, and then Beef said, "Wait! Hold on." He started playing something on the keyboard. "Yes, that totally fits."

"What?" P.A. asked.

"Bitter Blue?" He looked at me, "For the last CD, we tried recording this song and just couldn't get it right, but that thing you just played is perfect. Play it again." I did, and he started playing along and after a few times around, he said, "Go up to G," we did, "and then D... now A and pause." We paused, and on the beat I went back into the bass chord progression and David came in on drums and we all played that around a few times. It was beautiful, open, mellow. But it was big too. It could resound. We stopped for a minute.

"Nice feel, man." David said.

"Yeah, I see what you're getting at Jason. I'll sing it this time."

And a new song was born, resurrected, but still new. I wasn't even in the band yet, and we were writing songs. It felt so awesome in the moment that I hadn't realized the significance, but we talked afterward of how the five of us had a good vibe, how we connected musically, how the song seemed to take shape of its own accord. I should have suspected something then, but I didn't. I just had the song in my head. It was a soft one but every bit as good as "Athabasca" and "Biggest Storms." I thought that with such songs Sightseer should be the next thing, the new Seattle sound, but I didn't take it a step further and think that I might be part of that.

"You okay there?" Lightfoot asked on stage as sound came back. I smiled. They were asking me to commit to the band, to publicly avow my dedication to Sightseer. We all had a few drinks in us, and a few songs into the set, were feeling the combined buzz of alcohol and live music and all that was good in the world. Things always look good from up on stage with a bass in hand, a beer or two on the amp. I took a sip of one and said the only thing I could.

"Yeah, I am, and I do."

There were some more cheers, glasses raised and emptied. Lightfoot shook my hand, bumped my shoulder. "You don't know what you've gotten yourself into."

And he was right. I was agreeing to join a band, to enter into a five-person marriage, and even though I'd been in many bands throughout my life, I didn't know at all what I was getting into. I still don't, but the best things are like that. The future is dull only when it's certain, and now here I am a week later in the band, promoted from substitute to full member. We finished our set fifteen minutes ago and are waiting for Furniture Girls to go on. In the lull between bands, a middle-aged guy approaches P.A. and David. "That was stellar!"

"Thanks," David says. They shake hands.

"Glad you liked it."

"How much are CDs?"

"Ten dollars."

"I'll take two."

The guy buys his two Sightseer CDs and goes back to his seat at the bar. He sits next to an overly thin woman in a purple tank top, gives her a CD, puts his arm around her, and then they drink of their drinks, Miller Lite tall boys. I drink of my own, a Blue Moon. David comes over to where I am and sits down.

"This is what music is supposed to be. I'm glad you're with the band.

"Me too."

"We need to write some more songs now and capture the feeling."

"We will."

I pat him on the shoulder. We're a Dave, a Rob, two Jasons, one P.A, Sightseer. We're a band on the road. Maybe this is what I'll tell those nurses years from now. I'll mention this night, the music, the words, rather than a woman. I'll try to get the other hospice patients to join along in a chorus of "Bitter Blue" as I pluck it out on the low-quality acoustic guitar in the common room.

> *But if you ever*
> *Come back I'll never*
> *Fall hook, line and sinker again...*
> *A crooked path is where I've gone*
> *a dead end road you lead me on*
> *Tell me something, tell me true*
> *We're you ever mine?*
> *Bitter blue*

CHAPTER 34

A FEW WEEKS AFTER the Tri-Cities show, I open my eyes and check the time: 8:01. Elena's asleep so I walk out to the sofa and sit down. I grab the acoustic but don't start playing because I realize that it made no sound when disturbed from its resting place. The pickup inside it didn't rattle, the strings didn't hum, nothing, and the bed didn't creak when I got up. I listen now, but there's no noise from the bedroom or the living room, or outside. I strain to hear something, anything, but all there is, is quiet. This could be it. I might be full, finally, of all the music I've been storing up.

I take a guitar pick from the table but still don't strum. I think about the equation instead, not $2 + 2 = 5$, but the other one, Einstein's, the one I thought about after the Julia Massey show. $E = mc^2$. I was wrong before. Things do not add up to more than the sum of their parts. There's energy, mass, transfer, release. There's always some sort of conversion, which in this case means more like $1 + 1 + 1 + 1 = 3.7$, or thereabouts, but that 0.3 gets multiplied by the square of the speed of light, and so an A chord can rock the world for all the energy it creates, for that's what sound is, a form of energy. Air moves. Mass moves, is moved, from one side of the equation to the other, and so it's even more true than I'd thought. Things as they are are changed upon the blue guitar.

And there's Sightseer. We've written one new song. We want to do more, but if that's all there is, then it's all there is. It's one more thing that wasn't there before, one more song that moves along the equation to light up lives, to power the universe. Those chords, A, A, D, they do it. They've done it.

I finger an A chord thinking of "Bitter Blue" and prepare to strum. This will break the spell or confirm it. Will I miss music if this is it? Do I have enough inside to last the rest of my life? I've forgotten the sound of some voices, details of life-changing nights. I can't remember the color of the sweater Rita was wearing atop the Space Needle, or for that matter what the old man had on. I just remember the imagined future words, "She was the one!" but that wasn't really true. She was only one of the ones. And what is she now? What are people who have fallen into our pasts? They are fragments. I recall the image of an upside down elephant tattoo but not its position. Was it left breast or right? I can't remember much of what I talked about with Genny while she ran a needle over my chest, and I thought of new beginnings, and maybe that's just as well. Otherwise I might linger on the idea of her, on the possibility that wasn't, on what I couldn't be. I could write poems about that night, but they wouldn't be biographies. They'd be memories, and those, like people, are fragmented things. And then there's Officer who seems part guardian angel and part wannabe friend and drinking buddy. The best thing about him, though, is that even with a badge, even with the power to judge, he does not. He protects. He understands, absorbs, absolves. He's definitely getting a shot next time I see him, if I see him. Who knows? Maybe he'll just keep following me home, or maybe his work will take its toll, maybe even the ultimate toll. But that's the way of it. Most connections do not last. They just get us through until something meaningful happens, something that takes us in new directions. That was him. He saved me on a night I did not deserve to be saved.

With Officer on my mind, I'm tempted to drive to McDonald's. I did it the night Katie was here. Why not? I could set a pot of coffee and then go pick up a couple breakfast burritos and hash browns, maybe some hot cakes and sausage, maybe even some champagne. It's always cause to celebrate being on the verge of playing an A chord, to know that I do know the sound, that I have it in my head. I think about the A minor that starts Kristen Ward's "Die of a Broken Heart." There's the F that starts Alabaster's "Hit the Ground Running," and the E that kicks off Like Lightning's "Disappear." The words go through my mind, "I don't want to disappear." I doubted my strength in that once, but no more. Now, I hear the chords under the vocal. G# F# E C#. I feel them. The Missionary Position's "All My Mistakes" starts on a lonely C chord with an aching melody, then up to a D by the end of the refrain: "And I think about what could have been and who I couldn't be." But my heart doesn't break now. It's rather lifted. There's that opening descending guitar riff in Sightseer's "Red Eye Haze" that resolves to an F# before kicking into A for the verse, "I woke up in a red-eye haze, been drifting through a thousand days." I've done such for a year it seems, but not this morning, not sitting here with guitar in hand and Elena in the bedroom. "I don't care if you go, and I don't care if you stay." I do care now, but I have the song too. There's the E, F#, G#, A at the end of Julia Massey's "Aghadoe," the outro bit. It repeats and builds with the phrase "Please forget me." The last A and the song fade out over Julia's high-pitched "me" and into near-perfect diminishment. I know these songs, these chords. I have saved them all.

I have saved them for all time.

I close my eyes and listen for the hum of the refrigerator. Nothing. No cars or dogs outside, no buses rumbling by, no Soju purring next to me. There is the painting of him there on the desk where the dragon used to be. He watches me while I write, and I do reach up to touch it sometimes hoping for a purr. I ready myself to play the still fingered chord, but then there are hands around my shoulders, hair on my hair, breath in my ear. I smile and strum, and the air moves, vibrates, blows in my face as if I'm throwing the ashes of a loved one into the wind. It's a little harsh, but a little joyous too, letting something go and getting something new in the process. I can hear all the music I've ever heard, all the music I've ever played, and the chords mix with the fragments, and the arms around my shoulders squeeze tighter, and all blends together, all voice and thought and song, the vibration of the guitar against my chest, the breath in my ear with its requisite goose bumps, the movement of lips and the words I imagine they say. It's fiction in a non-fiction world, love in a life of forgetfulness, music in a world without sound.

ACKNOWLEDGMENTS

Thank you to the following for their help and support in making this book happen: Allison Severinghaus (Moon of My Life), Clint Brownlee, Frank Anderson.

Thank you to the following bands and musicians for writing such great songs and for allowing me to use their lyrics in this book:

The Young Evils
http://theyoungevils.com/

Like Lightning
https://www.youtube.com/user/WeLikeLightning

Kristen Ward
http://www.kristenward.com/

The Jesus Rehab
http://www.thejesusrehab.com/

Star Anna and the Laughing Dogs
http://www.staranna.com/
Star is no longer with the Laughing Dogs, but they can be seen here from PJ20.
https://www.youtube.com/watch?v=cJ5qTxJnJvc

Alabaster
http://alabasterband.com/
Sadly, Alabaster has gone the way of Third Stone and is no longer together. Another reminder to get out and see local music while you can.

Sightseer
http://sightseermusic.com/

Furniture Girls
http://www.furnituregirls.com/

Julia Massey and the Five-Finger Discount
http://www.juliamasseymusic.com/

The Missionary Position
http://themissionaryposition.us/
Jeff and Ben are playing in Walking Papers (http://www.walking-papers.com) now, but the Missionary Position is still playing and recording.

Third Stone
https://soundcloud.com/davemusic-1/out-of-my-shell

Dave O'Leary and Critical Sun Recordings (http://www.criticalsun.com/) have released a CD of the music from this book. It is available online at https://themusicbook.bandcamp.com/releases

Proceeds from the sale of this music—either via individual track or the whole album—will be donated to the Wishlist Foundation (http://wishlistfoundation.org/), a non-profit, fan-run organization dedicated to supporting the charitable endeavors of Pearl Jam.

Dave O'Leary is a writer and musician living in Seattle. *The Music Book* is his second novel. His first novel, *Horse Bite*, was published in October 2011 (Infinitum), and he has also had work published in the *Monarch Review, Slate.com*, and the *Portland Book Review*. Visit his website at www.daveoleary.net. Photo by Stacy Albright, stacy-albrightimages.com.

MORE TITLES FROM
INFINITUM PUBLISHING

Horse Bite by Dave O'Leary

Horse Bite is the story of Dave and his efforts to find a bit of permanence in the balance of the things we create and the things we do to sustain ourselves. At its core, Dave's tale is one of monster G chords, poetry, booze, goodbyes, and the chance at that which matters most of all, the heart of a woman.

This All Encompassing Trip by Jason Leung

Jason Leung is no rock star but he lives the life of one while following Pearl Jam on tour around the world, establishing a unique family of friends along the way. These extraordinary bonds and the adventures that emerge from them are the basis for Jason's story and This All Encompassing Trip!

Killer Sleepover by Eddie Lance

The career of Fast Eddie Fingers was running on fumes. More and more, he finds himself reminiscing on the newspaper articles he wrote long ago. Eddie decides that he needs one last front page story that will allow him to retire with pride. As Eddie reviews some of the stories he's written, he orchestrates a brilliant plan that will tie up the loose ends of four, still-wanted serial killers. Will he succeed? Will he become a modern day hero?

Picture in a Frame by Jennifer Sando

This is a photographic story of an Adelaide photographer's mission to shoot a portrait of her music hero, Pearl Jam frontman Eddie Vedder. It shows how a journey that started with a vision became a reality with the power of social media, the law of attraction and faith..

Visit **infinitumpublishing.com** for more information.

CPSIA information can be obtained
at www.ICGtesting.com
Printed in the USA
FSOW02n0358210617
35421FS